# Praise for Leo Dark's *Lucifer Sam*!

"Leo Darke has created a heavy metal nightmare made of hard-driving prose, a dark sense of humor, and a jovial nod to 1980s horror fiction. There's sex, gore, and suspense to spare, and it all unfolds to a heavy metal beat. An enjoyable read."

—Ray Garton, author of *Crucifax* and *Ravenous*

"Just like the punk rock era that it so finely evokes, Darke's tale is edgy, dangerous, thrilling, unpredictable, and scary. Lucifer Sam rocks. Hard."

—Stuart R. West, author of *Twisted Tales from Tornado Alley* and *Ghosts of Gannaway*

"Death Metal has a new vanguard band—and a literal meaning. This band's music is truly Killer."

—Mallory A. Haws, The Haunted Reading Room

**Other titles by Leo Darke**


*Lucifer Sam*

# PANDEMONIUM

**Book One in the *101 Ways to Hell* Series**

Leo Darke

A
Grinning Skull Press
Publication
PO Box 67, Bridgewater, MA 02324

# DEDICATION

To Mum and Dad. I'll see you both again some day. Much love.

# CONTENTS

# Part One

# The Guide Book

# Chapter One
# I Hate Pink Floyd t-Shirt

Billy was listening to an album of Pink Floyd cover tracks when the aggressive thumping at the door roused him from his chair.

He'd nicked the CD off the cover of the latest edition of *Mojo;* or rather, it had eased itself away from its meager gum fastenings and into his hand. Practically fell off. Listening to it now, to the various bands' interpretations of "Wish you Were Here" on this Tuesday in mid-April, he was reminded of two things: how much he loved the original tracks, and a t-shirt once worn by Johnny Rotten. He forgot all about these conflicting lines of thought when the ferocious banging on the door made him move to the laced net curtain to peep out. Another random thought occurred to him as he did so, about being caught "peeping," this one courtesy of material from Mickey Flanagan, the cockney stand-up comedian—because the lace didn't completely cover the left-hand corner of the lounge window and the "peepee" could see Billy peeping from his position outside the front door.

The sense of calm created by the music, vanished. He knew this visit must have something to do with Aura before he even reached the window and saw the thug standing there.

The man was in his early forties, stocky, wearing a scruffy, brown hoody and dirty jeans. His face was brutal and slightly deformed in a way that was difficult to pinpoint; there was something about the cast of the features that didn't sit quite right. And as he glared at Billy through the pane of glass, his expression certainly didn't hint that he was calling round to check the meter. The man jerked his head toward the door. *Open it, you fucker.*

If the man had something to tell him about Aura, then Billy wanted to hear it, despite his feeling that the man wasn't bearing good news. As he stepped into the short hall to open the door, he wondered if he'd pushed it just a little too far with her. As soon as he opened the door, he knew he had.

The man's dark hair was tousled and messy. It looked like he had a blotch of moss growing on one cheek, but it was probably paint, as he looked like a painter and decorator, albeit one potentially born in Innsmouth… His slightly askew eyes were menacing and dark.

"You Billy?" The voice was guttural, and a thick country accent dragged at the words.

Billy nodded, a clench of unease right in the middle of his gut. The Pink Floyd tribute album was still playing (a band he'd never heard of called Beak had reached "Welcome to the Machine").

The thug cleared his throat. "I'll tell ya this once. Don't try to contact Aura no more. No calls, no messages, nothin'." He ticked off the instructions on his fingers as he spoke.

Billy stood there in his socks and an insubstantial Judas Sinned t-shirt and bristled. "I just want to know she's all right," he protested. He sounded like a stalker, even to himself now, though he knew it wasn't like that.

The thug took a step closer. "I'll say it again: you keep away. You don't try to find her, you don't try to contact her."

He wasn't going to get any info out of this oaf. Billy's anger overcame his desperation to know more. "Who the fuck are you coming to my house and threatening me?"

The thug moved with terrific speed. He actually growled in fury as he lunged at Billy with demented eyes. The shock of the charge took Billy completely by surprise. He was bowled over and landed on his back in his own hallway while the thug slammed a big army boot down on his chest, effectively pinning him there. The man had wigged out big time. He tried to rain punches down on Billy's face and would have caused some real damage were it not for the narrowness of the hall impeding his blows. Unfortunately, the close walls prevented Billy from rolling away to either side, too, trapping him on his back beneath the boot that was now grinding viciously into his chest. He managed to deflect the majority of punches with his own hands, which just infuriated the thug even more.

The man was grunting and cursing as he gave in to his inexplicable hatred. "You cunt, you *cunt*!" he spat repeatedly as he stomped and punched. Billy strove unsuccessfully to push upward against the weight, "Shine on You Crazy Diamond" playing now through the open door to the lounge. Maybe the thug, like Rotten before him, hated Pink Floyd, too. Maybe Billy should have been playing the Cockney Rejects instead. At least he would have been in the mood for a scrap. As it was, he was only conscious of three things now: what in the name of hell the neighbors would be making of all this and what state his designer t-shirt would be in after the unprecedented wear and tear. The third consideration bothered him the most however: for Aura to send this animal around to warn him off (and there didn't seem to be any other explanation than that she'd sent him), he must have seriously pissed her off. There could be no going back after this. And that hurt more than anything this psychotic ape could do to him, and it also drained any desire to fight back. His anger and inability to accept the abruptness of her distancing herself from him had resulted in this. The flurry of unanswered calls he'd made to her mobile number certainly could be construed as unreasonable—and desperate. Nobody liked desperate. Billy had never before done desperate. This is what it tasted like. This was the fruit it bore. Billy was ashamed: this was conclusive proof that he'd blown it for good. She obviously never wanted to see him again.

"Get the fuck off me!" Billy managed to gasp as the boot continued to bear down on him, cutting off his breath. Then, a little more lamely: "The neighbors will have called the cops by now!"

The thug didn't respond to either utterance. His fists continued to try to mar Billy's unremarkable good looks, but the close walls continued to hamper him from getting a proper swing. Billy grasped the man's boot and tried to twist it off his chest, but his position gave him no leverage. "You *fucking* cunt!" the thug elaborated on his previous litany, and then suddenly lifted his boot and turned to go.

Billy pushed himself up on one elbow, stunned by the whole unpleasant, albeit surreal, experience. The man was about to step out of the house, his back to Billy. Billy jumped to his feet, adrenaline coursing through him, and shoved the man from behind, propelling him through the doorway. "Get the fuck out of my house!" he yelled this time. It was the thug's turn to be caught by surprise, and he stumbled over the doormat, allowing Billy to slam the door after him.

He stood there panting for a minute, trying to understand everything that had just happened. He jumped as a terrific crash jarred the wooden door in its jamb. That heavy boot had been put to good purpose again. Billy tensed, waiting to see if his assailant would repeat the kick, but there was silence from outside.

His thoughts were manic quicksilver crazy. He had not been prepared for a fight. He was in his socks, for God's sake! And Pink Floyd was not the most aggressive of soundtracks. He certainly didn't feel inspired to chase out after the man. But he knew he had to.

He darted toward the closet, searching for his All Saints mock army boots. He shouldered his way into a leather jacket for added measure, finished doing up the laces, and made for the door again, collecting a poker from the fireplace as he went. Surely the bastard would have disappeared by now, he hoped (and was that why he had taken so long to do up his boot laces? Was he actually just a coward who didn't deserve Aura in the first place?) and yet simultaneously didn't hope. With the thug gone, his last connection with Aura would be gone, too.

When he opened the door, there was no sign of the malevolent visitor outside on the street. But Billy could see his next-door neighbors approaching along the pavement. So they had missed the entire show then. That was something, he supposed. He really didn't want to have to explain why he was brawling with a stranger in his own doorway. The neighbors on the other side of Billy's terraced house were always out during the day, so that didn't matter.

He crossed the street to avoid the approaching neighbors, conscious of the poker clutched in his fist. He marched quickly to the side street on the right, wondering if the thug had nipped down there, but apart from the back of an old pick-up truck disappearing round the corner at the end, there was no sign of anybody.

He hesitated, realized his breath was pent up after the fury of the attack, and released it. He honestly felt more disappointed than relieved. Aura was gone. He'd lost her forever. All the phone calls to her voice mail over the last two weeks, the messages he'd left—his concern and agitation increasing with each one, until the dreaded "desperate" kicked in when she hadn't replied to any of them—had left him here, on this street corner with no answers, an aching chest where a size ten boot had ground, a bruise on his chin from the constant flailing fists, and a poker in his hand. What a hero.

He turned and made his way back to his house. The tumult of emotions the violent visitor had unleashed was beginning to ebb. The shock fading, replaced by despair. That was it then. Should he hate her for sending this (speed-fueled?) slightly deformed crazy to his house? Could he hate her? *Did he even know her?* The answer to that had to be no. He had no idea where she lived or any detail about her past whatsoever. The last time he'd seen her, two weeks ago in the elegant grounds of Tortworth Court, she had run away inexplicably. But if this attack proved one thing, it was that she had appalling taste in acquaintances. He remembered that afternoon, dusk creeping over the mansion house and the ornate gardens…and recalled what else he'd seen there among the gathering shadows of the trees. He remembered his unease, too. *No, it had been real FEAR, not unease; don't hide from the truth, sunshine.* He had been distinctly scared. And now this: violence and strangeness seemed to follow Aura around. Perhaps he was better off rid of her after all.

If only it was that easy, he told himself as he withdrew the keys to his house. If forgetting could only be that easy… His neighbors were letting themselves in next door. He nodded politely, his attention distracted by the dirty boot print on the white door. Was that to be Aura's legacy? Was that all he had to remind him of her charms? That, and the whistle of course… He could hear it now, as he closed the door behind him, and his overworked heart kicked into overdrive for the second time that day. The CD had run its course, and the house was otherwise silent, apart from the tuneless warbling. It was faint today. Sometimes it seemed to be coming from right behind him, loud and sharp, and, of course, there was never anybody there when he turned around. He froze in the hallway, the same hallway where ten minutes earlier he'd been sprawled on his back defending himself from a manic assailant, and listened to the indistinct whistle. It was always the same three notes, protracted, eerie, relentless. Right now it was trembling on the edge of inaudibility, wistful as a half-remembered dream, fading, fading… gone. He breathed again, the tension that seized him each time he heard the whistle easing away. There had been far worse times. He could handle it in the daytime. It was a very different matter when he heard it alone at night…

This was Aura's other legacy, of course. The one that had followed him since he had first met her, and which was beginning to drive him mad. The jury was still out whether the whistle was all in his head, just like the budding relationship with Aura seemed to have been.

He sat in his armchair and wondered where it had all gone wrong.

# Chapter Two
# Not the AA Guide Book to
# 101 Best British Walks

She was standing in the travel section, looking at a guide book to British Walks.

Billy had never seen her or the book before, and his attention was aroused immediately. Not by the book—he worked in a bookshop all day every day for God's sake and was surrounded by the buggers—but by the beautiful creature holding it.

She was slender as a water nymph, tall, maybe five-eight. Long, sleek legs in tight blue jeans and knee-length fawn boots. Her poncho was fawn, too, swaddled around her slight figure as if she was really feeling the late March chill. Her long, blonde hair fell in waves around her elfin face. She felt his gaze on her even from ten meters away and looked up.

Billy felt a shock vibration jolt him, as if he'd just stumbled into a live cattle wire. Her eyes held his for a moment, kaleidoscope-blue flecked with a mosaic of gray. The gaze was lost and wild, and even in that first moment of meeting, he saw the conflict there, an excitement mixed with sadness. She smiled shyly at him, dropped her gaze back to the book. Billy was already moving, stepping briskly toward her, no idea what he was going to say, just more convinced than he'd ever been about anything in his life before that he had to go and say *something*.

He paused at a loaded trolley that was next to her, waiting for the travel bookseller to shelve its contents. She looked up again and flashed that winsome smile, and Billy could see that her teeth were white and slightly sharp, although the side molars were slightly (ever so *slightly*) uneven. Now that he was close to her, he could see that her nose was a trifle prominent, too, though not unattractively so. It was shaped in a seductive curve rather than being oversized. And anyway, what was it they said about imperfection? It accentuated the beauty of everything else or some such bollocks. But it did in her case. It really did. And she was, startlingly, self-consciously beautiful.

Billy rested both hands on the edge of the trolley, trying to affect a nonchalant air. Now that he was here, he was a fish gulping on a beach. Stranded by foolishness, totally out of his comfort zone. Her electric eyes didn't waver, scrutinizing him…measuring him. But for what? But it was more than that, too. There was a quality to those eyes that stirred more than obvious attraction in him, teasing away at something beneath the surface of his memory that had been long buried. He could see the same suggestion of recognition in her gaze, too. But that was ridiculous. He'd never seen her before in his life.

"Hello," he said after the silence began to become unnatural, even if, for some reason, not awkward.

She smiled again in answer, her cheeks showing the slightest hint of a blush.

He wrenched his gaze away from hers and looked down at the hardback book in her hands instead. It looked old and battered, and he guessed it must have been in the shop a long time to be in such a well-used state. Her right hand obscured part of the title, but he could make out most of it: *The Olde British Guide to 101 Walkes through…* The rest was hidden. Were the extra E's a sign of when it had been written or just a postmodern affectation, he wondered. The book was fat, the dust jacket tattered, and she was holding it open at Walk No. 21, he noticed.

"Walk 21… Where does that take you?" he asked, and immediately felt foolish. It was his turn to blush.

Again the long, measuring gaze before she answered. And when she did, her voice was quiet and soft, with the slightest tremor of a West Country burr. "I expect it will take you exactly where you need it to."

He laughed. What kind of answer was that? Was she a little touched? Instead of deterring him, however, this hint of eccentricity only intrigued him more.

"And what does that mean?"

"It means whatever you want it to."

*Ooookayyyy.* He grunted in amusement. "Enigmatic, eh?"

She tilted her head coquettishly. "Me, or the book?"

Where the hell did he go from here? Everything she said seemed to pull the rug from under his feet. He realized a female member of the staff was watching them chat from the till by the door, but he refused to acknowledge her. *Julie, damn her.* Always watching him, flirting blatantly and sometimes inappropriately, and while normally he received her attentions gracefully but with no real interest, right now he really didn't want her interfering. In an effort to make it look as though he was helping a customer and not trying it on with an attractive female, he reached for the book as if to offer the blonde girl some advice.

"May I?" he said.

She handed it over readily enough without a word, and he glanced at the page she'd been studying.

## WALK NO. 21. DEEPEST, DARKEST SOMERSET

Beneath the title there was a paragraph of text written in old-fashioned English, followed by a sketchy map of a circular walk, and beneath that, a step-by-step guide on how to follow the route.

"Interesting, isn't it?"

He looked up. She stepped around the trolley to peer over his shoulder at the book, and he breathed in her scent. A faint aroma of blossom clung to her. It stirred his senses, quickened his pulse, and again, there was a vague memory associated with it that was just out of reach.

She took the book from him, closed it, and looked up earnestly. "It's very old. How wonderful to find such a book in a shiny, new shop like this."

He was still trying to catch a glimpse of the rest of the title, but again, those beautiful, slender fingers were obscuring it.

For lack of anything better to say he mumbled, "It *is* very old. Obviously been thumbed through a lot. Looks more like an old library book than something we would stock. I shall have to order in some newer copies." As conversational gambits went, this one was pretty dull, so he pushed on with: "Do you walk in Somerset a lot then?" It was better than "Do you come here often?" but only marginally.

"Oh, yes. I spend all my time in deepest Somerset."

He felt another thrill at the delightful accent that furred her words. He suddenly longed to hold her, to breath that May blossom aroma in deep, and nuzzle the long, pale neck. She was so close he could snatch her in his arms right now and not care about what anyone thought. Not even Julie, who, he noticed, was still watching them, a look of intense irritation on her face.

"Maybe I'll take a walk there myself," he said.

Her smile dropped, and she stared at him earnestly. There was confusion in her eyes now. She pursed her lips. "Yes," she said hesitantly. Her gaze fell for a second. "Maybe you should."

"Maybe even Walk number 21," he added.

Her eyes locked on his again. There was no trace of playfulness now. She looked deadly serious. She said nothing but held his gaze until he looked away, puzzled by her intensity. Over the blonde's shoulder, he could see Julie moving around from behind the till, her attention still fixed on him and the girl, her expression dark. Over in the Sports section, Jerry was watching them, too, a cynical sneer on his face as he paused in his shelving task. The blonde was oblivious to the reaction she was causing amongst Billy's colleagues, however. She stepped away from Billy and over to the tall stack of Travel books. She popped the book into a vacant slot in the British Isles section (next to an *AA Guide to Country Walks*, he noticed) and turned to face Billy again. The smile was back, shy, tentative.

Julie Everly was watching Billy alright. Oh yes. The *fucker!*

Didn't take much to distract him, did it? Blonde hair, good legs, and blue eyes. In fact, everything Julie *herself* had. What was so special about this tart, she wondered as she moved out from behind the till, ignoring the old lady who was approaching with a book to purchase. She stepped closer to find out exactly how much flirting was going on. The bastard usually saved it for Julie, even if (being *brutally* honest with herself) she knew deep down he wasn't that interested. Didn't stop him from responding to her insinuations and obvious desire for him, though, did it? He'd given her enough signals that one day he might give in and take her out. Julie had persuaded herself that the only reason he'd deferred 'til now was because she had a boyfriend. But hadn't she made it clear what a waste of time and space this particular boyfriend was? She'd certainly told Billy enough times, for God's sake. How he never paid her attention, never took her anywhere, never treated her. Just came home from work and watched sports on the TV. What kind of relationship was that? Julie wanted more. She sensed that in Billy there was real potential boyfriend material. Billy wouldn't settle for watching the soaps and maybe once in a blue moon (or even once a fortnight, if she was lucky) slipping her a quick one before falling asleep, as if the act had bored him into unconsciousness.

She saw him break off his flirting with the "special" customer as he became aware Julie was watching him, and she marched quickly over to where Jerry, the tall, skinny Scouse was making a poor imitation of a bookseller shelving stock.

"Look at him," she hissed. "Bastard hasn't done any work since she walked in."

Jerry smirked. "Don't blame him. She's a belter."

Julie glared at him. "What's so special about her?!"

"Let me see..." Jerry paused dramatically. "Sophisticated, slim, great legs, long, blonde hair—"

"*I've* got long, blonde hair!"

"—pretty."

Julie gaped at him. That hurt. "You wanker!"

"That I am," Jerry agreed cheerfully, a wicked grin on his face. "And proud of it. But to be honest..." he trailed off as he studied Billy from across the shop. "I don't know why you're so into him. He's not exactly Josh Hartnett." Indeed, he wasn't. Billy was in his late thirties, tall enough, slim enough without being skinny (unlike himself, Jerry thought ruefully), and his face was pleasant and reasonably good looking, and yes, he still had his hair (unlike himself, Jerry thought even more ruefully.) But really, he wasn't all *that*. "Face it Julie," the Scouse continued cruelly, "he ain't interested."

"Fuck *you*!"

"No, thanks. We already did that, remember?"

"You really are a twat, aren't you?"

He smiled smugly at her. "I think you've got a customer."

She turned to see the old lady waiting patiently at the till. She sighed and stormed over to serve her.

Billy stared at the mysterious blonde. He didn't know what else to do or say. He couldn't move, couldn't think of anything beyond this beautiful girl who seemed to trigger so many impulses inside him, some of them completely inexplicable.

"What's your name?" he said simply. His attempts at flirtation were gone. He was serious now, as serious as she had been a moment ago when he mentioned the Walk. He *needed* to know.

"Aura," she said, and then she was gone.

It wouldn't be the first time she would walk out on him, and he would soon become familiar with her disappearances. That is, until the final, most devastating one of all. But right now, it felt like the sun had died in his world. He watched her leave the shop, walking past Julie without looking back, and everything in this corporate bookstore suddenly seemed meaningless and mundane.

She was gone, and Julie was heading for him instead. What kind of poor substitute was that? Then, ashamed of his lack of charity, he summoned a smile for his colleague. To his surprise, she turned her head away, blanking him, and strode purposefully away across the shop. Going to report him to the manager for flirting with pretty customers maybe? *Jealous mare.*

Billy sighed, and then he remembered the book. He crossed over to the shelf where Aura (and wasn't that a great name?) had replaced it. For a moment, he couldn't find it. There was the *AA Guide to Country Walks*, but next to it was a book on farming. Maybe he hadn't watched carefully enough when she put it back. He stepped back and scanned the rows of books. All sorts of walking guides—circular paths around Bath, around Bristol, even around Portishead, but none dedicated to Somerset. And they were all paperbacks, too. Not a hardback in sight.

He scratched his head. Weird.

Slightly confused, he turned away from the Travel section, ready for his lunch break.

It was as he was crossing the shop that he heard the whistle for the first time. It was faint, almost submerged under the classical music playing over the shop's speaker system, and he didn't think too much about it. It was probably some old fool whistling out in the central hub of the Galleries, the shopping mall complex the bookshop belonged to. So he promptly forgot all about it and hurried over to the staff room door before any customers could stop him with a request.

An hour later, as he let himself back out onto the shop floor, his stomach full of tomato soup and cheese sandwiches, he heard it again. A little louder this time.

He searched around for whoever could be producing it. The shop floor was fairly busy with Friday afternoon shoppers, but he couldn't see anyone whistling.

The flat, tuneless warble seemed to be coming from over by the Erotica alcove, where the dirty old men hid to read the pornographic photography books (Frank, the portly security guard attached to the shop had caught a middle-aged man actually pleasuring himself there once; it was no wonder the female staff were calling for the section to be moved to a more conspicuous location), but when Billy leaned over the balcony on the raised section overlooking the alcove, there was nobody there.

A little disconcerted, Billy put it to the back of his mind and headed for the Travel section again, thoughts of Aura more appealing than those of a bodiless whistle. He was determined to find the book now that lunch was out of the way, and this time, it didn't take him very long to track it down.

The classical music pumping around the shop came to a stop as the CD was changed, and in the sudden silence, the whistle was clearer, louder. It seemed to be coming from all around him, the three protracted notes changing interminably. Probably an electrical fault with the speakers, he decided and focused his attention on the book, the spine of which he could now see clearly—right next to the *AA Guide to Country Walks*, where it should be. He pulled it out carefully and glanced at the cover. It bore the illustration of a path meandering through typical English countryside, the meadows and hills simply sketched. But it was the title that riveted him. The piping whistle swelled in his ears as he read it:

THE OLDE BRITISHE GUIDE TO 101 WALKES
THROUGH…

And if he'd expected the location to be Somerset, he was in for a surprise. For some reason (maybe it was the creepy whistling), the word that was no longer concealed by Aura's slender fingers chilled him right down to the marrow. It was probably a publisher's whacky attempt at humor, maybe referring to the difficulties experienced by ramblers finding the right paths through overgrown terrains. Probably. Maybe. But (and he couldn't, for the life of him, explain why) he didn't think so.

The word Aura had hidden was HELL.

# INTERLUDE ONE

# ROMAN BRITON, 364 AD

"Enough of your complaints! We have a job to do, so let's do it before this squad is whittled away even more by Celtic demons."

The squad of battered and filthy legionaries regarded their centurion with distaste that bordered on rebellion. If it hadn't been for the fact they were stuck in this heathen island of dark forests filled with creeping, savage Britons and no way of returning to their homeland, they would have long ago gutted their leader with his own *gladius*.

The squad originally consisted of ten legionaries. The troop's original leader, the *Decanus* with whom they had exercised and drilled, not to mention shared every night in their squad tent for the last eighteen months, had been replaced for this mission by a more experienced centurion, and they were missing their erstwhile commander with each hour they had to spend in this new bastard's company. He wasn't a bad man, and that was his problem; he was far *too* dedicated. He obviously believed in this crazy suicide mission, probably because he had one eye on promotion. They'd already lost three men in sneak attacks, and while that wasn't the centurion's fault, it was clear to everyone but him that this mission was doomed to failure.

They glared up at him now as they sat on the damp grass and rocks of the small clearing, shivering from the cold and the gloom and the incipient threats of attack from the depths of the forest.

Laccus Sciro, a stocky, swarthy legionary with a foul temper and a cruel sense of humor, regarded the tall centurion with barely guarded contempt. Of course, this quill pusher of a centurion hadn't allowed them to light a fire. Their old *Decanus* would have. He would have brought an amphora of good Roman wine along for the trip, too. Which was probably why the poor bastard had been replaced with this Ceasar's arse-licking fucker instead.

Sciro turned to the soldier beside him, ignoring the centurion. "A real fucking mess," he muttered darkly, not quite loudly enough for the officer to hear. "This bastard's leading us to certain death. We just going to take it?"

His friend, Antoni Martus, shrugged, glancing at their leader hostilely. He was lithe, with sneaky features and a prominent nose. He spat in the grass without answering.

"What was that, Sciro?"

The centurion stepped toward the bulky legionary, one hand on the hilt of his sword. His face was set and hard. He would not take *any* more bullshit from this pack of lazy scum.

Sciro glowered up at his leader. "Nothin'."

The centurion stiffened. This was just another example of their disrespectful attitude toward authority. If they were back in camp and a common infantryman had addressed his officer in such a manner, he would have been cleaning the barracks for three months. Why the hell had they given him this bunch of insolent, not to mention indolent, gamblers and whoremongers to do such an important job? It was almost as if the *Pilus Prior* who had delegated them for this mission had known it was doomed to failure and didn't want to waste his best men. But what did that say about the centurion? He believed in this job even if nobody else did, and he was going to do his damnedest to prove the *Pilus* wrong and complete the mission as planned.

He kept his hand meaningfully on the sword hilt. There was a long silence while the two Romans glared at each other.

Eventually, Sciro lowered his eyes. "Nothing… *sir.*"

"Then get on your feet. Now!"

The seven legionaries climbed up slowly and reluctantly, their bodies tired and aching from the long march through this hellish forest and the incessant cold and rain.

Sciro was last up. He withdrew his sword from its scabbard as if to check it was clean and dry. His eyes met the centurion's as he did so, and they locked gazes for another handful of seconds. The officer's hand was still on the hilt of his own weapon. The other soldiers fell silent, watching the conflict of wills eagerly, wondering who would make the first move.

Sciro grinned wolfishly and then slowly, so slowly, sheathed his sword in its scabbard. He scratched at the two days' worth of stubble on his jowls and watched as the officer nodded abruptly, then turned away to continue the march.

He led them on through the dripping trees. Mostly oak and ash, thick boughs and trunks making the darkness of night that much darker, more threatening. Painted Celts could be lurking behind every bole, waiting to skewer them with their primitive javelins and swords.

Sciro, last in line, was no longer grinning as he glanced furtively around him at the impenetrable gloom. He hated Briton. Hated it with a passion. No wonder the indigenous people were so wild and barbaric, so utterly savage. They lived out their brutal existence squatting in mud huts and praying to dark Gods while Sciro's countrymen back home erected magnificent palaces, temples, and cities that were glorious testimonies to their advanced civilization. What did these pigs have that could rival those achievements? He gritted his teeth. Megalithic monuments and arcane stone circles. It was pathetic, and it stirred a deep hatred in his soul. If it hadn't been for the stubborn refusal to accept Roman civilization into their lives—to accept *sophistication*, for fuck's sake—he could have been deployed back to Rome years ago. Back to the warmth, the wine, the food, the women of Rome.

He thought of the women here. Mud streaked, clad in filthy, stinking furs, their hair crawling with lice, their teeth snaggled (if they had any), their bodies gristly and sharp-boned. It was no wonder some of the legionaries turned to each other for sexual comforts. Not that Sciro would ever stoop to *that*, of course. He would wait until he got back to Rome, and then he would spend all his *sestertii* on the elegant ladies of the most beautiful city in the world.

But right now he was squelching through mud, with a biting wind penetrating his tunic, his head aching from lack of sleep, his balls itching from wet leggings, and wishing the centurion would trip in the dark and fall down one of the various clefts and gullies that riddled this endless forest. Now *that* was an idea…

Ahead of him, the puny form of Aurelius Piccano halted momentarily to adjust his sandals, causing Sciro to walk into him. *Clumsy fuck!*

Sciro was tempted to push him over in the mud as the smaller soldier knelt to refasten his buckles, but he resisted the urge. He shouldn't waste his aggression on his friends… He patted the legionary on his head as he passed him. "You can pull rear duties now, Piccano, you useless prick," he said in what, for him, was an amiable tone.

Piccano straightened swiftly, blanching at the idea. "The centurion picked you, Sciro," he argued petulantly, his small, round face puckered up with anxiety.

"Fuck you, and fuck *him*," Sciro replied, walking on and leaving the smaller man to look nervously around and (especially) behind him.

At the front of the troop, the officer had heard the mutter of voices and glanced back to see what was causing the commotion. Hadn't he told them enough times to keep silent while they were on the march? Their enemies were all around them. These really were the most clueless cowherds he'd ever seen. He certainly wouldn't dream of calling them soldiers. He halted the file of legionaries momentarily with a raised hand, making sure the disturbance at the back was finished before beckoning them forward once more. Sciro, of course. Always Sciro. The way he'd played with his sword, openly mocking his officer—openly threatening him. The centurion half expected to wake from one of their infrequent rest breaks to find the evil bastard squatting over him with that sword blade resting against his neck.

As far as missions were concerned, this one really *was* going all the way…

…to Hell.

# Chapter Three
# Closing Time

It was closing time, and Billy was glad of that. The last customer was ushered out by the portly Frank, and as usual, the "loss prevention officer" (hey, Frank, fancy title for a security guard) nipped off sharpish, leaving three members of staff to close everything down.

Those three members consisted of Billy, a stout, former football hooligan turned philosophical bookseller named James, and the truculent Julie.

Billy wished he could have locked up on his own. At this time of the evening, he just wanted to get the hell out, not have to put up with Julie's weirdness or James's constant chatter. But tonight there was another reason he wanted a bit of privacy. He'd been thinking all day about the book Aura had been reading. He'd been too busy serving a flurry of Friday afternoon customers all eager to snag a good book for the weekend to get around to checking it out properly until now. He could see James up on the raised area where all the Mind, Body, and Spirit bullshit was, tidying up the mayhem customers had left it in. He couldn't spot Julie anywhere, thankfully.

He crossed to the Travel section, half expecting not to be able to find it again like earlier, or heaven forbid, discovering it had actually been sold. But no, there it was, in plain sight, wedged next to the AA guide book. He was pulling it from the shelf when Julie appeared from the customer orders office and, spotting Billy, immediately made a bee-line in his direction.

Billy groaned to himself but looked up with a forced smile.

It wasn't that he disliked her. How could he dislike someone who so obviously thought he was wonderful, even if he couldn't, for the life of him, work out why she felt that way. She was only 25 after all, and Billy was 38. There was a world of difference between them in terms of tastes, interests, and general character that could not be put down solely to the age gap. Her constant attentions toward him were kind of flattering, but they were, at times, a bit cloying, too. And she was very persistent. Like right now.

She glanced at the book in his hand, and irritation creased her freckled brow. She obviously remembered who had been looking at it earlier. Julie was pretty enough, Billy couldn't deny, in an anodyne, underfed, prickly kind of way. Her blonde hair was thin and a little lank despite the curler she obviously used to energize it. Her eyes were faded blue, sharp as a seagull's, as was her pointed nose. He wasn't really attracted to her—or maybe only slightly (he'd once almost kissed her at a colleague's leaving do, but that was after a fair few pints). If he might have relented before, however, the arrival of the ethereally beautiful Aura into his life had really put paid to any chances of anything happening between Julie and Billy now. She looked like a faded black-and-white photograph next to Aura's Technicolor glory.

"What's so interesting about that bloody book?" she asked him, unable to disguise the note of petulance in her voice.

He shrugged, feeling caught out and a little cornered. He wished she would leave him alone. He felt a needling compulsion to investigate the book and whatever secrets it might hold.

She scanned the title and laughed mirthlessly. "Walks through Hell, huh? Sounds like a pleasant way to spend a Sunday afternoon. You planning to take your new friend for a stroll?"

He ignored the sarcasm, then indulged in some of his own before he could stop himself. "It's six-thirty, Julie. Your boyfriend will be expecting you."

Annoyance flared up in her pixie face. The end of her pointed nose crinkled. "You trying to get rid of me?" Then she added her own spin to his words, a spin that appealed to her, however far-fetched it might be. Her expression brightened. "You're jealous, aren't you?" She reached out a bony hand and touched his bare arm (he was wearing a standard branded corporate t-shirt emblazoned with the name of the bookshop franchise). When he didn't flinch, she took that as encouragement and stroked his skin in what she guessed was an erotic fashion.

"There's no need to be, you know," she said, lowering her voice huskily.

Billy detected the note of passion in it, and despite himself, he felt a little aroused. God, he was a man after all! Yet he gently pulled away and glanced at his watch demonstratively. His urge to check the book out properly was stronger than any lust Julie might stir in him, especially now that Aura had arrived on the scene.

"Time to close this baby up," he said jovially. He could hear James thumping down the stairs from the raised area. Julie heard him, too, and that spurred her on.

"You know there's someone in this shop I really like, don't you?"

Billy felt trapped. "Julie," he began, but she put her hand on his chest to stop him.

"Listen to me. There's someone who makes me feel more alive than I've ever felt before. Every time I hear him speak, I want to kiss him. When he's serving on the till and calls for the next customer, he always shouts out the same thing and..."

He almost laughed. "What thing?"

She smiled, and her hand moved down his chest a little, a subtle caress. "He calls out, 'Yes, please,' and..." She chuckled and flushed. Her cheeks looked like freckled bacon for a second. "And I go all weak at the knees..."

"Weak at the knees, eh?" James popped his head around the tall shelves of the Travel section and smiled broadly, his round, frameless spectacles reflecting the fluorescents above. "Who's causing that? Not Billy the Kid again, is it? When are you gonna make an honest woman of her, Bill?"

"For fuck's sake, James! Haven't you got a home to go to?"

"Too right. As soon as you two love birds have finished flirting, of course. Don't let me stop you though."

"Nothing for you to peep at here," Billy told him.

"James, you're a prick," Julie snapped angrily.

James beamed. "Is that any way to refer to your Assistant Manager?"

Julie shook her head in irritation and walked off toward the staff room.

Billy cleared his throat. "You might as well clear off, too, James. I just wanted to sort one more thing out and I'll follow on."

James glanced at him curiously. "What you up to? Not like you to linger after time."

Billy averted his gaze. "Just something I forgot to do earlier. You don't want to miss the start of the England game do you? Just leave me the keys. Won't be long." Billy knew exactly what buttons to push to decide it for James. He handed the shop keys over and turned to leave. "Cash drawers are all in the safe. And don't forget to check Goods In, for fuck's sake. You know what happened last week." Last week involved a rather daring but ridiculous plan by a rival bookshop owner (although, in this case, it was a stall on St. Nick's Market) who decided it would be a brilliant idea to hide in the parcel unpacking room until after the shop had been shut and then help himself to a sack load of free books. It wasn't so much that he forgot about the alarm as he was convinced he could get away quickly enough with his booty before anyone responded to it. If it had been left up to Frank, the shop's corpulent security guard, then he would have been right. However, he forgot one essential thing—the shop was part of the Galleries Mall shopping center. Every alarm alerted the 24-hour security staff for the whole complex, and they hadn't eaten as many pies as Frank over the years.

"I'm heading there now," Billy told James, and he walked across the shop, still clutching the guide book. He was aware of a curious niggling in his mind, almost like an urge for a fix, like a junkie wanting to be alone so he could find a vein. A silly analogy, he told himself, but the sense of compulsion stayed with him as he hurried to Goods In. He was just pushing through the double doors into the unpacking room when he caught sight of Julie out of the corner of his eye. She had her coat on and a grim expression and was heading for the main doors. He breathed out, and then the doors swung closed behind him and he was alone in the shop.

James had already killed the canned music, so the shop was eerily silent. Billy crossed to one of the PCs on the long desk and placed the book next to it, intending to check out the ISBN and gain a little more information about the Guide. He nudged the "stock analysis" key on the board and turned to pick up the book again. He frowned, scanning the back, then flipped open the inside cover. He flicked through to the publication info page, his frown deepening.

No ISBN. That was unusual. But not unprecedented. No barcode either. Just how bloody old was this book? It looked like one of the old books he used to take out from his local library back in the early eighties. He remembered a copy of the *Everyman Frankenstein* that had looked every bit as battered as this.

Even the pages were yellowed, for God's sake. But then maybe that was the intention, the faux antique-look marketing to match the kitsch title, which he could only assume was a postmodern attempt at humor.

Except this book looked anything but postmodern. And absolutely nothing about it hinted at any intentions toward humor on the part of whoever had compiled it. He examined the publication page more carefully. Published by Hobbemarke House, Somerset. The publication history was a real eye-opener: *first edition published 1610, derived from older texts.*

For the second time since he had found the book, a coldness spread inside him. He actually looked over his shoulder, something he hadn't done in many years. The Goods In room suddenly seemed larger than normal, with too many corners not illuminated by the one small fluorescent. Stacks of empty cardboard boxes and metal racks of books were obscured by gloom at the furthest end near the fire door.

He turned back to the PC and pulled up the book search page. He keyed in the title of the book and waited while the slow machine worked its wonders. Or didn't, in this case. There was no mention of *The Olde Britishe Guide to 101 Walkes through Hell* ...

He refused to be beaten. He *needed* to know about this book for some reason. He checked the cover for the editor. Of course, there wasn't one listed, not on the flyleaf or title page either. He keyed in Hobbemarke House and came up with a similar blank.

He returned his attention to the book, and flipping through it again, a brief preface caught his eye:

> *The Wayes marked in this Booke Are not for*
> *All, though all those who touch it must follow them.*
> *Those who tread them would do well to tread them wisely.*
> *Trust unto the markers, though they may alter...*
> *For the Pathes may change for those who walke them.*
> *Lest ye not enter a wilderness of the mind, tread softly, tread with care.*
> *Man is lost... May you each find your Waye.*

The light flickered and then went out.

He was plunged into complete blackness. And silence. Even the hum of the computer had been cut off. He could hear his own breathing, though, and it sounded way too loud.

"Fuck," he said to break the quiet and bolster his nerves. Then something else disturbed the silence. Faint at first, then growing in volume, as if whoever was whistling was approaching the Goods In room from across the darkened shop.

Three notes in a descending key, long and trembling, pausing as the whistler took in a breath, then resuming, becoming clearer. Billy could hear the tuneless drone right outside the doors now. He stepped away from the desk, groping toward the wall beside the doors, intending to find the switches that operated the shop's lighting system, realizing as he did so that even if he managed to find them in the dark, they would not respond. He stumbled over a box of half-unpacked books left in the center of the floor and fell to one knee. His gasp of breath was loud in the sudden silence. The whistling had stopped. He strained his ears, remaining in a kneeling position, but all he could hear was the tinnitus in his left ear and the thumping of his heart.

Then the whistle started up again from just behind his right ear, as if whoever was responsible was leaning over him in the dark. Billy cried out and lurched to his feet, heading for where he hoped the double doors were located. The whistle followed him, *reached for him....* Billy's shoes clattered over the concrete Goods In flooring, but he heard no other footfalls pursuing.

He burst through the doors, and the haunting whistle was with him, just over his shoulder. It stayed with him as he scampered through the pitch dark of the shop, colliding with tables, spilling the immaculately piled books onto the carpet. It stayed with him as he blundered into the Erotica alcove, completely clueless as to where he was going. He felt the tight cul-de-sac of books pressing around him, the whistle trapping him from behind. The three notes grew more urgent, more violent in tone.

Then they stopped. And Billy's tinnitus was again the loudest sound in the shop.

And the lights flicked on.

And everything was normal again.

Everything was *normal* again.

# Chapter Four
# Shoplifter

Billy didn't fancy going back to the shop the next day.

He'd lain awake all night, and for the first time since he was about 12, he had slept with the light on. He lay in bed and waited for his Batmobile alarm to go crazy, all shrieking brakes, wheels, and sirens, but in the end, he reached over to switch it off before it even activated.

He stood in the shower like a dead man, drooping, unresponsive. Breakfast was overdone toast as usual (one day, he really would remember to adjust the heat setting, but that wasn't going to be today). He drank his coffee without tasting it, his thoughts a confused and turgid mess. The events of the night before clouded his brain. He didn't want to think about the whistling, but it dominated his mind. What it was, what it meant, and why it should be persecuting him were questions he couldn't begin to answer.

And then there was the seemingly more mundane mystery of the book. For some reason, the Guide lurked in his consciousness, refusing to go away. If he tried to rationalize it, then it seemed his preoccupation with the volume was out of proportion. It was just a book. Who cared if there was no ISBN, barcode, or even evidence that it existed in the shop's computer records? Who cared if the title still unsettled him? It was just a title. The fact that the whistling had commenced around the same time he had first seen the book probably accounted for him giving it the undue attention he was. That, and the fact it reminded him of Aura.

Aura. The one thing that had gotten him out of bed this morning was the hope (and let's face it, it was pretty slender) that Aura might return to the shop. But why should she? Did he really think she would be so impressed by his corporate t-shirt and minimum wage that she'd come back for more?

Billy had scored a handful of girlfriends in the past. None of them had cared about him enough (or vice versa) to stay. He had gotten used to his solitary existence: just him, his library of superhero movies, and his pet piranha. The piranha was called Ferox (after a crazy Italian cannibal film he saw once at a mate's house), and it was the only thing that *had* stuck by him over the years, though the fish didn't have an awful lot of choice in the matter. Ferox had seemed like a good idea at the time—back when *Piranha 3D* was wowing folks at the cinemas. Now the "ferocious" fish just floated in a tank of dirty water that Billy really should change, looking morose. The two were a perfect match.

He left his house and walked down the road toward the city center. The Bristol traffic seemed louder than usual, every horn and siren filling his head to an almost painful degree. The constant rush of vehicles on Totterdown Bridge made him nauseous. When he finally reached the Galleries, he was almost grateful to enter the subdued atmosphere of the shop, even if the barely restrained aggressiveness of Frank's sneer was the first thing he saw.

"You look like shit," the security guard welcomed him.

"Thanks, Frank." *Go fuck yourself, you fat, lazy bastard.* This was one of those mornings when he was very close to vocalizing his internal commentaries. Dangerous. He punched in the entry code and entered the small staff room. Julie gave him a smile that he struggled to return. Sitting down was dangerous, too. Would he ever be able to get up again?

The manager, an irritatingly hyperactive knobhead from Exeter by the name of Tom, spotted him as he rinsed his mug under the tap. "Are you locking up tonight, Billy?"

He nodded. Bad mistake. The contents of his skull rattled emptily. He blinked up at the tall, sprightly manager with sleepless eyes.

"Well, in that case, please don't forget..." Tom began slowly and reasonably before unleashing the storm: "TO SWITCH THE FUCK-ING ALARM ON THIS TIME!"

Billy rubbed his eyes. Nodded again.

"Loser," Julie chided jokingly.

"Oh, and by the way," Tom continued, "you look like shit."

"Thanks," Billy mumbled, and got up to start his shift.


The first person he spotted on the shop floor was Cyril Peck, a well-known shoplifter and general pain in the arse. When he wasn't nicking the stock, he would be sidling up to the staff to discuss his other major passion: *Doctor Who*. There weren't many obsessive, shop-lifting Who fans around, so Cyril was generally tolerated as something of a curiosity piece. He had been barred from the shop at least twice, but with the management changing every six months or so, he always managed to slip his way back in—and slip his way back out again, usu-ally with a pricey tome tucked under his raincoat.

Billy groaned. He could *really* do without this today. But Peck had already spotted him and was eagerly waving a WH Smiths bag at him.

"The new monthly's just out," he said, spray flecking Billy's cheek as he showed the bookseller the cover of the new *DOCTOR WHO Mag-azine.* Cyril was in his late forties, thin as a whippet, with a perennially cheerful expression on his face. His graying hair was long, curly, and unwashed. His clothes were charity shop Best. He'd once worn a pair of cords from Age Concern for a week (he came in the shop most days) with the handwritten price tag still attached to the belt loophole. The rest of the staff thought it funny not to point it out, in the typically arrogant and self-superior fashion bordering on hostility that consti-tuted their customer service. Billy had been away and didn't find it funny when he returned to the shop and discovered what the others were laughing at. He pulled it off Cyril as soon as he saw it. Frank called him a killjoy bastard, but Billy could live with that. Frank was a seething cauldron of prejudices. The only thing holding him back from dedicating himself to one particular right-wing ideology was not knowing whom to hate the most. He was an ex-squaddie who had views on everyone and everything, and none of them favorable. He joked with you like he was your best buddy, then as soon as you turned away, he had five different kinds of knives embedded in your back.

"Frank let you back in then, Cyril?" Billy said tiredly, nodding politely at the magazine.

Cyril put the mag back in its bag and shrugged. "I think he can't be bothered chucking me out anymore, to be honest, Billy..." He winked and gave a cheeky smile. You couldn't help liking him. There wasn't a nasty bone in his body. If it wasn't for his predilection for nicking stuff, he would have been received more amicably in the bookshop. The man had a problem, and that problem was kleptomania; he'd admitted as much to Billy. A female member of staff once asked him if he'd tried counseling. Cyril had laughed. He didn't have time for that nonsense, he told her; he was way too busy nicking stuff. It really was a compulsion with Cyril.

"Get a hobby, Cyril," Billy told him, trying to get past him.

"Oh, I've got hobbies," the shoplifter said. "I love Sci-Fi, and healthy stuff too, like cycling—when I can find a bike, that is."

"You don't find bikes, Cyril, you nick them. And not to ride either, just because you don't have any choice. Just for once, be good today and try to act like every other customer. And that means leaving the shop without something tucked under your jacket."

Cyril chuckled and let him go. Billy wandered hopefully over to the Travel section. Aura wasn't there. Nor was the book. But that's because he'd left it in Goods In the night before, of course.

He felt a little sick as he remembered what had happened there. He really didn't want to go back into the unpacking room. But that was irrational. It was daytime now, and he wasn't alone in the shop. There were at least six members of the staff and a handful of customers around. Besides, what *had* happened last night? A power cut, that was all. And some weird sonic anomalies, probably caused by the air-con backing up.

*But the air-conditioner had cut out along with the power, hadn't it, Billy?*

Whatever. Everything had a rational explanation in the cold light of... etc., etc.

*Except, what if there wasn't a rational explanation? Not even the hint of one? What then? If it wasn't the speaker system, and it wasn't the air-con, then what the fuck had caused that weird fluting whistle?*

Billy knew it hadn't been a mechanical fault. The sound had been too human while not being human at all, if that made sense. No, it didn't make sense. None of it did. The whistle, the book... Aura.

No; that was the one thing that *did* make sense. She made all the sense in the world to him. And though he'd only met her the once, and that very briefly, she seemed to him right now to be the only thing worth thinking about.

He entered Goods In, and there was the book, right where he'd left it on the desk. He picked it up, unable to resist glancing nervously around the gloomy room as he did so, and hurried out again.

When he got to the Travel section, Aura was waiting for him.

He stopped. He could feel his mouth drooping, but his brain wouldn't send the right signals for him to close it again.

She smiled, and the shop grew brighter. She was like an incandescent candle, and he was a doomed moth, helpless, unable to do anything but flutter in to his own destruction, even if he didn't know it right then.

"I see you've got my book. I was looking for that..." Her words were all country purr and sexy tease. Her smile was more confident today, though there was still a hint of conflict in her eyes. Or was it just shyness?

Billy finally closed his mouth. Then promptly opened it again, but to use it this time: "*Your* book?" He looked down at the mysterious hardback in his hands. "Yes, I suppose it *is*, in a way..."

She was holding her hand out to take it, and he was just about to pass it to her when Cyril intervened.

"That looks interesting," he said, and took it out of Billy's hand. "You know how much I like a good walk." Billy had been too stunned and excited to see Aura to even notice the older man approaching.

"Hey!" Billy tried to grab it back, but the eccentric shoplifter had turned and was heading toward one of the customer sofas in the corner near the customer orders room. "Don't worry," Cyril called over his shoulder, "I won't nick it!"

Billy was about to follow him when Aura put her hand on his bare arm. Julie had done the same thing yesterday, and he'd felt himself retract, like a snail into a shell. This time his arm felt like it was on fire. His flesh tingled like a live wire had buzzed it. A deep wave of pleasure pulsed through his entire body. She looked up at him with those ambiguous blue eyes, and as he felt himself drawn into them, he experienced the same sensation he had the day before; he knew these eyes, he'd always known them. He'd always known Aura. He didn't understand how that could possibly be. It just was.

"It doesn't matter about the book," she said softly. "I didn't come here for that."

Her hand was still on his arm.

"No?" was all he could manage.

"No."

"I feel like I've met you before, maybe a long time ago…," she said, as if she were reading his mind. The wave of pleasure took him again. Talk about synced. She was either somehow guessing his thoughts from his expression and playing with him or…

*Or what?*

"Get a grip, Billy Boy. You're supposed to be on the main till now."

Yet again he had failed to register anyone else's presence apart from Aura's until they were practically in his face. Tom was standing with his arms crossed, watching him with a quizzical expression on his face. Then, all smarm, he smiled at Aura and added, "Unless he's helping you find a book, that is, madam…"

Aura smiled ever so briefly back at the manager. "No, I've found exactly what I want..." She started to go, and Billy hated his manager right then; he hated the shop too, and everyone in it.

But then she turned, and the smile was just for him, not Tom, not the shop: it was all for Billy. "I'll be waiting for you outside when you close...if you like?"

He grinned like a fool. It took him a moment to speak. "I like. I finish six-thirty..." She nodded and left the shop as abruptly as the day before, taking that smile with her. The shop lost its brightness appreciably. Tom, watching him, arms still folded, had a look that was half approval, half disdain on his face—quite a difficult feat to accomplish, Billy thought as he grinned sheepishly at his manager and walked toward the main till.

Cyril was oblivious to all this as he sat on the leather sofa with *The Olde Britishe Guide to 101 Walkes through Hell* open on his lap. One of Cyril's many hobbies (of which shoplifting was only the most compulsive) included collecting rare books, and this tatty volume certainly seemed to belong in that category. He'd perused Bristol's second-hand bookshops countless times in search of rarities, and this one looked like it would be more at home in a Charing Cross antiquities specialist than in a corporate store that dealt only with new stock. Whatever its rarity value, Cyril was having it. There was something fascinating about the book...

He scanned the publication page curiously. First edition published 1610... it didn't say when this edition was published, which was odd in itself. He'd never heard of the publisher either. He flicked over to the index page. He wasn't much of a walker, but then that really didn't matter. It was the book that mattered.

The area covered by the Guide was quite diverse, and that was rather strange, too, he thought. Most walking guides tended to concentrate on one area: Wiltshire or Devon, for instance. This one didn't seem to care how far apart its various hikes were. There was even one that covered the East End of London. Another following the longest road in England, the A38, which stretched from the northern counties right down to Plymouth in the south. *That* would be some walk... The only walk that could be classed as local was No. 21. He flipped through the pages until he found it. Deepest, Darkest Somerset.

If truth be told, Cyril had begun to feel a little strange as soon as he opened the book but had passed it off as a buzz of excitement at finding something so obviously unique and unusual. But as he examined the book further, he became aware of an increasingly compelling sensation that he could only compare to his urge to shoplift, and this particular urge was compelling him to keep hold of this book and discover exactly what made it so special. The buzz became a feverish desire, a burning need to read on.

He scanned the passage of antiquated text and glanced at the crudely drawn circular route. The start point was a village Cyril had never heard of called Payndom, and the entire circular walk was six miles in total. That didn't matter though because Cyril had no intention whatsoever of walking it. What he had said to Billy about his hobbies including cycling had been a complete lie. Billy was much happier in front of a classic black-and-white episode of *Doctor Who* than filling his lungs with the stink of the country. Yet he examined the route carefully, the various landmarks sounding exciting and picturesque to him, increasing the beat of excitement that had coursed through his blood as soon as he opened the book.

After a few moments, he closed the Guide. He didn't even bother to check if any of the staff were watching him as he slid the volume under his rain jacket and walked slowly out of the shop. If any of the booksellers had happened to notice him walk out, they would have been puzzled by the blank look on his usually jovial face, but nobody saw him go.

# Chapter Five
# Cornucopia

Billy didn't take his time closing the shop. He also left it to James to enter Goods In and activate the alarm located inside the unpacking room. He wasn't about to risk the same thing happening to him as the night before.

But in all honesty, he was too excited to feel afraid. He heard Julie's chatter as she closed down all the till PCs without listening to a word; it was just white noise. He carried the till trays stacked with the day's takings over to the manager's office, punched the code in with his right hand while clutching the three tills piled on top of each other with his left, and pushed through the door, then knelt down beside the large safe.

He popped in the numbers and spun the dial. Shoving the tills inside, he slammed the safe door and was on his feet again and through to the staff room in half the time it normally took him.

Julie looked up in surprise when he emerged on the shop floor in his long, black coat scarcely sixty seconds afterward, heading for the main door.

"Night, then!" Julie called out sarcastically.

"What's the rush?" James asked, emerging from Goods In, obviously unaffected by disembodied whistles. Billy barely noticed that, nor did he ponder on the fact that he hadn't heard the whistle at all today; he was far too busy thinking about what lay ahead.

"See you tomorrow," was his only acknowledgment to both of them, and then he was pushing open the door, heart riding high in his chest and…

And she was waiting for him, just like she said she would be.

She was wearing the same poncho he'd seen her in for the last two days, and he wondered how she managed not to look cold in the late March evening. A gorgeous smile was on her lips, and he resisted the urge to kiss them right then and there. He smiled back instead, glowing with excitement.

"Where shall we go?" he asked, heart pounding, yet not feeling awkward at all.

"Where do you normally take your dates?" she said softly, and he felt himself aroused without her having to even touch him. *Dates??!*

"Is that what this is?" he asked impishly.

She merely smiled and reached out to take his hand.


When Julie emerged half a minute later, he was already halfway up the street. She stopped as the door slammed closed behind her and was still standing there when James emerged shortly afterward, rattling the keys in his big podgy hands.

"What's up, babe?" he asked jovially, his eyes twinkling as ever behind his round lenses.

She ignored him, and he followed her gaze. Billy and Aura were turning the corner at the top of the street, hand in hand.

James laughed. "Lucky bastard. Doesn't hang about, does he?"

Julie angrily tightened her scarf around her thin neck. "I wonder what Tom would have to say about him fraternizing with customers," she said waspishly.

"I don't think he'd give a fuck," James answered, zipping up his leather jacket. "As long as he's not shagging her in the shop." He laughed loudly. "G'night, babe."

She ignored him, her back to the Assistant Manager. If James had seen her face, he might have felt a little sorry for Billy.

Julie began to slowly follow the couple up the street, her eyes hard and small, her mouth pursed tightly.

Billy took her to the Cornucopia. It was only a five-minute walk from the bookshop and was an old-fashioned pub, an endangered species in a city full of American- and European-style bars that had steadily encroached on the old city's historical integrity over the last few years. He also liked the Cornucopia because it had secluded nooks and dark corners where he could sit in relative privacy.

She asked for a glass of red wine, and he bought a Merlot for her and a pint of Hobgoblin for himself. The pub was quiet this early, and he had no trouble finding a good table hidden away in a secluded nook. Aura smiled provocatively at him as she sat, and he leaned forward on his chair, glowing with happiness.

She didn't seem in a hurry to say anything, so he took a sip, cleared his throat, and began with, "You said you think we've met before…a long time ago. I have the same feeling. A very strange feeling that I can't explain. *Do* we know each other?"

Her eyes regarded him steadily. The smile withdrew. There was a seriousness to her tone as she answered. "You feel strange? Yes, I suppose you do. The reason you believe we have met before is, of course, because we have."

He sat back, puzzled. "Really? I *knew* it! When, and where, and how the hell could I forget?!"

She sipped her wine and didn't reply, but her kaleidoscope eyes continued to hold him. *Like a bluebottle caught on flypaper*, he thought, and almost laughed at the absurdity of the idea.

"I like you…" she said suddenly, avoiding his question. Her lips parted a little, and he saw the white teeth glistening, and his arousal chased away his ridiculous imaginings. She was strange, yes. But who cared? She was absolutely gorgeous. He knew he was staring, and that didn't matter either. He took in every detail of that perfect, imperfect face: the beauty mark that someone less charitable might have called a flat mole on her right cheek, the slightly protuberant nose that was seductive as hell, the sharp cheekbones, the pointed, elfin chin, the wariness of those fantastic eyes.

"I like you, too," he said simply. And there didn't seem to be any need to say any more. Yet there was something he needed to know. "But you haven't told me *where* we met before. It must have been a long time ago, or I sure as hell would remember. Was it when we were children or something? Were you my first girlfriend? I remember holding hands with a blonde girl in pigtails when I was in year four. That wasn't you, was it? I can't remember her name. She moved away a year later. No, come to think of it, I saw her on Facebook recently, and she doesn't have blonde pigtails anymore. Or even blonde hair." He was babbling, desire and the sheer joy of her company making him lose his sense of everything. He needed to keep his cool. He really didn't want her to think he was a prick. "You don't look like a pigtail-type of girl to me…" Brilliant. He didn't even know himself what that meant.

She continued to stare. Her hand reached across the table to touch his, and he felt another jolt of sheer pleasure rip through him. *Boy, if he could bottle that sensation, he'd make a million.*

"You're not going to tell me, are you?"

She allowed a little smile at that and withdrew her hand.

"Where we met before, I mean. Can you at least tell me where you live? You sound like you're from around these parts." Even more brilliant. Now he was telling her she sounded like a country bumpkin, even though the burr of her accent combined sex and sophistication in equal parts, and none of those parts remotely suggested cows and milk churns. Her smile widened, however, so she obviously hadn't taken offense. He decided to let it go for now. He took a gulp of his beer as something else occurred to him. "That book you were looking at… You said it was *your* book. What did you mean by that?"

A shadow moved behind her eyes momentarily. She sipped her own drink instead of answering. If she hadn't been so damn attractive, he would have been vaguely annoyed. He watched her twirl a lock of her golden hair and felt the excitement almost too much to bear.

Eventually, she sat back and said, "It might be more correct to say it was really *your* book."

He chuckled. "And that makes everything clearer, of course!"

She pursed her lips and looked up at him suddenly. Her coyness simply turned him on more. He controlled his rising desire with another gulp of beer.

She was staring at him hard now, her expression serious, oblivious to his levity. "Have you looked at the book yet?"

Her solemnity was catching. "Yes, I've looked at it, and very unusual it is, too." *A bit like the girl who showed it to me.* "I've never seen it in the shop before, and I can't trace it on the system, which is weird." A thought occurred to him, a strange one, but somehow that was appropriate. "Did you bring it into the shop and leave it?"

She didn't look away. "Why would I do that?" she purred.

He laughed awkwardly. "I don't know. It's just... It's very old and doesn't seem to belong in our shop."

"What are you saying? You think I am old and don't belong in your shop, too?" Her voice had momentarily taken on a more playful manner, which melted him, although her eyes retained that enigmatic blend that seemed to mark out some kind of internal conflict he'd noticed when he first looked into them. Just as abruptly as it came, the playfulness vanished, like a stone dropped into those deep blue eyes to disappear without a ripple. She almost whispered the next words. "You think it is my gift to you?" She looked away, frowning, as if about to speak more and deciding better of it.

"I don't...know," he answered lamely. Something else occurred to him, something that seemed stranger and far more disturbing to him than the book. He didn't know why he should mention it to Aura, beyond the sheer coincidence of the phenomena commencing around about the same time she first came into the shop, but before he could even consider the appropriateness of the question, it was already out there: "Tell me... Have you heard anything odd at all when you've been in the bookshop?"

"Odd?" She breathed the word. Her eyes were distant now. She took a sip, and the wine glistened on her lips.

He struggled to regain his thread. "Yes. Since I met you, I've been hearing strange noises…" Okay, that was beyond embarrassing. Not only did he sound like he had graduated with a Diploma in Derangement, but his words could also be perceived as a potential accusation of some sort. *Idiot!*

"What kind of noises?" She looked toward the bar, and Billy was aware that the young barman was eyeing her appreciatively. He felt a flare of jealousy and sat back in his chair, deciding he was probably frightening her off. But was she really checking out the barman, or avoiding the question? The frown was back.

"Whistling," he said, wanting her attention returned to him. "I've heard whistling noises in the shop." Reducing what had been a genuinely frightening experience to such simple terms sounded ridiculous, however, and he felt his cheeks burn. "Nobody else hears it," he added. *Great. That didn't sound schizophrenic. Not at all. Big turn on for her.* But at least her eyes were back on him now, and they were electric. He sensed danger in the blue shock of their depths: danger and an answer. Fear was there, too, but it was gone in a heartbeat, and the disarming beauty of her gaze overwhelmed everything. "It doesn't matter. I'm just glad you're here."

And that's when Julie entered the pub.

She stood just inside the door, watching them both. Billy spotted her straight away, and he sighed with frustration. Aura followed his gaze but seemed as disinterested in the new arrival as she had been in the barman.

Julie made no move to approach them, nor did she head for the bar to get a drink. *If she only realized how weird and unattractive her behavior was,* Billy thought with real irritation.

"Your friend wants to join us?" Aura asked innocently.

"No, she really doesn't," he said vehemently, rising from his chair. Julie matched his frown and began walking across the bar toward them.

Aura was on her feet now, too. "It's alright, honestly. I have to leave now anyway."

"What?" Billy was utterly dismayed. "But you've only just got here. And you haven't finished your drink…"

She gave him a little smile, picked up the glass, and drained the contents in one, managing to make the action feminine and alluring as she did so. She let out a little gasp of breath and moved around the table to kiss him on the cheek. Julie hovered a few feet away, a crazy look on her pinched face. Billy ignored her, the dismay turning to anger toward his colleague.

Billy wasn't letting her ruin his evening. Impulsively, he reached both arms around Aura's waist and pulled her to him, kissing her firmly on the lips. He didn't push it, and she didn't resist, and as he let go of her and stepped back, her eyes seemed to spark with the same excitement he felt coursing through him.

"I'm free Tuesday afternoon… I'm only working a half-day…if you want me to take you somewhere…"

"Somewhere," she breathed almost mockingly. She glanced at Julie like she might look at a stopped clock or a faded painting on a wall and then back at Billy with a half-smile. The wild look was still in her eyes as she said, "Somewhere sounds good…" And then she was walking toward the door past Julie, her hips swaying with a wholly natural sexiness as she did so.

Julie was staring at him, her jealous bitterness obviously overriding any sense of embarrassment she might feel at her intervention. Billy ignored her, calling after Aura. "You don't have my number!"

She turned briefly, hand on the door. "I'll find you," she said. "Outside your shop…"

"Yes! Tuesday… One o'clock!"

She was gone.

It was only then that he turned to face Julie.

But his anger was already dissipating. He was going on another date with Aura, and that was really all that mattered. So he finished his pint in one gulp while Julie sat herself down in the seat so recently vacated by Aura, and then he slammed the glass down on the table and shrugged into his coat.

Julie said nothing. He could read it all on her face. Disappointment, hurt, the anger still burning there. He didn't have room in his life for all that bullshit, so he winked at her ironically, patted her shoulder, and said, "Call your boyfriend. I'm sure he'll buy you a drink." And then he, too, left the pub, feeling fantastic.

It wouldn't last.

# Chapter Six
# I'll Whistle as I Come to You...

That was the night the Whistler came. As bad nights went, this was up there with the very worst.

Billy had cleaned his teeth, staring in the toothpaste-flecked mirror at his reflection, wondering how he'd managed to get so lucky.

His blue eyes were fired with an enthusiasm for life that had been distinctly lacking for a long, long time. His long face, normally drawn and weary, was rejuvenated. Billy glowed. Even his hair shone.

He climbed into bed and reached languorously for the bedside lamp, switching it off and plunging the bedroom into darkness. He lay back beneath the sheets and thought of Aura. He imagined holding her in bed with him, the smell of her warm body next to his, the wonderful, soft country purr of her voice in his ear. He imagined her head on the pillow, her whirlpool eyes staring into his...

He was never going to sleep if he kept this up. He turned to the illuminated digits of the Batmobile alarm clock on the bedside table. 12:05. He didn't feel remotely tired, damn it! He turned on his right side, then his left, but neither side helped sleep come. Aura filled him. His mind and body tingled with the idea of her. She liked him; she had made that clear. That she was beautiful was without question. Elegant, intelligent, articulate—those, too. So what the hell *was* wrong with her, to make her interested in him? He flipped sides again. Shit. He was sounding like Frank now. That was the sort of putdown ever ready on the portly security man's lips. Fuck it. *Sleep, you fool.* A quick peek at the time: 1:30. Jesus. Up in just over five hours. Sleep…

Eventually, he slept.

The house was quiet. The cemetery beyond the back garden was quiet, too. No fox or owl to disturb the peace, so rare in the center of a sprawling city. No car alarms being triggered accidentally or otherwise. No late-night revelers shouting out in the dark. Just…

Just the whistle…

Faint. So faint at first. Tickling the edge of Billy's dreams, so, at first, he thought it was part of them. Then climbing up the scales of audibility as the Whistler climbed the stairs of the house. Could Billy hear footsteps slowly and heavily thumping up the steps, now pausing outside the door of his bedroom? Sleep, Billy, you're dreaming…

His head lifted from the pillow in a violent jerk. He *could* hear it. He could hear it right now. The footsteps had stopped, but he could still hear the whistle. It drifted in and out of key, first quiet, then louder, shifting from a haunting, desolate plea to a spiteful glee, wild and violent.

Sweat slicked Billy's naked body. He could not move. His eyes were adjusting to the dark, but not fast enough. The bedroom was pitch black. The whistling stopped.

Had it gone? Billy gasped in air, having forgotten to breathe. He tried to force his body into a sitting position, but it would not respond. Fear paralysis gripped him. Silence. Utter, total silence.

His eyes made out the outline of the door now, and he was sure he had closed it when he came to bed. Now, it was open a crack. His hair pulled at the roots, as if an invisible hand were tugging at it, so tightly did his scalp contract. Terror riveted him to the bed. The door was opening.

He was shivering uncontrollably. His body tensed in preparation for one mighty leap out of bed. The door continued to swing slowly inward. The darkness of the hallway beyond was absolute, but his eyes were straining through it, and with every second, he was finding more detail.

Something was standing in the doorway, almost indistinguishable from the night. A black shape, a figure, and if he kept on staring, it would take on more form.

His shaking reached new, uncontrollable heights. His left arm managed to free itself of its paralysis and groped for the bedside lamp, knocking over a glass of water left there from three nights before. The sound made him jerk spasmodically and freed him from the spell of terror. He sat up and twisted toward the table, his left hand fumbling for the light switch, his naked back turned toward the door for one agonizingly vulnerable moment as he did so.

Then his hand found the button and the room was filled with blinding light.

He screwed his eyes shut against the glare, his heart exploding in his chest. Opening his eyes again, he stared at the open doorway, his breath coming in fragile gasps.

The doorway was empty.

It took him a further moment or two to summon the courage to climb from the bed, to step ever so carefully toward the door. Forcing himself forward, he leaned against the door jamb and peered out into the hall.

The hall was empty.

As were the stairs. And after he had spent the next ten minutes thoroughly examining every shadow in every corner, he began to hope the whole house might be empty, too.

The front door was locked, as it always was at night. The back door bolted top and bottom. By the time he had searched every cupboard and closet he could think of, he had come to the conclusion that, apart from the miserable fish in its tank, he was, in fact, absolutely and entirely alone in his mid-terraced house. There was no Whistler. Had there ever been? Had he dreamed the entire incident? So had he also dreamed the whistle in the packing room at work then? *Of course not.* Both experiences had been as real and *tangible* as anything else that had occurred to him throughout the day.

He climbed the stairs again, pausing outside his door, as if expecting to find his bedroom occupied, then entered and shut the door firmly.

His shivering had died away. But the three sinister notes of the whistle had not. Not in his mind. They would stay there, on the edge of his hearing, long into the night.

# INTERLUDE TWO

# ROMAN BRITON, 364 AD

They lost Aurelius Piccano half an hour before they reached their destination.

One minute he'd been behind Sciro, constantly glancing nervously around at the impenetrable forest as the troop marched onward, the next, he was gone. Sciro had gotten used to the jangling and creaking of Piccano's buckles and armor behind him, and the sudden cessation of the sound was the only thing that alerted him to his compatriot's absence.

He shouted out to the rest of the troop to halt. The centurion marched back to the end of the line to confront him, obviously suspicious of another rebellious motive for the delay.

"We lost Piccano," Sciro said simply. His sword was out as he surveyed the dark vegetation that closed in around the path.

The centurion acted immediately. His sword was in his hand in one swift movement. "Stand fast in defensive position!" he ordered his men. It was an unnecessary instruction; his men were already back to back in pairs, swords at the ready. They may have been an undisciplined, lazy bunch of shits most of the time, but their training had obviously penetrated their work-shy brains at some point. The centurion walked back along the path the way they had come, stealthily, looking for signs of an attack. A hundred yards down the trail he found blood on the foliage, dripping along with the rain from the leaves. There was more on the path. Piccano's helmet lay in a thicket of nettles beside the path. There was blood on that, too.

He scanned the undergrowth. The trees were pretty much impenetrable here, and he could hear nothing above the dripping of rain. Sweat ran down his forehead from under his helmet, while more slicked his grip on the gladius. His men were equally still, the tension etching their faces along with fatigue.

The attack had obviously happened within the last five minutes. The centurion thought quickly. They were nearing their destination now. This had been the first interaction with the natives in almost a day. The method of attack was different, too. Previously they'd been charged by screaming primitives waving makeshift javelins; there had been no attempt at stealth. This was different and far more unsettling. He couldn't see or hear the enemy. Was the change in tactics down to a different tribe being responsible? One that was guarding the Roman patrol's intended destination? The centurion didn't know, but he was determined not to lose another man.

He strode back to the waiting legionaries. "Keep your swords at the ready at all times," he instructed in a low voice. They stared back at him with open fear in their eyes; even the thuggish Sciro looked cowed. "And keep your eyes open for any sign of a presence. But do not break ranks to pursue." He knew his men were due a rest, but they couldn't possibly stop now, not with the threat of death lurking all around them. And they had to complete the mission.

The troop continued forward, the centurion at the head. Sciro found himself at the rear again, and he didn't like that at all. The legionary directly in front of him kept turning round to check if Sciro was still there, and he didn't like *that* either. He didn't like what it implied.

"Ferrus," he hissed at the grizzled legionary in front of him.

The legionary swiveled his head around again. He was nearly fifty, and this would be his last tour of duty in Briton. He had a villa and a plump wife waiting for him on the outskirts of Rome, and he desperately wanted to see them again. "What?"

"Twenty sestertii if you swap places." Sciro kept his voice low to prevent the centurion or any potential hostile from hearing.

"Fuck off." Ferrus continued ahead, the conversation closed as far as he was concerned.

"Thirty…"

Ferrus paused and looked around again. "You don't have thirty sestertii." Ferrus was likewise whispering.

"I've been saving."

"You're a lying, cowardly fuck; we all know you spend every sestertius on whores."

Sciro began to rummage in the pouch on his belt as if looking for the money. Then he abruptly pushed past Ferrus, shouldering him out the way as he squeezed in front of the older legionnaire.

Ferrus watched him do it with astonishment. He stood still for a minute, watching the bulkier legionary scurry to catch up with the rest of the troop, who were rounding a bend in the path. He felt the darkness and emptiness pushing against him from behind, but he refused to give in to his fears and turn around. He was the most experienced legionary in the squad and the most disciplined. He was not going to give in to fear of the dark, even if he knew that dark was potentially crawling with hostiles. "You liver-less scum, Sciro," he hissed and was about to trot forward to seize the duplicitous legionary by the belt and haul him back when he heard a faint noise to his left.

A rustle. That was all. There was no wind, no breeze at all. The rain had abruptly stopped a short while ago. There was nothing to account for the sound. Ferrus whirled, sword clenched tightly. He strained his eyes trying to penetrate the wall of darkness on the left side of the path.

When it came, the attack was from the right side, from directly behind Ferrus. As the most experienced member of the squad, he should have called ahead, signaled his suspicions to the others, but his fury with Sciro overrode his caution. He didn't even hear the rush from behind until a crooked stone dagger as sharp as any Roman gladius cut across his neck, just below the strap of his helmet. His eyes bugged down at the filthy hand clutching it, at the warts peppering the skin. His shout was a gargle of blood. His own life fluids were pumping over those warts now as the dagger hewed away at his carotid artery. His sword arm flailed madly but met no resistance. Ferrus fell to his knees. His eyes glazed, dimly seeing another figure emerging from the foliage ahead to seize him, but his vision was too red to discern much of anything anymore, and Ferrus was taken, his last thought not of the plump wife and the villa he'd never see again, but of how Sciro had avoided a fate that was by all rights his.

When Ferrus didn't follow them round the bend in the path, Sciro knew at once something had happened. This time he kept quiet. He wasn't going to alert the centurion to the fact he was responsible for Ferrus's absence by stealing his position in the procession. And why should he? It was survival of the smartest in this wilderness. So he didn't breathe a word until Martus, who was now in front of him, glanced back and noticed the missing legionary. He halted, eyes focused on Sciro, eyes that were full of naked fear. "Ferrus…?

Sciro made a show of turning round to look for his comrade. "He was right there a moment ago," he hissed.

Martus called ahead and the troop froze for the second time while the centurion once again came back along the line.

He glanced at Sciro. "What happened? I thought you were on rear duty."

Sciro shrugged. "You know Ferrus… He likes to live on the edge."

The centurion glared at him. Then he signaled for Martus to accompany him down the track. "The rest of you stay here. Any sign of hostility, call me."

With an unhappy Martus behind him, the centurion trotted back around the bend, already knowing he would find nothing…

Nothing but blood.

Blood on the path, blood on the leaves.

They were being toyed with. Whittled down one by one.

He scanned the thick trunks of the oaks and birch, peering around every bole that was visible in the dark, straining his eyes, craning his neck to look up into the branches, just in case the enemy was lurking up there.

He motioned to Martus to follow him again, and they rejoined the rest of the squad. They looked at their leader with desperation. This was the biggest challenge of his career. If they had been on the point of aggressive rebellion before, they were now thoroughly cowed and looked to him as if he were their last chance on Earth of getting out of this alive. Even Sciro appeared terrified, but he also looked like the only one who still wanted to argue.

"We have to keep going," the centurion told the men. "We have to do this."

"What the fuck for?" Sciro growled, his voice betraying his fear. "You're leading us to our deaths, and you know that. We should go back now."

"No!" The centurion's voice was firm. "We go on. We finish this. We go back, we die. They're behind us, not in front."

"You don't know that," Sciro persisted, and the centurion had to admit that was the truest thing the surly legionary had said all day. "There's probably more ahead." He turned to the others. "We ain't gonna make it if we carry on."

The centurion straightened, struggling to assume the mantle of a seasoned, battle-hardened leader. They were listening to Sciro, and it appeared as if they were ready to break at any moment. This was the centurion's moment. The time he proved his mettle as one of Caesar's finest. He would show them how a Roman centurion acted in the face of adversity. This time his voice was raised deliberately. He didn't care if the enemy lurking in the shadows heard him now. This was make or break.

"You listen to this coward and you're dead already. I promise you I will lead you on to victory in this war against the primitives. We will accomplish our mission and return to Rome, not only as heroes but with Caesar's gratitude clinking in our money belts. We march on to glory; we retreat to certain death. Which is it to be, legionaries of glorious Rome?"

He studied their faces. One or two of them looked undecided, but the majority seemed to have been bolstered by the speech. They stood taller, and there was a glint in their eye. But maybe that was down to the sestertii he'd mentioned. And Sciro… Sciro was looking at him with hatred now. He'd called him out, and everyone knew he was craven now. The realization that the stocky brute had somehow been responsible for Ferrus's death was spreading.

He had them.

"Then let's finish what we set out to do." Without waiting to see if any of them were moving, he strode determinedly forward.

The five surviving legionaries followed him.


When, after another half hour of trudging, they emerged from the forest and found themselves on the verge of an open stretch of plain, it came as a huge relief to the weary men. There had been no more attacks, and this, coupled with the centurion's motivational speech, had revived their flagging spirits. The centurion called a halt, and the legionaries sat down in the tall grass with much relief. They drank from the almost-drained containers at their belts. Food had run out hours before. The centurion sat, too, removing his helmet to feel the gentle breeze that had sprung up and cool the sweat in his hair, but he kept his eyes on the fringe of woods behind them.

Judging from the darkness of the sky, dawn was still a way off yet. Stars and a sickle moon brightened the expanse of breeze-tousled grass that stretched away from them. Half a mile or so to the east, another expanse of trees clumped together, albeit far smaller than the dense forests they'd marched through for the last two days. The centurion studied them as he rested his aching bones, a frown on his face. So there it was: the objective of this blood-splattered mission. The Pilus had called it a grove, but it looked bigger than that epithet implied. The "grove" consisted of more beech and oaks, some of them—those occupying the center of the extensive copse—towering over the rest. The centurion examined it from a strategic viewpoint, weighing up the density of tree cover, the room to maneuver and fight, and estimating the probability and efficiency of an ambush.

He had five men left, six including himself. Not great odds, but they would have to suffice. He climbed stiffly to his feet and replaced his helmet, which was still slick with perspiration. The crest had twigs and bits of leaves caught in the bristles. He brushed them out and called to his men. Reluctantly they stood, Sciro last of all.

Ahead lay their fate. Death or glory?

The next hour or so would decide which.

# Chapter Seven
# Walk No. 21

Cyril got off the bus at Payndom.

He barely knew where he was or what he was doing. All he knew was that the old guide book fascinated and compelled him to do what was, for him, a wholly irrational act. Cyril Peck did not go for walks in the countryside. He was an urban dweller, happiest indoors with a good Sci-Fi movie on the TV or poring over his collection of rare books. He liked to be surrounded by people, for he was a sociable fellow—even if his shoplifting urges were anything but. He liked streets of homogenous houses, petrol stations, carpet shops, and the scent of petrol and uncollected trash. He had never been fond of open spaces, trees, and grass. *So what the hell was he doing out here, in "Deepest, Darkest Somerset"?*

He had no idea.

He'd left the bookshop and headed straight to the bus station to plan his journey for the next day. He'd asked at the inquiry counter, as he couldn't see Payndom on any of the route signs that guarded each bus bay. The fat woman behind the counter had eyed him with disinterest and consulted her computer.

"Never heard of it," she had told him flatly as she keyed in the name. After a few seconds, she looked up again. "And neither has the computer."

"Oh dear," Cyril had said, panic rising inexplicably. "But there it is on the map," he'd said, pulling out the book, flipping to the relevant page and proffering it through the open inquiry hatch for her. "Look..."

She'd glanced at the book and scratched her nose. "How old is that, I wonder," she retorted.

"Please, there must be a bus that goes near it."

She'd blinked at him. He'd caught her glance at the unopened packet of BLT sandwiches on the shelf next to her hatch. A frown of deep deliberation, then she had sighed in resignation and lifted the telephone in front of her. "George?" she'd said when the connection was answered. "Buses to Payndom, mate." A pause. "No, neither have I. From the map I've been shown, looks like it could be somewhere in the middle of nowhere, somewhere east of Weston." Then, "Yeah, that's what I'm thinking. Alright, cheers George."

Cyril had waited expectantly.

"The route supervisor hasn't heard of it either, but he thinks you might get somewhere near it on the Weston bus. Number three sixty. Every half hour."

He'd thanked her and left, excitement rising. He'd thought of going back to the bookshop and stealing an OS map to double-check if she was right, but the urge to get home and study the book again had been too strong. He would have to trust what the fat woman had said.

And the fat woman, or rather George, had not led him astray. When he boarded the 360 at 11:15 the next morning, the driver eventually allayed any fears he still had. "Payndom?" He looked confused for a moment, was about to shake his head, then his eyes cleared as if a long-suppressed memory had been restored. "Yeah, I think I know it. I'm pretty sure it's on this route. I think you'll find a stop just outside the village somewhere. Never had nobody wanting to go there before. Three fifty, mate."

Cyril paid and took a seat in the middle of the bus. He felt like a child on a school trip. He also felt confused. Why was he doing this? It was so uncharacteristic. He pulled the book out of his old rucksack (it had been his father's, and probably dated from just after the second world war, and never got used normally; in fact, this might be its virgin voyage with Cyril) and flipped through to Walk No. 21.

He rubbed his forehead as he squinted at the map. He felt cold and hot all at the same time. He hoped he wasn't coming down with a fever. The bus bounced and vibrated as it left Bristol behind and clattered along the A road through increasingly open countryside.

It was a beautiful morning. Sunlight blinded him as he looked up to check he hadn't missed his destination—although the driver had promised he would call Cyril when he got there. The shine accentuated the fur of dust and dirt on the window, which made looking out more difficult. He scratched his chin distractedly and went back to the map.

According to the book, the Walk started at a stile just outside the village. The bus stop was presumably situated a few hundred yards further away on a country lane that deviated from the A road they were now on, though, of course, it wasn't marked on the antiquated map. He would just have to trust the driver, he decided and tried to relax.

Relax? He couldn't possibly relax until he found the stile and started the walk. It was niggling at him, a compulsion that was as pressing and inexplicable as his own need to shoplift. He glanced nervously around at his fellow passengers, as if they might be jealous of the rare find he clutched in his hands. Apart from Cyril, there were only four others on the bus: two elderly ladies chatting morosely to each other up the front, a drunk-looking. middle-aged man with an old jacket and a stained, open-necked shirt just across the aisle, and a young male student further back. The drunkard worried Cyril the most. Suppose he too got off at Payndom and followed him? He might know that the book was special. He would try to steal it.

Cyril closed the book and hid it away in his rucksack. He cleared his throat and stared ahead, careful not to catch the red-faced man's eye. He tried to focus on the driver, anxious not to miss any utterance that might mean he was supposed to alight.

The bus stopped at Cleve. The two old ladies got off, and the bus trundled on. Ten minutes later, the bus pulled over at the junction of a B road. B road? It was more of a tiny lane. Cyril peered through a patch of grime on the window, and what he saw made his heart leap. A very old wooden finger sign pointed down the lane, and on it, in faded letters crumbled by time, the words: PAYNDOM. Cyril lurched to his feet at the same time the red-faced man did the same.

"Your stop, mate," the driver turned around, pointing at the lane through the windscreen. "This is the closest we go. I'm pretty sure there used to be an old bus stop round here at one time, but no one ever uses it nowadays."

Panic gripped Cyril. He clutched the seat in front of him as he stood in tormented indecision. The red-faced man was moving forward along the bus. Of course, he was going to get off and follow Cyril.

"You getting off or what?" The driver looked annoyed now.

"Y-yes." Cyril stepped out from his seat and moved unsurely down the aisle toward the driver. The red-faced man suddenly stopped in front of him, blocking his way.

"You gettin' off as well, Terry?" the driver asked, a sly smile on his face. "Think you've had a drop too much, mate. Been at the sauce early today, eh?"

The red-faced man looked at him blankly, then bent to peer ahead through the windscreen. Cyril saw the bottle of Bells Whisky tucked in the pocket of his jacket. "For fuck's sake," he said in a slur. "Wrong stop. Why dincha tell me, Stan?"

"I just did, ya barmy bugger. Go and sit down again and let this gent off."

The red-faced man turned to look blearily at Cyril, then staggered sideways into a seat and rested his head on the back of the seat in front. Cyril smelled the alcohol as he passed him.

He thanked the driver and alighted.

He watched the bus go and suddenly felt very alone. The realization that he really didn't know what on Earth he was doing struck him more forcibly, and he resisted the urge to run after the bus. Then it was gone around a corner, and the grumble of its engine faded, too.

He became aware of how very, very quiet it was.

Cyril was used to noise. Traffic, horns blaring, tires screeching, people shouting, phones ringing. Here, there was none of that, and it made him feel very small and very vulnerable. He peered at the lane as it sloped down into the shadow of overhanging trees. Go down there? Why? Why in God's name would he do that?

He glanced back up the main road in the direction he had come, but there was no other traffic. He scratched his nose nervously. Looking again at the lane, the urge picked his feet up and moved him in a brisk walk along the rutted tarmac before he could argue with himself any further.

Under the over-arching trees, it was dark despite the late morning sun. The branches cut off the light effectively, and his shoes echoed too loudly for his liking. Anyone could be lurking in the gloom. Cyril focused on the small patch of daylight ahead that signaled the end of the foliage tunnel while his shoes kept going, carrying him on. Soon he was out in bright sunshine again, blinking, and the Somerset countryside unrolled before him.

Cyril was not one to appreciate the swell of gentle hills and the darker green of woodland that formed the backdrop to the small village of Payndom waiting for him on the other side of that dark tunnel. But an excitement quickened in him regardless. He could see the bridge that carried the lane over a stream, just as it had been on the map. He hurried on, barely glancing down at the chortling stream beneath as he crossed the bridge, his eyes fixed on the first few houses ahead of him.

He saw the stile.

The book, no matter how old, had not lied to him.

His pace slowed as he neared the start of Walk No. 21.

Doubt returned. He glanced at the quiet village. The main street looked deserted. He saw the sign of a pub, though he couldn't make out the name from this distance. Probably everyone was in there.

His shirt was slick with sweat. Well, it had been warm on the bus. He wanted to take the book out and study it one more time before proceeding but was afraid somebody in the village might see him. *And what did that matter? It wasn't as if they could possibly know he'd stolen it, was it?* But that wasn't what was bothering him. Nor was it that someone might want to take the valuable item. He'd stopped worrying about that now. No; something more troubling was eating away at him, and he couldn't put his finger on what it was. Was it the fact he was over twenty miles from home and had no idea why he felt so compelled to be here? Possibly. But there was also another fear. Deeper, stronger than any he'd ever felt in his life.

He felt like he was going to die.

The rucksack was heavy on his back, although the only contents were the book, a bottle of ginger ale, and a Cornish pasty. Or was it his body that seemed suddenly too weak? *Too weak to resist the compulsion forcing him on, that was for sure.*

Without another glance at the village, he stepped onto the stile and swung his left leg over to the other side.

He jumped down into a meadow and followed the path that cut across it, just like the map in the book had directed him to.

The sun was hot on his head, making it ache. Or was it the confusion of thoughts causing the unpleasant pulse? He felt queasy, and his lips were dry. He wanted to stop and have some ginger ale, but the urge inside him wouldn't allow it. He had to keep going. No stopping yet. Not until he had crossed the meadow to the iron gate on the other side and pulled his sweating body up and over that and down to the path in yet another meadow.

This path stretched ahead for a few hundred yards before passing a ruined cottage embraced by weeds and nettles, just as the map showed him it would. He glanced behind him. The meadow he'd just crossed was empty. He could hear no signs of activity from Payndom. Ahead, the bright sun obscured the view, but when he shaded his eyes, all he could see were woods beyond the cottage.

He trudged as far as the ruin before stopping. This time the compulsion relented enough for him to sit on a stone fallen from the broken wall and lug out his ginger ale.

He gulped at it hungrily, then twisted the cap back on and replaced it in the bag. He removed the book and studied the map. He had completed Step 1 on the Walk. Step 2 began at the cottage, and the written directions in the text told him he would soon be entering Lord's Wood, all that remained of the once-mighty forest that had covered this part of Somerset. The brief paragraph above the map told him of wild boar and stags that inhabited the forest, but Cyril didn't want to hear about those things; he was nervous enough without the possibility of encountering a maddened hog in the gloom of the trees. He knew he was being stupid. Wild boar had become extinct in England centuries before. But hadn't they reintroduced some in recent years? He was sure he remembered reading that somewhere.

He found his attention wandering to the weed-choked cottage next to him, and he wondered who might have lived there once upon a time. Well, by the look of the neglected ruin, it didn't seem like the fairy tale had had a happy ending. Not his business. He had work to do. *Work?* Cyril hadn't done an honest day in a decade. Disability benefits had seen to that. He suffered from a nervous disorder (or so his doctor had described it, although, to be honest, Cyril had laid it on a bit thick when describing his symptoms) and any undue stress or social interaction caused panic attacks. He couldn't believe he'd managed to shirk employment for so long on so tenuous a diagnosis, but Cyril took the prescribed pills every now and then, and if he felt guilty about not contributing to society, he never shared it with anyone.

But right now it did feel like the stress was causing an unpleasant reaction, and he wasn't even anywhere near the Job Center. His sweating had increased, as had the headache. He scratched at a rash that was now spreading on his cheek, and he breathed in deeply in an attempt to calm the nausea and threats of panic that were building. After a few more deep breaths, he felt better.

He got to his feet, and the compulsion closed in on him again, stiffening his resolve. He followed the path toward Lord's Wood, and if the panic flared momentarily, he didn't let it stop him again until he was walking into the shadow of the first oaks that fringed the woods.

The sun was taken from him almost immediately, and the cold pressed in. The path twined ahead around the mighty oaks, bullied on both sides. He managed to get ten yards in before the fear halted him again.

He sat on a tree stump and groped for his ginger ale. He'd finished the bottle before realizing it, and the usually eco-conscious Cyril dropped the empty container on the ground without a thought. The urge was almost like a voice now, calling to him. *Get up. Keep going…*

So he did.

It got darker. It got quieter. His footsteps crunching on twigs and scuffing stones were the only sounds. No birds in Lord's Wood, it seemed. He penetrated further, into the heart of the woods. It wasn't too dark to see; after all, it was early afternoon now, and the sun was strong above the branches, but it was gloomy, and several times he stumbled over a protruding root or caught his raincoat on brambles.

It wasn't too dark to see the figure ahead of him, either.

Cyril stopped, but his heart carried on, faster, louder.

The figure waited beside a falling shaft of sunlight, dim and vague, standing as still as Cyril, watching him. Whoever it was wore some kind of long, dark robe with a pointed hood covering his head. The shadows of the woods obscured his face. He held a long wooden staff in one hand, the clutch of twigs at one end carved and sharpened until it resembled a large claw. The figure might have been a strange variation of a monk, and his immobility, together with the evil-looking staff, brought more fear to Cyril's timid heart.

Cyril looked back the way he had come.

There was another figure a hundred yards behind him, blocking off his retreat. The same black robe and peaked hood, although this one clutched a short object in one fist that glinted in the splinter of a sunbeam.

Cyril faced forward again, terror rising, but the figure with the staff had gone. Cyril whirled, hoping the one behind had disappeared, too, but he was still there, watching silently.

"Can… Can I help you?" he stammered pathetically.

No answer.

The robed figure began to advance slowly. Cyril saw it was a dagger in his hand. Not an ordinary dagger, but a long and strangely crooked one, made from stone. It was as weird and nasty as the wooden staff.

Cyril began to stumble forward along the path, his heart punching his ribs.

He passed the spot where the first figure had been, half expecting it to step out from behind a tree trunk. When nothing appeared, he dared a look back. The figure with the stone blade continued to advance, taking its time, its face hidden by the cowl and the dark of the woods.

Cyril emitted a sob and lurched on, following the twisting path through the dense forest, praying he would come to the end and feeling irrationally that that was never going to happen.

But it did happen. After ten minutes or so of stumbling onward, his breath tearing at his lungs, he eventually saw the oaks and birches begin to thin, and glorious sunshine appeared ahead. He could see a section of grassland beyond. Relief gave him the strength to turn again.

The figure following him had disappeared.

Crying now, Cyril made it to the edge of Lord's Wood and collapsed in the grass. He vomited, great heaves squeezing the air from him until he had ejected the contents of his stomach, which was mostly ginger ale.

But the sun was warm on his head, the breeze soft and refreshing, and soon he began to feel a little better. He slowly got to his feet, staring back into the dark woods.

When nobody emerged, Cyril's breathing stabilized, and he turned to survey his surroundings, wondering how he was going to get back to the bus without going through those dreadful woods again.

He stood on the verge of a great sweep of grassland patched with scabs of broken earth and stone. Half a mile away to the east, another cluster of trees grew, smaller than Lord's Wood, and beyond that, he could see the grassy ramparts of what looked like an ancient settlement. To the north and south, rolling hillside and more woods, but not a house in sight, and certainly no road.

What on Earth was he going to do? While the initial blind terror was starting to subside a little now that he was in the open sunshine, the shock of his experience with the two figures was not going to leave him so easily. Who the hell were they? They hadn't looked like monks so much as…

But that was stupid. Druids wore white and danced around Stonehenge at the summer solstice. They didn't chase people through woods all dressed in black. And they didn't threaten people with stone daggers.

Whatever they were, he had sensed instinctively they wished him harm. And he was still far too close to Lord's Wood for his own comfort. He began to move away, his steps impulsively following the faint path that cut through the grass in the direction of the large copse on the horizon. But why go there? The copse looked equally as dark and sinister as Lord's Wood had been. He knew without having to check that the path in the guide book led through the copse (he remembered it being marked simply as "The Grove"), but why the hell would he want to follow the route now, after his recent fright? Better to head north and try to skirt Lord's Wood and find a way to double back to Payndom.

Yes, that made sense.

But the urge was back in his head, and the urge wouldn't let him.

It pushed him on toward that Grove, as if he really had no choice in the matter. And to be honest, from the moment he took the guide book from Billy's hand and sat down to read it, that was absolutely how it was.

Cyril Peck knew he was heading to his death. Deep down he *knew* that. But could he have stopped himself?

Not a chance.

He was nearly at The Grove now. He could see the mighty oaks, ancient and lightning-stroked, welcoming him to their conclave. And then he was in.

The trunks dwarfed him. Bark had peeled and been blasted away by centuries of storms. Gaping hollows ruptured the boles, pockets of dark large enough to conceal a man. The urge fought his panic and won; he would go on, to the heart of this Grove, and discover its secrets. Because that was why he had come, wasn't it?

Not to die. He definitely hadn't come to die.

He didn't want to die. There was some considerable part of Cyril Peck, beloved Galleries shoplifter extraordinaire, that was still aware of everything that was happening to him, and that made it all so much crueler because he couldn't stop it from happening.

He came to the center of The Grove. Here, there was a fair-sized clearing filled with fallen tree trunks and glorious sunlight. Cyril stepped forward like a man in a dream and let the rays warm his body. The oaks here were the tallest of all, giant, twisted monsters that circled the clearing.

Cyril took off his rucksack and withdrew the book. He opened it to Walk No. 21 and saw that the circular path on the map now ended at The Grove. The rest of the path, and Cyril's future, had been erased.

When he saw the hooded figure with the staff appear at the far side of the clearing, he was barely surprised. He knew without looking that the dagger man would be behind him again. But he hadn't expected a third to appear from the bushes to his left, taking up position beside a tree. Coils of bramble garnished the robed body like a wreath. In one hand he held a branch like a weapon. It was loaded with a cluster of vicious thorns and jagged green leaves. *And something even more vicious than thorns—flint shards whetted on stone to razor sharpness bound by twine to the bristling twigs.* The red berries nestled amongst the leaves in no way diminished the branch's threat. It looked like a flail, as used by a particularly cruel Green Man.

Despite the brightness of the sun, the faces of all three were still in darkness under the hoods.

Cyril turned, a dead man moving, and saw, almost as if in a dream, that Dagger Man was right behind him now, a mere couple of yards away. The figure raised the knife, and Cyril saw warts peppering the sickly flesh of its fist.

Cyril wondered what would happen to his collection of rare books, his trove of *Doctor Who* DVDs, and whether he might get to see his long-dead mother again.

Then the branch flail took him across the right side of his face, the thorns and flints gouging away flesh and one eye, and Cyril began to scream.

He fell to his knees as the flail ripped away at more of his features. The Black Druid with the dagger circled him, then leant forward to drive the stone blade into Cyril's screaming mouth and out through the back of his throat. The guide book dropped from his twitching hands onto the path. Cyril seemed to be reaching for it as he fell forward, his blood spouting over the cover.

Two of the figures caught his toppling body and dragged it across the clearing. They draped the corpse face up on top of a flat, ancient stone lying amidst the brambles. The druid with the staff held it high in silent celebration.

The figure with the dagger began to hack at the still-jerking body of the shoplifter.

Soon the green glade was red.

The grass, the leaves, the thirsty soil, all red.

A mile away, on the A37, the 360 bus returning from Weston Super Mare passed the lane with its quaint sign pointing to Payndom. The driver glanced across at the dark tunnel that led down to the village and eased his foot down on the brakes, as if half-expecting to see the nervous-looking fellow with the gray hair and rucksack waiting by the roadside.

Then he changed gear and accelerated away round the bend and was gone.

# Chapter Eight
# Gone

Aura was waiting outside the shop for him, just like she had said she would be. She'd brought a beautiful day with her, too. A soft breeze touched her long blonde hair, and her white wool cardigan glowed in the sun. She blew him away, and all the weirdness that had been troubling him, too. The Whistler at his bedroom door? Gone, like the hallucination it so obviously was. With her smile, she banished it.

He was aware Frank had followed him to the door, curious as to why the bookseller was in such a good mood. So when Billy leaned in to kiss Aura's cheek, he knew full well he was putting on a bit of a show for the security guard. He didn't need to turn round to see the astonishment or envy on Frank's chubby face. He knew it would be there. Billy had done *good*…

He breathed in her fragrance as he leaned in, and it was like the first buds in spring. He felt his body stir with excitement. She took his hand, which just ignited him even more.

"So where are you taking me?" she asked, her eyes electric with expectation.

"Somewhere special," he told her cryptically (hey, he could do enigmatic, too!) and led her up the street to the Galleries NCP.

Five minutes later, she was sitting in the passenger seat of his purple 1974 Beetle, and he was driving through the car park exit as the barrier lifted on what promised to be a fantastic day.

He drove north out of the city, a Cult CD playing softly. They did not talk much. Aura seemed content just to sit back and listen to the music and gaze out the window, a thoughtful (slightly melancholy?) expression replacing the initial smile. But then every time Billy had seen her, there had been a strange hint of sadness in her eyes. It was part of her mysterious appeal. He was happy just driving with her.

Thirty minutes later, he left the M5 and took a minor road. Aura glanced at him curiously as he drove through the picturesque Cotswold countryside, finally pulling into a drive where a big sign declared they had arrived at Tortworth Court.

The long drive took them through an avenue of firs until finally the full splendor of the Victorian mansion was revealed, solid and imposing, elaborate with Tudor influences, and if Billy had hoped it would impress her, he was not to be disappointed.

"Very grand," she said, giving him a little smile.

He pulled up outside the pillared entrance and got out to open her door.

He felt exhilarated. He'd always dreamed of taking someone special to this magnificent mansion, now converted into a luxurious hotel. They entered the lofty hallway, where rather dull portraits mingled a trifle uncomfortably with surreal and expressionist landscapes on the walls. Aura glanced up at the oils of country scenes with some appreciation; he noticed, however, that she had no time for the staid depictions of former owners of the Court through the centuries, glowering down in their wigs and velvet. Billy took her into the bar and ordered two glasses of Sauvignon Blanc. Then he led her out of the building again, across the graveled forecourt, and through an arch in a tall hedge.

Aura stopped as they came under the archway, her eyes wide with wonder.

"It's beautiful," she said, taking in the wide terraced lawn furnished with white latticed chairs and tables. Stone steps descended to a larger expanse of lawn and some exquisitely landscaped rose bushes. To the right of this lawn, sculptures formed an avenue leading into woodland that covered the rest of the Tortworth estate.

"Glad you like it," he beamed. He led her to one of the chairs and took a seat beside her, sipping his wine and exulting in the view, glorious in the early afternoon sunshine.

It was warm and peaceful, and apart from the occasional waitress or gardener walking past, they were quite alone. Blackbirds called cheerily from the woods. A fountain sculpted to form a large stone petal in the center of the lawn threw sparkling water into the air. Billy had never felt happier.

"I know so little about you," he began; despite the beauty of the setting, he was unable to tear his eyes away from her profile as she gazed at the view.

"And yet you know everything," she replied without looking at him.

He laughed. "Enigmatic to the end."

She turned quickly. "Don't say that." The sadness was more pronounced.

He felt suddenly afraid and didn't know why. His happiness began to curdle. "What d'you mean?"

"The end..." She chewed her lip and reached out for his hand.

"I don't understand you half the time."

She gave him a wan smile.

"Are you all right? I mean, is there anything wrong with—" A sudden thought as banal as it was upsetting occurred to him. "Are you married or something?"

Her laugh was curt and a little cynical.

"Does that mean yes?"

She stared at him with those kaleidoscope eyes. "You don't have to worry about that."

"Then what *do* I have to worry about? I can tell something's bothering you—"

She interrupted him, "You're kinder than I expected you to be—"

He started to speak again, but she reached out and touched his lips with one finger. "More gentle."

"You don't know me," he said when she removed the finger. "I'm a beast really—"

She leaned forward and kissed him softly. He put down his glass of wine and pulled her to him, their lips crushing together with increasing eagerness. Then she was breaking away and reaching for her glass.

Billy sat back in his chair and took a gulp from his. His senses were reeling; he didn't know if he was the happiest he'd ever been or the saddest. Everything about the mysterious Aura was confusing; she promised ecstasy and despair at the same time, and he couldn't understand any of it.

"You're a good man," she said and turned to him again, her right hand reaching out to stroke his cheek. The sadness lingered in her eyes, although her lips parted as if she longed for another kiss. "This isn't right. It can't be."

"What isn't right?!" His frustration was getting the better of him. "Why the drama? You either like me or you don't. And if you do, what's the problem? Why do you have to look so sad about it?"

Her hand dropped away. She gazed out across the lawns.

"Remember a day," she said eventually, her voice far off. "One dawn more than a thousand summers away. I remember a man. I remember his face. The sun was rising on what we did."

He waited for her to explain that riddle, though now his frustration was waning. A new fear had entered his mind: Could she be unwell? Her conversation was so removed, her behavior fractured and contradictory. Could she be suffering from a mental illness? He took a bigger gulp of wine. And with no warning, a memory came to him.

It struck him with such force he jerked in his seat.

*Sunrise… Aura at dawn.*

Her words had triggered an association as powerful as it was elusive; he knew instinctively that he *had* known her before. He just didn't know when, or how. The sadness had intensified in her eyes as he, in turn, touched her cheek and drew her around to face him. He felt an urgent need to capture this moment, which suddenly felt so horribly fleeting. Her body was tense, as if she would spring from her chair any second and be gone. He stumbled for things to say that might keep her from the disappearing act he felt was imminent. He pulled out his cell phone.

"Give me your number." His heart was sinking even as he spoke with the conviction she would not have a phone, or she would pretend not to.

"You cannot keep me," she answered. "I should have known this was wrong. Evil. I'm *not* evil…" Now there were tears glistening in her eyes.

"Please," he said, despair clawing at him. "You're not making sense. Of course, you're not evil. You're beautiful—the most desirable girl I've ever seen. At least let me take your number. Give me that one thing before…" *Before what?* He was making as much sense now as she was. The sun was glorious, the lawns radiant, the fountain sparkling, and he had just kissed a beautiful girl. He would have felt on cloud nine, but for the shadow. And that shadow was more than one thousand summers long.

And what the hell did *that* mean?

But now Aura was reaching into the pocket of her baggy, woolen cardigan, and there was a mobile in her hand. She looked at it as if she were unsure what it was or how to use it. "I found this… To connect with you…"

*Found* it? But it felt like he had no time to even care that her words were beyond his understanding any more. The "connect with you" part was all he needed to hear. He took it from her before she could withdraw it. It looked old and scratched, a good few years out of date. He thumbed the largest button at the bottom of the clunky phone, and the small screen blinked into life. His fingers moved swiftly, locating the green phone symbol and pressing the stiff button. It took him seconds to enter his own number and press the green call button. All the time she watched him with a curious detachment, as if he were performing a weird spell.

When his own cell rang, he checked the incoming number; then, with a slight abatement of the dread that had filled him, he switched it off and handed her phone back. She dropped it in her pocket without a word.

The sun was dipping over the trees to the west now. She looked wistfully at the woods, then suddenly she was jumping up and pulling him with her. There was a new determination on her face, as if a decision had been reached

She ran with him along the terrace to a smaller flight of steps on the western corner. The path at the bottom led them into the trees, through the avenue of fine art sculptures until the trees grew thicker around them. She slowed her pace, though her grip was still as urgent. She followed the path until they came to a bench in a small clearing hidden from the mansion and the curious eyes of gardeners and maids.

He thought she was going to sit on the bench, but to his surprise and delight she knelt on the soft grass and pulled him down beside her.

She pushed him down on his back and rolled on top of him, her lips closing on his, soft, pressing. He felt her tongue tease inside his mouth, and he responded, his body flaming. Her lips molded perfectly to his, their tongues entwined. Then he was moving his mouth from hers, reluctant to leave the softness but eager for more delights. He nuzzled her long, white neck, teeth edging playfully along the skin. He felt her hands slip under his jacket and shirt, cool on his flesh, stroking his chest. His own hands slid up her back under the cardigan and thin top, and she was sitting upright astride him now, looking down on him, almost haughty with lust.

His fingers searched for a bra and found none, and his excitement gained momentum. His hands slid around her slender body and up, locating the small breasts, the nipples pushing out eagerly to meet his fingers, his palms. He sat up to meet her, undoing the cardigan, his loins aching with need. The cardigan fell open, and he lifted the purple top beneath, rolling his face softly against her exposed breasts, breathing in the smell of them, exulting in their warmth, the gentle swellings driving him on to a peak of desire.

He was about to close his lips around her right nipple when he heard the whistle.

It drifted out of the dense trees ahead, faint, but unmistakable.

His body jolted with shock. Aura's spine arced in unison. She was pulling away from him and scrambling to her feet. He leaped up, shocked by the sudden intrusion of that horribly familiar sound, and also *by the fact Aura was reacting to it with equal fear.*

It came again, the three long notes, more urgent. Louder this time. *Getting nearer.*

She was staring into the depths of the woods as if expecting something to emerge at any moment. Billy was startled to see how quickly the sun was now setting. Dusk crept through the trees toward them.

"You hear it, too!" He snatched her hands in his, and she faced him. Her eyes were wide with despair and terror.

"They're calling *him*!" she hissed, squeezing his hands tight. "But it's not time!" She jerked her head around to search frantically over his shoulder. *She was expecting someone.* Shadows filled the gaps between the beech trees.

"It's too soon!" she shouted, her voice cracking. Now she was beseeching the dusk and breaking free of his grip to confront the woods that stretched away from the house. "Not yet, please... *please.* It's not time!"

Billy stepped forward again helplessly, utterly bewildered by this latest turn.

The whistle emerged from the darkness forming thickly now between the trees. The tone changed slightly from the terrifying searching key of a moment before, taking on the gloating note Billy remembered from his bedroom. Billy's heart iced over as he listened. His scalp contracted. He wanted to reach out for Aura again, but the whistle had paralyzed him.

"They're *here!*" Aura whirled toward him again. Her face was ghostly in the twilight. Tears tracked down her ashen cheeks. "You've got to go!! *You've got to go NOW!!!"*

Behind her, three figures emerged from the dusk.

Indistinct shadows blending with the dark, Billy sensed more than saw them. Before he could register any details, Aura was flinging herself onto him, embracing him desperately, wildly. Her lips crushed against his one last time, and then she was running away, into the trees, into the darkness—*toward them...*

He started to move after her, slowly at first, then running until the path petered out and he was stumbling into beech trunks in the dark, bark peeling away under his hands. Brambles caught at his jeans. He panted in the silence.

The whistle was gone.

And so was Aura.


After an hour of groping through the darkness, losing his way in the deceptively large woodland that formed the western perimeter of the Tortworth Court estate, he realized he had actually only succeeded in performing a torturous circle when he eventually found himself back at the avenue of sculptures.

He had tried to ring her cell phone, but, of course, there was no answer.

He walked stiffly back to the table at which he had sat with her a mere hour or so before, when the sun had shone and everything might have been glorious, and collapsed in his chair. Their glasses had been collected long ago. Lights from the mansion lit up the lawns below him. The only sound was the occasional slam of a door from the hotel and the soft whisper of the fountain.

He sat for a while—it could have been hours—thumbing the dial icon on his cell screen repeatedly, and reaching only silence.

Eventually, he got up and walked back to his car.

He sat in the driver's seat and looked up at the looming expanse of Tortworth Court. He'd always wanted to bring someone special here.

He hadn't expected to lose them here, too.

# Chapter Nine
# Meadow Talk

And that's how Billy met, and then lost Aura.

Over the next two weeks, he phoned her every day. He left numerous messages on her voice mail that kicked in always after the same number of rings. He'd counted them enough times. Eight rings and then the tone. His depression worsened each time he rang.

In the final message he had left, he told her he would find her no matter what it took. He would search for her, and he would not give up. The next time he tried to ring (and every time after that), he got a recorded message declaring the number was no longer in service.

He'd been so close to contacting the police on numerous occasions, but each time he changed his mind at the last minute. He thought of the whistle and those indistinct shadows in the woods that accompanied it, and while they filled him with a deep sense of unease, he knew he wouldn't be able to translate that dread to a copper behind a desk. It seemed entirely Billy's job to find her, and he would.

Who were those figures, and what did they want with Aura? She seemed to know them, and while she was undoubtedly afraid, her fear had seemed more for his sake than her own. He kept coming back to her words… *"It's not time…not yet! It's too soon… They're calling HIM…"* Billy's imagination worked overtime about whom Aura could possibly have meant by "HIM." A husband? An abusive lover? Had he sent his friends to retrieve her? And what on earth could she have meant by her exclamation, "I'm *not* Evil"? Billy had tortured himself for days over that one.

He heard the whistle several more times in the fourteen days after Aura disappeared. Mostly at work, faint when the shop was busy, loud and taunting when it was quiet. Nobody else heard it; he didn't need to ask them. He'd heard it at home, too, of course, and those were always the worst times. It had visited him fairly frequently since the occasion when he'd heard it outside his bedroom door; often, he would hear it taunting him from the foot of the stairs while he lay rigid in bed, waiting for the Whistler to climb the steps like that first time. Once he'd woken sweating in the night, and the whistle was beside his ear in the dark. Quiet and spiteful, goading him, luring him…*to do what?*

Sleep became fitful, if he managed to get any at all. When he wasn't lying awake waiting for the whistle, he was thinking of Aura.

Then, when his concerns for her were escalating to a point where he found himself hovering near the police station in the city center every lunch hour, and communication with his colleagues at work had broken down almost entirely—his mood black and surly—he was given a sign that Aura had at least received his countless messages.

The sign came in the form of a knock on his door, and a psychotic thug came to call.

The psychotic thug walked slowly back to his car after his little visit to Billy's house. He felt proud of himself. She would be pleased with him. He'd stamped on the problem and made it go away. The bookman wouldn't bother Aura again.

Aura…

Even the sound of her name in his thoughts filled him with desperate longing.

He hadn't loved much in his brutish life, but Aura was the one thing he would never be able to give up, at least in his heart. And yet he knew she wasn't for him. That was not how things were ordained, he knew that. He wasn't stupid enough to mess with it. With *them*…

Yet he would do anything for her.

*Anything.*

His head ached with the things he would do for her. He felt a dull fear, too. Because what he had done *was* solely for her, and he knew that he had risked everything doing it. If *they* found out… A cold dread curdled his stomach. They must not find out.

He climbed into his dilapidated pickup and drove away from the bookman's street. He kept driving until the city was gone and his head stopped aching at last. The country was reaching for him, calling for him, and he would soon be home.

But first, he had to see Aura. Had to tell her how well he had done. She would be pleased. He knew that.

He parked on the outskirts of his home village, next to the stile. His excitement about seeing Aura grew, but so did the unease. He vaulted heavily over the stile and began walking quickly through the grass of the meadow. He climbed the far gate more slowly, his breath a little labored. He blamed it on the warm weather; he was still fairly young and not overweight. *It wasn't fear…*

He sat on top of the gate for a moment, looking first toward the ruined cottage a hundred yards ahead, then at the distant Lord's Wood. He couldn't see Aura even though this is where she said she would be waiting for him… but there was nobody else around either. A ragged scarecrow stuck on a pole in the middle of the field, but that was all. He glanced nervously behind him, at the village. Quiet as ever. But he shouldn't stay sitting on this gate—he was clearly visible for miles around. He leaped down, landing with a grunt, and ambled over to the cottage.

The sun glowed on the broken walls. Inside the ruin, all was still. He peered into the gloom, crushing nettles with his work boots.

"Is it done?"

He whirled in shock. Aura was behind him. But where…

"You scared me…" he said feebly. "Didn't see you coming."

"As long as you scared *him*…" she replied softly. She was ravishing in a coat of dark velvet and black jeans. Her hair was a vibrant blaze of gold.

He felt his breath stop as he looked at her. For this girl, he would sacrifice everything…

"I taught him good," he boasted after a few seconds. He gazed at her with open adoration. "He won't bother you again." He clenched his fist demonstratively.

"I hope you didn't hurt him." There was a note of anger in her voice.

He frowned. "I did what you asked. He got the message."

"I didn't ask you to hurt him!" Her face was anxious now. "What have you done?"

His heart sank. She didn't care he had trampled on the bastard and scared the life out of him. She was only worried he might have damaged the bookman's sweet face… His frown deepened.

"Do you know what I risk for you?"

"I asked you to warn him off, not to harm him!"

The man sighed. "Don't worry. He's not damaged."

She glared at him as if to make sure he was telling the truth, then her expression relaxed a little. "Let us hope he understands to stay away. I would not like to use other measures."

The man looked at her sharply. "I can't do no more. If *they* knew what you had me do today—"

"I cannot let them!" Her eyes were fierce with determination.

The man smiled slowly and bitterly. "You knows you must…in the end."

She averted her gaze and began to turn away. The man took a step after her, his passion for her and the pain of her disinterest making him desperate. "They will make you suffer iffen you don't go to him again! Is it… Is *he* worth that? And while I hate you to be near him, I knows you must… I could not bear it if they found out what you done," he said pathetically. "What you got *me* to do!"

"They will not find out," she replied, then looked back at him over her shoulder. "Unless you tell them."

"I would *never* do that! You knows I care as much for you as that fool in the city!"

She nodded and turned away. He started to follow her, but something caught his eye. He had noticed the scarecrow in the center of the field earlier. It seemed to be nearer now. He squinted against the sunlight. Why would a scarecrow be here in this meadow anyway? There were no crops...

He shielded his gaze, but the glare of the sun prevented him from making out much detail, apart from the fact the scarecrow seemed to be wearing a long, black garment when he was almost sure it had been dressed in a tatty tweed jacket before. A long, black robe, like...

The scarecrow was definitely nearer. Only a hundred yards from the cottage now. He was sure it had been hanging from a wooden pole earlier, too... Now it seemed to be standing without any support, and it was holding a long staff. He felt a trickle of dread.

The man turned round to see if Aura had noticed.

Aura was gone.

He peered into the gloom of the ruined building. Nettles and weeds and a dead crow, nothing else. He blundered around the side of the building to the back wall, which was still relatively intact. She was not there. Behind the cottage, a thick line of trees stretched away to eventually join Lord's Wood. Had she disappeared in there? She must have. She came and went like the wind, he knew that. She'd left him. Left him alone with...

The scarecrow was fifty yards away.

And now he realized the disguise had been lifted from his eyes. The figure had no need to hide any longer. It had heard everything, even from across the expanse of meadow. It *knew*...

The man began to run back toward the iron gate. His breath, labored before, was now catching in his chest, slowing his ability to run.

The gate was fifteen yards away. If he could just get over there and across the shorter field to the village… Surely he'd be safe there?

He carried on stumbling forward, his boots catching on tussocks of grass and threatening to trip him. He dared not look back.

The gate was ten yards away.

He felt a shadow block out the sun.

He kept running, heart squeezing his chest.

He made the gate. He launched himself up onto the first rung, the metal clattering under his weight. His hands clutched the top bar, and he began to heave himself over.

He felt a coldness behind him, as if the sun had died.

He had his left leg over the top of the gate now, his back to the meadow and whatever was pursuing him. He was wheezing in terror. He lifted his right leg to swing that over, too.

A hand latched onto the belt of his jeans, then yanked him off the gate as if he were a child.

He tumbled backward, the sky spiraling, and hit the turf hard. The rest of his breath was knocked from his lungs. He lay on his back, grunting with pain, gazing up at the blue sky, unable to move for a second.

A figure stepped into view above him, the hooded head bent to look down at his prone form.

The man tried to rise. The figure placed a foot on his chest, pinning him down in the grass. He gaped at the ancient boot restraining him. It was fashioned from old black leather, split and eroded. His gaze traveled away from the boot, up the long, dark robe to the inclined hood. The sun shone inside the hood, and he saw what was revealed there.

The man found breath to scream at last.

The "face" partially hidden by the hood had no eyes. In fact, it had no features whatsoever. Thick, black fur covered the huge, upturned cloven hoof that occupied the place where a head should have been.

The man started to cry. *Aura had led him to this. He should never have let her persuade him with her witch ways. He should never have given in. She was promised to another, and, of course, they would NEVER let a common villager like him have her…*

He tried to speak, to reason with the horrific head. She had worked her magic on him, he wanted to say. He never had no choice... But words were dry. He could only sob. The goat's hoof inclined a little more, as if he were being judged.

The right "hand" moved into his field of vision.

More black fur covered the claw holding the staff. The villager's eyes fixed for a moment on the lock of blonde hair tied incongruously around the wood of the haft, then shifted to the other end of the staff. Here, the bristling but sturdy branches had been whittled into curved spikes that resembled long, wickedly sharp talons.

Goat Hoof lowered the staff almost reverently toward the man's face.

He watched it come down.

The carved claw touched his forehead, tapped it gently, then plowed viciously downward, the hooded figure leaning forward to apply all its inhuman strength.

The wooden spikes gouged down through the flesh of his face, rupturing the man's eyes like tomatoes caught by the tines of a fork. The nose was ripped free, lips shredded, half the teeth in his lower jaw jabbed out in the process.

Blood jetted into the air, pattered down on the grass.

The man from the village screamed like hell.

He was screaming IN hell.

All for Aura.

*It was all for Aura!*

The staff lifted, then came down to rake through the gore, like the claw of a mechanical digger coming down to rip at a patch of stubborn earth.

The man stopped screaming. Stopped moving, too. His face had been demolished. But still, the staff continued its work. Goat Hoof caressed the man's chest with the wicked prongs, then began to tear through his jacket and the flesh beneath. A loop of intestine was clawed loose and flung aside into the meadow. More guts coiled around the sharp wooden tines were wiped clear on the top bar of the gate. The figure continued to savage the villager's chest until it exposed a deep cavity and excavated all the intestines.

The figure hooked the claw into the hole, worked it until it had a purchase, then began to drag the corpse behind it as it moved toward Lord's Wood.

When both Black Druid and corpse were far enough away, a crow swooped down onto the blood-soaked grass of the meadow. It had spotted the ripped-out eyes lying amongst the clover like gruesome golf balls. It pecked hesitantly at one of the eyes, head flicking from side to side to make sure it could enjoy its feast in safety. The crow waited until the figure had dragged its burden into the dark fringe of the woods before swallowing the morsel in a rapid series of gulps, then fluttered over to the other eye.

Two more crows alighted. They fluttered around the first, trying to get some of the treasure. One of them flew off to the gate and landed on the top bar, where a coil of intestine still lay draped over the metal.

Apart from the delighted cawing of the crows, the meadow was silent and peaceful in the spring sunshine.

*Aura saw it all.*

*From her prison inside the ruined cottage, she saw the druid destroy the man who had helped her.*

*She could do nothing. She was trapped here until they needed her. Unseen by the human eye, like a ghost caught in a beam of sunlight, she waited silently among the nettles and weeds.*

*The druid had banished her here with one gesture of the staff. The lock of her hair tied around the haft compelled her. It was useless to resist. She knew they would not let her out again until it was time. They had sensed her reluctance to continue luring Billy in the clearing at the manor house and had intervened before she betrayed them. They had banished her to this ruin in the whisper of a breeze, but at least she had been able to move a little outside the tumbled walls and conspire with the villager. Now the druid had used his staff again with more constricting results, and she could not even do that.*

*She saw the man die and knew she could do nothing further now to prevent*

*Billy's coming.*

*One of the crows flew to land on top of a broken wall, its beady black eye fixed on her for a moment. Then it fluttered away to join its fellows as the sun began to dip toward evening.*

# Chapter Ten
# Staffroom Shenanigans

Julie had witnessed Billy's decline over the last two weeks with a mixture of joy and frustration.

For God's sake, surely he couldn't have liked the silly bitch that much?!

He hardly knew her! He had been with her on two dates! Come on!! Pathetic.

She must give *really* good head or something! That was the only way Julie could account for Billy's despair since losing her.

Losing her? Been dumped, more like. When Julie asked what had happened to Aura, Billy had refused to speak about it at first. But Julie was a girl of infinite wiles and possessed a variety of conversational gambits devised exclusively to wheedle information out of love-lorn and foolish men. She was an expert. She knew *all* the ways.

She knew Billy had been dumped from the very next day after his ill-fated date. Frank had told her all about Billy kissing Aura outside the shop—of *course*, he had! Frank loved gossip more than any shop-girl Julie had ever known. And besides, he knew it hurt Julie, and that gave Frank additional pleasure, the wanker.

So when Billy came in looking all lost and hopeless the next day, Julie had known the score immediately. She had set her plans in motion from that moment onward: first, to find out exactly what had happened between Billy and Aura, and then to work her way into his affections instead. She had accomplished the first objective without too much resistance for a girl of her talents. Billy's pain had to find an outlet, and Julie was nothing if not a sympathetic listener, even if it did take her a few attempts (not to mention a few days) to get the truth from him.

Yet she had the feeling he was not telling her everything. They had an argument on the date, and it was over. End of. But Julie suspected there might be a third person in the relationship. Billy even hinted as much, but she had gained all she could. He had relapsed into brooding silence on that particular subject—and every other subject for that matter.

So that was that, and the first step in her plan was accomplished.

It was the second step that was taking the longest...

But she would persevere. Julie always got what she wanted.

And then one Wednesday, just over two weeks after Billy had been dumped, events took a turn in her favor.

He came into work looking more haggard than usual. He looked confused, defeated, had dark rings under his eyes. She knew he hadn't been sleeping lately, but now he had aged visibly. He stared at her without seeing her when she asked what was wrong with him. There was a look of deep hurt in his eyes.

"You've heard from her, haven't you?" she asked him outright as he hung his coat up in the staff room. He looked through her.

She seized him by both arms.

"Get a grip, man. She's not coming back. Face it."

He seemed to notice her for the first time. "No. I know that now. She's...gone."

"Have you seen her?"

He shook his head slowly. "No."

"Then why do you suddenly seem so sure today she's not coming back after pining for two bloody weeks?"

He moved to the sink, blindly following his customary routine, filling the kettle, grabbing his mug from the cupboard.

Just when Julie thought she wasn't going to get any more out of him, he spoke. "She sent someone to tell me to stay away. She really doesn't want to see me anymore." Yet he still managed to make it sound like a question, as if he were still doubting the finality of his statement. *Asshole!* Still, Julie would make damn sure she drove all doubts from his mind.

"Hoo-bloody-ray. The penny drops at last." She followed him to the sink and put one hand on his back, stroking gently. "So maybe we'll finally have the old Billy back, eh? And maybe he'll even put in a decent day's work?"

*And maybe I'll get him to fuck the hell out of me very, very soon…*

He put down the mug, not having even used it, and without another word, he walked out of the staff room and onto the shop floor.


Tom met him as he emerged.

"You look like shit," the manager greeted him. "Travel section needs shelving. Let's see how fast you can get her done. Pronto Billy-o." Tom grinned inanely and patted him on the shoulder as he swept past.

Billy pushed a trolley laden with books into the Travel section. That wasn't his designated work area, but more and more lately the shelving that should have been done there by Richard Colesley, the Travel bookseller, was being left to pile up. Dick Coleslaw (as Frank uncharitably referred to him) was more intent on following Tom around with his tongue lodged firmly up the manager's arse for brownie points than doing the work he was assigned to do.

Billy hadn't looked for the guide book since the last time Aura had been in. He didn't have the heart and had avoided the Travel section. He tried not to glance over at the shelf where it usually sat as he moved around the large alcove.

He remembered Cyril Peck snatching the book from his hand as he talked to Aura. *Don't think about her! Don't picture her in your stupid head!* The sly bastard had probably done a bunk with it.

Then, as if an invisible thread were pulling him toward the book, he gave up all pretense of ignoring it and strode directly to the shelf. *Might as well check*, he thought distractedly, see if it had been re-shelved, or whether it had indeed been purloined.

He found it straight away and eased it out from the shelf. He felt the blood under his fingers before he saw it. Dried, crusted spots of rusty red patterned the cover. He frowned, scratching at one of the patches, then sniffed his finger. Who the hell had spilled blood on the book? Cyril was the last person Billy had seen read it, and come to think of it, he hadn't seen the shoplifter since. He took it across the shop floor toward the staff room, intending to wash the cover, and bumped into Richard, who was chatting to Tom near the door.

"Is that one of my Travel books?" the pompous thirty-nine-year-old asked, peering through his glasses at Billy with open hostility. Richard was a book snob; if you weren't reading all the latest Booker prize winners, you were beneath him. There were quite a few booksellers with this attitude. Billy stuck by his pulp crime thrillers and loathed Richard and all he stood for. Richard embodied a particular breed of bookseller that condescended to the great unwashed public, imagining they were intellectual sophisticates because they worked in a bookshop. Billy even railed against the term "bookseller"; they were shop assistants, pure and simple. Get the fuck over yourselves.

Billy ignored him, punching in the code on the door.

"Did you hear me?" Colesley's voice took on a more aggressive note.

"I never hear you," Billy said and pushed open the door, slamming it in the Travel bookseller's face.

Julie was still in the staff room. Did she ever do any work?

She was washing her mug as he entered and put it aside to give him a sudden embrace. It took Billy by surprise, and he did not fight it this time. The warmth and closeness of a female suddenly very welcome right now. She looked up at his face, and he thought she was going to kiss him. Her eyes looked hungry and cunning, as always.

"What's the book?" she wanted to know, and he released himself to look for a cloth, hiding the volume from her view as he did so, instinctively not wanting her to see it.

"Blood on it," he mumbled by way of answer, picking up a tea towel and moistening it under the tap. He dabbed at the cover with his back to her while she watched him curiously.

"Your *blood?*"

"Dick Coleslaw's, if he gets in my way again." He scrubbed away at the spots.

"He's a tit. A stuck up prick, you know that. Ignore him."

Billy would have agreed with her wholeheartedly and might have applauded her partisanship but for the fact Julie said the same thing about *everyone* in the bookshop. She hated all of her colleagues apart from Billy, and he knew she only wanted him on her side to prove she had at least one friend. And to fuck him, of course. Her promiscuity was as pronounced as her general hostility.

But right now none of that mattered. Billy dried the book and started back across the room.

"Great conversation," Julie said, following him closely. "We must do it again…"

Billy didn't hear her anymore. He was opening the door to the shop floor and thinking about the book.

Somehow, the book took his mind off Aura now that he had it in his hands. Or rather, it at least stopped his desolate thoughts about her. He didn't know why. The same urge to investigate the book that had driven him a couple of weeks ago when he first met Aura was taking hold of him again. He resisted the urge to flip it open and take a detailed look at the Walks inside. He would save that for later.

Richard followed him into the Travel section.

"You haven't done much," he pointed out, staring at the full trolley, arms folded.

Billy replaced the book on the shelf. "What do you want, Dick?" he asked quietly without turning around.

"Don't call me that." The travel bookseller came up behind Billy, glaring at him through his glasses with piggy little eyes. He hated being called Dick. He had a rectangular head, like a block of wood, and a staid, permanently pompous look on his face.

"Go away, Dick," Billy said, facing him slowly. "Before I lose my temper."

"Are you threatening me?"

Billy stared at him in silence for a moment. What the hell had got up the bland bookseller's ass today? He searched his memory for anything he might have done or said to offend Colesley. He had been surly to everyone over the last fortnight, that was true, and maybe Colesley (who, along with Billy, was the longest-serving bookseller in the shop) saw this as an opportunity to get rid of what he saw as his nearest rival for promotion. Not that Billy gave a toss about promotion. Not now, not ever. It wasn't until Julie suddenly appeared next to Colesley, having heard the tail end of the conversation, and stretched out a hand to rub Billy's shoulder that he began to realize what else might have caused the other bookseller's hostility. The silly sod actually fancied Julie *himself!*

He shook his head. "Get out of my face, Coleslaw, or I'll shelve *you* along with your books…"

Colesley took a tentative step closer, while Julie watched with interest bordering on sexual excitement. He was about the same size as Billy, five-ten, maybe twelve-and-a-half stone. But Billy knew without even considering it that he could kick Colesley's ass all the way to hell and back, if it came to it. He would welcome the chance to blow off steam.

"You're useless!" Colesley spat. "Everyone here knows it. All you do is swan around in a daydream, chasing female customers—and staff! I'm going to make sure Tom knows exactly how useless you really are." He began to turn away. Billy laughed in his face. This was too perfect an outlet for all his frustrations. He actually *wanted* this right now.

"And you're a pompous, conceited jackass," he told Colesley, a grin spreading as he spoke. "And I would *love* to pick you up by the seat of your baggy corduroys, carry you over to Tom, and let you do just that—right before wedging you as far up his arsehole as I can fit you. You wouldn't even need a map to find your way out again either, you've been there so many times."

Julie laughed, thrilled. "Is this how booksellers fight?" she trilled. "You're both so…so *polite!*"

Jerry ambled over, hunting down a *Travel Guide to Spain* for a customer. He took in the situation immediately. "Calm down, kids," he chirped. "You'll both get sacked in a minute if Tom sees you, ya daft bastards. And there's a queue of customers over on the main till. Didn't you hear me ringing the bell?"

Colesley swung round immediately at the mention of Tom's name and followed Jerry back to the counter. Billy laughed again mirthlessly, and Julie rubbed his shoulder again. "You're *baaad,*" she cooed, one eye winking at him suggestively. Before he could move away to help Jerry on the till, she gently restrained him.

"You locking up with me tonight?" she asked coyly.

He nodded, and her hand moved down to stroke his chest.

Billy felt the wildness ebbing a little. He would have smeared Colesley all over the Travel section. The fury had been mounting. He knew it was all down to losing Aura, this blackness that had descended on his soul, this desperation that needed catharsis in some way. Violence had just seemed the easiest option. But now it looked like Julie was offering another one… He thought of Aura, her sensuous beauty. Her kaleidoscope eyes. Then he looked at the far plainer Julie and slowly removed her hand, although he smiled humorlessly as he did so.

Julie couldn't get the last few customers out quickly enough.

She watched Billy carefully as he locked the doors, making sure he didn't slip out with them. James was carrying the tills through to the manager's office. He wouldn't hang around, she knew. The trick was to make sure *Billy* did.

She came up behind him. Her hand snaked up under his black t-shirt, stroking his naked back as he worked the bolts. He jerked and turned around, his face blank.

She pulled him toward her in an embrace. She was surprised when he let her. She kissed him lightly on the lips. "Forget her," she hissed. "She's not coming back. She's not real anymore. I *am...*"

He was still staring at her as though he could see right through her to where James was re-emerging from the staff room door, already wearing his leather jacket.

"Oi, lovebirds, stop that!" He grinned his usual cheeky Jack-the-lad grin and tossed Billy the keys. "Gotta dash, kids. Bristol City at home to Doncaster tonight. Don't do anything I wouldn't do..." He winked as he passed them, then paused and chuckled. "Actually, knock yourselves the fuck out. I would in your shoes." He nudged Billy and nodded at Julie.

"Thanks, James!" Julie objected with mock dismay. Billy said nothing. He put the keys in his pocket.

"Do you mind switching on the alarm in Goods In?" Billy asked her after James had gone, a strange look in his eyes.

She put her arms around him and kissed him again on the lips, a little more suggestively this time. "Why don't we just leave the alarm for a minute?" She smiled up at him provocatively. She noticed he didn't push her away this time. She grabbed his hand and began leading him toward the staff room. Her heart beat a little faster when he followed slowly without objecting.

She punched in the code and dragged him inside. They were alone in the building. She had been waiting a long time for this.

He stood silently in the middle of the staff room, a thousand-yard stare on his face.

*Why was he such an enigma all the time? Did he think he was the sodding James Dean of booksellers or something?* She laughed at her own analogy and sat down on the leather sofa, pulling him after her.

He was like a block of wood. He was looking at her, but she had the infuriating impression he wasn't seeing her. *I bet he's wishing he was with that bitch! Bet he's picturing her face instead of mine... I'll just have to show him what a real kiss is.*

She pressed her lips against his. At first, he didn't respond, but as she increased the urgency of her kiss, she felt his tongue react to hers.

She broke the kiss and pulled her t-shirt over her head. She saw his eyes move over her body. She thrust out her breasts at him, conscious that they were pretty diminutive. The lacy black bra would work him, though…

But just in case… She unhooked the bra and let it slide down her arms and onto the sofa seat. Then she reached out, took both of his hands in hers, and guided them onto her breasts. Still no reaction. She rubbed his hands over her breasts, massaging them, her nipples pert against his palms. She leaned in to kiss him again.

"I'm here," she whispered through parted lips. "I'm *real*…"

She stood up and began unbuttoning her jeans. She slid them down her pale thighs, stepped out of them, while he watched her dully. *For fuck's sake! Look like you're enjoying it!*

"I don't put on this show for just anyone you know," she said petulantly, kicking her jeans away and standing before him naked but for her black knickers. "I bet Dick would love to be in your position right now…"

Billy smiled slowly. It was the first acknowledgment he'd given that she was in the room with him. "Shall I call him?"

She sighed and reached out to pull him off the sofa. She tugged his t-shirt off and began nuzzling his chest, while at the same time undoing the zipper on his jeans. She groped inside the fly for his cock, gratified to see that there was a sign of life in there at last. She slipped her hand in his briefs and closed it around his thickening shaft, easing it out from his fly.

She knelt in front of him and flicked her tongue over the head, then licked the base of his shaft, moving her tongue up the length of him slowly before closing her mouth over the head. He stiffened. She unbuttoned his jeans and tugged them down, then took her mouth away long enough to slide his briefs down. She darted a look up at him. His eyes were closed. *Better not be imagining HER doing this!*

She slid her lips down his shaft once, then back up and reluctantly released him again. She stood up to remove her own knickers before leaning over one arm of the sofa, back toward him, pert ass in his face.

She imagined the mess they would make on the leather seats and grinned at the thought of Tom or Dick sitting on them tomorrow morning.

Still with her back to him, she reached behind to seize his cock, gently pulling him against her, guiding it toward her moist, throbbing pussy. She groaned with pleasure as the tip entered from behind. His penis hesitated at the entrance of her hungry sex, but her guiding hand urged it on until he was fully inside. He began to thrust, and she arched her back, face turned over her shoulder to watch him. She began massaging her own breasts as he pumped. His rhythm was building now, and she gasped aloud as her own passions soared.

And then he was withdrawing abruptly. He began pulling on his clothes while she could only blink at him stupidly, turning round to sit on the sofa, more frustrated than she thought she ever could be.

"What the fuck … are… you… *doing*?!!" She felt like bursting into tears. No man had ever walked away from her like this before.

He was fastening his jeans, face turned from her. "I'm sorry," he muttered. "It's not you…"

"Oh, I *know* it's not me!" She felt her cheeks, which minutes before had been burning with lust, now inflamed with fury. "It's you who has the fucking problem! But then, maybe that's not what you meant, is it? It's not *her*, that's what you really wanted to say, wasn't it, you pathetic bastard?"

She threw his t-shirt at him. He caught it and pulled it over his head. He leaned over and kissed her cheek. She slapped his. Hard. He got his jacket and stood there watching her, still sitting naked on the sofa.

"I just couldn't do it," he said quietly. "I really am—"

"Don't you fucking *dare* say you're sorry again!" She picked up her bra, put it on, still flushed with anger and shame.

*I'll get you for this, you prick…*

When she had finished dressing in silence, he followed her out of the staff room. He gestured toward Goods In. "Could you?"

"Fuck you. Do it yourself. What, you scared of going in there alone? Pussy." She watched him hesitate, then walk toward the swinging doors that opened onto the unpacking room. She thought about storming out now, but a curiosity to see why he was so obviously averse to entering the room made her watch until he came out again. He looked a little pale, but also relieved. Relieved? What the fuck did he expect to happen in there? It wasn't as if she was going to rape him...

"Good night, Julie," he said, opening the main door. He reached forward to kiss her cheek. Impulsively, she seized his head in both her hands and kissed him aggressively. "That's just to show you one last time what you're missing," she said, and left him to lock the door behind them.

As she walked up the street toward the bus stop, her anger and resentment began to cool. She looked back once to see Billy finish locking the door and drop the keys in his jacket pocket. She smiled bitterly to herself. *Nobody fucks me around, you shit. Let's see what Tom thinks of your closing-time escapades...*

The smile stayed with her all the way to the bus stop.

# INTERLUDE THREE

# ROMAN BRITON, 364 AD

They entered the grove, swords in hand.

The centurion led them, eyes strained for any sign of hostility.

He wondered, certainly not for the first time, if the Primus Pilus knew just how dangerous this job was. Sending ten men (now six) into this heathen wilderness to locate and destroy a nest of pagan worshippers. Not the best strategy. *But then, maybe they were just bait. Maybe they were just being used to identify the hostiles and calculate just how powerful they were.* He didn't like that thought. Not one little bit.

Rain dripped from the towering trees as they progressed along the rough path, and the centurion didn't have to think too hard to realize exactly how expendable they were. Look at the caliber of the squad he'd been put in charge of, for Jupiter's sake... If they didn't return from the mission, his superiors would have their answer and probably send in a century to eradicate the enemy. But if one squad could deal with the problem, even better. Resources were stretched, the centurion knew that; the savage Picts to the north of this forsaken hell of an island were causing all sorts of strife. The majority of Caesar's cohorts in Briton were deployed up there, keeping them down. The southern territories had been considered quieter, more civilized...until this particular pagan cult came to Caesar's attention...

All the centurion knew about the mission was that they had to locate the druid cult, and "eradicate their malign influence on the locals."

Druids! The centurion had thought the task sounded easy. Hunt down and kill a pack of philosophers and star-dreamers with long beards who indulged in snipping sprigs of holly and the odd bit of human sacrifice… He really hadn't expected this…

They came to a clearing, and the open space allowed them to spread out a bit more. It soon became apparent that they were not alone.

Someone was standing in the center, watching them.

The centurion raised his hand to halt the troop. The jangling of armor ceased. The centurion peered through the shadows, straining to identify the figure. Then she stepped forward into a moonbeam.

The centurion heard a couple of gasps from the men. There was an approving curse from Sciro, a snigger from Martus.

The centurion frowned disbelievingly, the sword still clutched in his hand. *It's a trap. Has to be. She's the bait.*

She took another step forward. Now he could see the long waves of silky blonde hair, the blue kaleidoscope eyes. Her face was refined yet elfin, her nose slightly curved. She wore a white fleece that covered most of her body apart from her long, slender legs, arms, and a hint of cleavage. She was a wild nymph sent by the Gods to lead them to heaven…or to hell. As yet he hadn't decided which, but considering where they had found her, was decidedly more in favor of believing the latter.

"I would give a thousand Sestertii to fuck that…"

It was Sciro's voice, the centurion knew that. He swiveled round to glare at the burly legionary, who had pushed his way forward to get a better look.

"Shut your mouth, Sciro," the centurion growled. When he turned around again, the nymph was closer. He felt his heart become molten gold just looking at her.

She smiled.

*Stay alert…* He had intended the warning for his men but found himself unable to speak. He could sense their restlessness behind him. If he didn't control them, things could turn nasty here…

Sciro was already pushing past his leader. His face was a mask of lust. He took off his helmet and sheathed his sword. "Come to Sciro, my lovely…" he breathed hoarsely. Some of the others laughed crudely.

The centurion saw how it was going to go. He moved rapidly in front of Sciro and placed the tip of his blade against the legionary's chest. "Get back, Sciro! I'm warning you…"

Sciro glanced at his officer. "Do you wanna know something, *centurion?* I've had more than enough of your fuckin' warnings." As he spoke the last word, he struck out quickly, knocking the centurion's blade aside with his left hand, then smashing his right fist into the officer's face. The centurion staggered back.

Sciro turned to Martus and another of his meaner fellow legionaries, a brooding giant called Bellari. "*Hold him!*"

They had seen how things were going, too, and they liked Sciro's option a lot better. They were hungry, exhausted, and scared, and they hadn't been with a woman in months. They wanted this.

The blonde nymph saw how things were going, too, and began to run. Sciro bellowed with glee and began the chase.

"Let her go, you idiots! Can't you see it's a trap?!" Martus and Bellari seized the centurion. He saw the wild look on their faces and knew reasoning was impossible.

Sciro caught her before she made twenty yards. He seized her round the waist from behind and slung her over his shoulder, laughing wildly. He stroked her naked buttocks where the fleece had ridden high. She kicked and struggled, a wild antelope for sure. He carried her back to the others, grinning crazily. The legionaries laughed coarsely, and one let out a filthy cheer. They had forgotten all about the danger they had encountered, the men they had lost. They had a beautiful, half-naked woman, and they were going to share her. Sciro would go first, of course.

Sciro spotted something in one shadowy corner of the clearing that was ideal for his purposes. He carried his prize over to the long, flat stone and lay her down on it. She tried immediately to get up. Sciro's fist stunned her. His lust and excitement pushing him to wild heights, he wasted no more time.

The centurion watched him rip the fleece from the semi-conscious girl and intensified his struggles. "You touch her and I swear I will kill you, Sciro!" he gasped. "You're a disgrace to the Legion. To *Rome!*"

"What shall we do with this bastard?" Martus called to Sciro. Sciro didn't even turn round as he finished ripping the wool from the lithe body draped before him. "Kill him," he barked, and knelt down on the stone to explore the nymph's body more fully.

Martus let go of the centurion, leaving the huge Bellari to contain him, and drew his sword. "Fair enough," he said, and plunged his blade into the centurion's body.

The centurion gasped, his eyes wide, staring at Martus with incomprehension at how things had gone so badly wrong for him, for his first important trial of leadership. He felt the shock of the blade entering him and the cold that rushed in with it. Martus's face began to recede as if down a long, black tunnel. Bellari dropped him to the path.

On the stone, Sciro was squeezing the nymph's soft breasts with his brutish, filthy hands. His tongue forced its way into her mouth, and she groaned as consciousness began to return. Sciro moved his head down her smooth belly, leaving a trail of saliva and mud behind. He slid his hands beneath her warm buttocks and lifted them slightly, nestling his stubbly chin between her thighs. He could hear the raucous cries of encouragement from the rest of the men as he slid his tongue into her.

It was then they heard the whistling.

# Chapter Eleven
# The Rapist


"Are you sure you want to go there, Julie?"

Tom looked at her steadily. She had never seen him more serious, and her resolve faltered just a tick.

"He forced himself on me, Tom. I swear it."

Tom sat back in his chair and sighed heavily. It was just after nine, and he should be getting on with all sorts of reports and stock management issues. He really didn't need this. Julie could read all that in his face, and the suspicion there, too. She knew he didn't believe her. She bit her lip and tried to look vulnerable and distraught. She worked on bringing up some tears, but that was way too hard.

"All right... Tell me exactly what happened," Tom said resignedly.

Julie took a deep breath, the venomous hatred she felt for Billy crowding out almost all rational thought, but she had spent all night rehearsing this in her mind, and she was going to give it her best shot.

"It was after closing..." she began, pausing demonstratively, hacking up a dry sob. "We were in the staff room. I was about to put my coat on and go home. And Billy..."

He leaned forward again. "Yes...?"

"He pulled me down onto the sofa with him and began...began touching me."

Tom frowned. "Did he hurt you?"

"He *raped* me!" She slammed her fist down on the desk.

Tom blinked, nodded his head slowly. "Go on..." he said.

"He tried ripping my t-shirt off and...and he put his hand between my legs, tried to undo my pants. Then he started undoing his, and... and he took his penis out."

Tom nodded again, weighing up her words. "You do realize this is a very serious allegation, Julie? And if you have any doubts whatsoever, you really need to tell me now. Without any solid proof, this isn't going to do either of you any favors, you know."

She felt his eyes studying her expression carefully, and involuntarily she looked away. Her sign of guilt angered her even more.

"He groped me without my permission and tried to rape me, Tom!"

Tom cleared his throat. "I have to ask you this, so please don't take offense. Did you offer him any encouragement at all?"

She glared at him as if he were mad. She really should have gone to the Royal Academy of Dramatic Arts, she congratulated herself.

"*No!*"

"Okay, it's just I needed to be sure, and you understand the police will ask the same questions."

"Police?" Her voice faltered. She felt a pulse of fear in her gut. She hadn't expected this.

Tom looked deadly serious. That frightened Julie, too. "Of course, the police will have to be involved. I should call them now. There will have to be an internal investigation within the company, too." He leaned back again in his chair, watching her very carefully.

She felt trapped by her own spite. She had just wanted him sacked; she didn't want the police involved. They would know immediately she was lying. Her visions of graduating from the Royal Academy with full honors evaporated.

"But first I'll have to look at the CCTV tapes," Tom said. "The police will want to see exactly what went on last night."

"But...there aren't any cameras in the staff room," she said, realizing as she said it how defensive she was sounding.

"No, but there are in all other areas of the shop. The police will want to examine footage of you both leaving the store to discover if there is any evidence in the way you were both acting to support your allegations."

"You...you sound like a policeman yourself, Tom." She heard the fear in her own voice. Fuck. She remembered kissing Billy by the door and knew it was all over. Why had she gotten herself into this? She knew she'd gone pale.

"That's because I *was* one, back in the day. Detective Sergeant down in Essex. Had to leave the force for medical reasons. Now..." He scrutinized her again. "Are you absolutely *convinced* you want to go through with this?"

Julie realized she was swallowing. *Couldn't look more guilty if you tried, you silly bitch.* Her plans suddenly didn't look quite so clever after all.

Tom came to her rescue. "Why don't you go away and think about it? Maybe take the day off." His tone suggested he would prefer it if she took the rest of the year off—indeed, never came back at all.

She got up from her chair. She really didn't know what else to say.

"Julie," Tom began quietly. "We're all aware you've got a crush on Billy. Please don't let it ruin your career. Sometimes you just have to accept it when someone's not interested. We can still all put this behind us if you're having any doubts whatsoever about whether you're doing the right thing here. Now..." His eyes assumed a kindly, avuncular expression. "Do you really want me to proceed with this or not?"

She shook her head briefly and walked toward the door, guilt, fear—and hell yes, even shame—preventing her from saying anything else.

Tom called to her as she opened the door.

"Oh, and Julie?"

She turned, unable to look him in the eye.

"Stay away from Billy. For my sake, if not your own."

She closed the door quietly behind her.

# Chapter Twelve
# The Somerset Triangle

But keeping away from Billy was not going to be so easy for Julie. The very next morning Tom called a staff meeting just before they opened the store.

Billy noticed she avoided looking at him and was thankful for that. He sat nursing a coffee while Tom ushered everyone into the staff room, all business-like and cheerful at the same time. He sat down on the most comfortable chair and smiled benignly.

"Don't worry. No redundancies this week!"

It was in bad taste, not unusual for Tom. There were constant threats of job losses from Head Office. The last cull had been the month before when they lost the official Goods In un-packer (they had to all share that job now) and a couple of part-timers.

Perhaps realizing he was treading on toes, Tom got straight on with the matter at hand. Billy thought Julie looked particularly tense. He didn't care. He couldn't worry about her feelings now.

"Some of you might be aware—and the rest of you might not care—that it's the tenth anniversary this month of our branch opening in Bristol." He'd been wrong; judging from the blank faces on all ten faces, just about *nobody* cared. Julie, if anything, looked a little relieved. Only Colesley nodded brightly, just to remind everyone whose ass his square head was firmly up. "Please manage to contain your excitement..." Tom added ruefully. "I know it's hard."

"Whoopdeedoo," Jerry said humorlessly.

Tom frowned at him, then carried on. "And Head Office has generously set aside part of this year's budget especially for us to celebrate it." He glanced back at Jerry to see if the morose Liverpudlian had anything else to add, but the bookseller obviously found his shoes more interesting.

"So what I want from you lot is ideas. What would be the best way to celebrate? A party in the store after closing? A party while the shop is open that involves the customers?"

Obviously, neither option appealed, judging from the silence that greeted this. Colesley decided to come to the rescue: "So when were you thinking this would take place, Tom?"

"Any time in the next month. It could be next week, or the weekend... It could be—"

"Next Saturday." Billy spoke without thinking. He had no idea why he spoke; it just came out. It had seemed important.

"Okay..." Tom shrugged. "Any reason?"

"No reason. Saturday's a good day to..." *Die?* No, that wasn't the word he was groping for. "...party," he finished quietly, making the word sound anything but. He was dimly aware they were all looking at him.

"Next Saturday..." Tom threw it out there. "Everyone on board with that? Sounds reasonable to me. Seeing as you're being so forthcoming today, Billy, have you any thoughts on how exactly we could 'party'?"

"Not yet..." His voice was distant, as if he were waking from a dream. "But I'll let you know."

"Excellent. You do that. Right, shop is opening in five minutes. So let's go make some sales. Remember to cross-sell at the tills, and remember mirroring. It works!"

"Mirroring, my ass," Jerry muttered as Tom got up. But the manager didn't seem to hear, or he ignored it if he did. He paused in the doorway and glanced at Billy as he rose from his chair.

"Billy? A word please…"

Billy followed him through into the manager's office.

"Close the door behind you."

Billy did so and sat down opposite the manager. He stared back at Tom, waiting. "I haven't thought of anything yet…" he said slowly.

"It's not about that." Tom looked a little hesitant. He fiddled with a pile of reports on his desk, then shoved them away purposefully. He fixed Billy with his serious business stare. "Are you aware that Julie has made a complaint against you?"

Billy took that in slowly. It didn't register as important. "No. What am I supposed to have done?"

"It was a serious complaint, and it needs discussing. I need to hear your side of the story."

He nodded, waiting. Tom sighed and told him about Julie's allegation. When he finished, Billy nodded again. "It didn't happen like that."

"So tell me how it *did* happen."

"She came on to me. I started to respond then stopped. She didn't like that." He sounded bored. "Can I go back to work now, or would you like me to leave the shop altogether?"

"Do you *want* to leave? It doesn't sound to me like you're that bothered."

Billy shrugged. "Like I said: it didn't happen that way. You can believe me… Or not."

Tom regarded him steadily for a few seconds. "I should sack both of you, you realize that? It sounds like something promiscuous took place on the premises, and you know that's strictly against company policy."

Billy said nothing.

Tom lifted his chin up importantly. "But I'm going to give you a break. Your work's dipped a little recently, and I know you've had some personal issues—nothing is private in here, I'm afraid—but as far as I'm concerned, that's all in the past. You made a positive contribution to this morning's meeting, and I'm just as positive you can contribute more. In fact, I'm going to put you in charge of organizing next Saturday's celebration. Consider it a punishment for screwing around in the staff room after hours if you like..." Was that a sign of *approval* on Tom's face? Billy stared back at the manager and imagined him as a bookseller learning the ropes down in Exeter and gradually working his way up to managerial level. Did that rope-learning include a few casual digressions away from career-building into more romantic escapades? Looking at the slim, narcissistic manager, Billy was pretty sure it did.

"So you don't believe her?"

Tom got up, signaling the chat was over. "Let's just say I think she was embellishing the facts and leave it at that."

Billy left Tom's office and headed straight for the Travel section. He hadn't been asked to shelve there today, but that didn't matter. He pulled out the book and, ignoring Julie, who was dallying in the Sports section chatting to Jerry, made for Goods In. It was 9:30 in the morning, and he did not expect to hear any whistling. What he did hope for was a bit of privacy.

Luckily, the unpacking room was empty. He sat down at the desk, the book next to him, and switched on the PC. Ignoring the stock systems, he fired up the internet instead. He picked up the book and flicked through to the publishing details.

He entered Hobbemarke House into a search engine and waited for a response. One entry. He clicked on it, and there was a black and white picture, copyright 1936, of a rambling mansion. Not much information. Nothing about it belonging to a publisher. But the address given beneath the bleak picture was a little more illuminating: Grove Lane, Payndom.

He picked up the book again almost feverishly and thumbed through the pages to Walk No. 21. There it was... the path started at Payndom.

Back to the search engine, and this time he entered the name of the village.

This time the results were a little more eye-opening.

Billy felt the room grow chill around him as he studied the entries. Something stirred on the desk next to him, making him jerk around in alarm. The A4 sheet from an unpacking report moved again, then fluttered to the floor. The air conditioner, idiot. He turned back to the computer, throat dry.

There were four mentions of Payndom in total. A small village in Somerset, established officially in 1411, but some of the information hinted there had been some kind of community in the location long before that. The search entries were brief and vague. The majority of them consisted of supposition and local rumor rather than historical facts, though there were a couple of newspaper articles and quotes posted in one.

Payndom had a little bit of a reputation, it seemed. At least, the surrounding area did. It appeared the locale had been the subject of missing person investigations several times over the last eighty years or so (and Billy strongly suspected the absence of reports before then presumably only indicated a lack of investigative resources and journalistic sophistication in those less media-driven times).

Billy rubbed his chin nervously as he read. "A veritable sinkhole of human disappearances," *The Somerset Gazette* had gushed back in 1933. The Bristol-based *Evening Press* had even got involved in 1963 with: "A deepest Somerset Bermuda Triangle where hikers, ramblers, and various visitors to the area have been noted missing for hundreds of years…" Knowing the *Press*, that probably involved a little bit of hyperbole, but Billy felt the chill intensify in the room nevertheless. Another snippet from one article caught his attention. It was very brief, not very informative, and seemed reproduced purely to add to the mystery: "a number of obscure public access footpaths apparently exist in the vicinity of Payndom that seem to defy all OS surveyors' attempts to reconnoiter them."

His eyes wandered back to the book still open at the Payndom walk. He felt the strongest compulsion yet to stride out of the shop with the book right now and follow it. His mind raced. Aura had been looking at the path. She had a Somerset accent… She had been particularly secretive about where she actually lived, but Billy suddenly had a worrying conviction that it might be Payndom.

But so what if she did live there? There had never been any real concrete proof of foul deeds in the area. No bodies had been reported as turning up. It was all Penny Dreadful speculation.

He remembered the three figures emerging from the shadows at Tortworth Court. He remembered the fear in Aura's face. His hands trembled as he lifted the book.

Julie chose that moment to enter Goods In. She knew he was in there, and despite everything Tom had said about staying away, she just couldn't. It was a suppurating itch she just had to fuckin' scratch. When she saw him holding the book, she recognized it immediately. The blonde bitch he was mourning had been reading it when he'd first met her, hadn't she? The barely suppressed indignation, hurt, and anger simmered close to the boiling point.

"What the fuck is *wrong* with you? You are seriously obsessed!" She watched him from just inside the doorway, scorn twisting her up inside, and probably twisting her face up, too, for that matter. "Ahhhh, just because *she* was holding it, you have to as well... How fucking sweet. How fucking nauseating!"

He ignored her and continued to study the book.

Now she wanted to slap him. The urge was all but irresistible. "Reading that won't bring her back, you dick!" Realization dawned. "Oh, I get it... It's your day off tomorrow, isn't it? What, you gonna go on her favorite walk, see if she's waiting for you?! You're not just fucking mad, you're pathetic, too!" She strode over and snatched the book out of his hands before she could even think about how crazy she might look herself. "You'll *never* see her again. Face it!"

The book was still open to Walk No. 21. Julie glared at it, her hands shaking with rage. Through the red haze, she saw the circular route, a few penciled Tudor-style houses representing the village, a clutch of trees representing Lord's Wood. The Grove was depicted with more trees and a flat stone drawn between them, accompanied by an "ancient monument" notation next to it.

And as she looked, the anger began to fade...

It was replaced by a new sensation: a tingle of unease. It played up and down her spine, a clammy finger, and then slipped under the protecttive layers of her mind. It tickled the itch to pursue and persecute Billy and made it even stronger, wilder: a more dangerous itch, a maddening compulsion.

When Billy tried to take the book out of her hands, she was strangely unwilling to let it go. With a more concerted tug, he snatched it from her.

Then he closed it and walked out without saying a word. She watched him go, and it took all her strength to resist the urge to follow.

# Part Two
# The Walk

# Chapter Thirteen
## Stalk

If she had studied herself in the rearview mirror, she would have seen a permanent scowl on her blandly pretty features. Her small, gray eyes were as bright and mean as a seagull's. Her hands rested on the steering wheel as she patiently watched the house across the street.

It was early. But what did they say about the early bird?

*This was one worm she wasn't only going to catch, she was going to...*

A frown was added to the scowl in the rearview. What the hell *was* she going to do to him anyway? And come to that, why the hell was she bunking off work with a sick call that she suspected Tom was actually quite glad to receive to follow someone she hated on a wild goose chase into deepest Somerset?

The frown stayed. She had no answer. She couldn't explain her compulsion. Was it hatred, though? Or was it obsession?

No. *He* was the one obsessed.

So... What was *she* doing exactly?

She squeezed the steering wheel of her boyfriend's Mazda angrily. All she knew was she had to follow him. She couldn't rationalize anything beyond that.

She glanced at the dashboard clock: 8:15. Suppose he'd already left?

No. She didn't think so. She knew exactly which house he lived in—she'd checked that out on the cover of his pay slip envelope—and the curtains facing the street were still drawn. *But what if he was in such a hurry, he didn't bother opening them?*

She bit her lip. Her stomach grumbled. She hadn't even thought about breakfast. Her eyes ached from the sleepless night she had endured. And that was his fault, too. She bit her lips harder.

The red front door in the terraced house opened.

Julie tensed, squeezing the wheel harder.

A fat, balding man emerged, pulled the door closed behind him.

Julie exhaled, her heart racing. The number on the door was 75. Billy was 73. She'd been focusing on the wrong door for the last fifteen minutes.

*This was ridiculous!* She should go back home, go to bed. This bastard was making her unwell.

She closed her eyes, trying to calm her breathing. And almost missed Billy step out of the door of number 73 and walk over to his Beetle parked at the curb. He was wearing a light leather jacket and some scruffy boots with a light rucksack slung over one shoulder.

She waited for him to start the engine. A cloud of noxious vapor coughed out of the rusty twin exhausts. *Twat! Doesn't even know how to keep his car maintained.*

When the Beetle had pulled away from the curb and was halfway down the quiet street, she started her own engine. The Mazda purred into life and followed slowly.

The Beetle turned right, and she followed down to the junction with the main road. The purple car swung left this time, and she let a car slip past before doing the same. Billy wouldn't recognize her boyfriend's car, but he might spot Julie's face in his rearview if she stuck too close.

He was heading up the Wells Road out of Bristol as she'd suspected he would. The Walk was in deepest Somerset, and this was the main route there from the city.

Did he really think he would find his lost girl? Sad fuck. Like she would just be strolling around the path every day—or hangin' out on a street corner in Payndom... Actually, that wouldn't be a bad guess. *And when exactly did she get so bitter?* She couldn't blame Billy entirely for her growing hatred of men. Her boyfriend was a useless, inattentive fuck, too. He farted in bed and thought that was funny. He took a dump when she was trying to have a restful bubble bath. He didn't go down on her anymore, like he thought she was dirty...

He didn't do a whole lot of things, which was why she thought Billy might bring some new magic and excitement into her life. She'd fancied him for a couple of months now. His polite disinterest in her had just made her more determined, and when it seemed the other day that at last he had succumbed—only to then push her away... (*in the middle of fucking her!*) She guessed that was the point of no return all right. He would fucking pay for what he had done, that was for sure... although strangely, that didn't seem quite so important anymore. She frowned again into the rearview mirror, and this time she saw her own expression—and also the tired, yet haunted look in her eyes. So exactly what *was* important now? Following Billy into Redneck County to spy on him hiking?

Again, she had no answers. She just knew she had to do this.

She realized her confusion had made her ease her foot off the pedal, and now a Mini Metro had nipped past and there were two cars separating her from Billy.

Bristol was behind them. They were following the sweep of the A37 through open countryside. To the right, a field of rape, bright yellow as a child's crayon sketch of the sun. To the left, soft hills and patches of lush woodland, undulating to the east in the direction of Bath. She ignored the beautiful scenery, eyes fixed on the Beetle, which she could occasionally see as he took a bend ahead of the other two cars.

They swept through Pensford, immortalized by the Wurzels in their Greatest Cider Hits. Wells was twelve miles away now. She knew Payndom was further than that. Right out in the sticks, from what she'd seen in the book. Strangely enough, when she tried to find it on an OS map in the shop, there had been no sign of it. When she'd entered Payndom in a search engine, she hadn't been able to find it there either.

It didn't matter. Billy had the map. He knew where he was going. All she had to do was follow.

After fifteen more minutes, the car immediately behind Billy turned off to Glastonbury. The Metro continued to follow the Beetle until the junction for Weston, and then that peeled off, too. Julie toed the brakes, dropping back. She passed the Weston intersection and continued onward, keeping a respectful distance between them. She had a suspicion he was too preoccupied to spot her anyway. He hadn't been himself for nearly three weeks now. Ever since he'd met that *whore*...

She squeezed the wheel and involuntarily revved the accelerator. The Mazda sped ahead, and the Beetle hove into view, almost filling her windscreen. She hurriedly took her foot off and let the other car gain distance again. Careful.

When the Beetle finally turned off the A-road and trundled down the leafy lane which an antiquated signpost (with a pointing finger for fuck's sake) indicated as leading to Payndom (see, it *does* exist!), it was nearly 9:30.

Julie saw the jaunty, little, purple car disappear down into the tunnel of trees and again pumped the brakes. She'd have to be careful now. Even the oblivious Billy might become suspicious if the same car that had tailed him all the way from Bristol also followed him into a no-horse village like Payndom—which *did* exist.

She dropped to twenty miles an hour and eased the Mazda down the lane. Even so, she was driving fast enough to almost miss the Beetle turning up what looked like a disused drive through the trees at the left-hand side of the road. She decided to carry on and park in the village and then walk back. The Beetle had disappeared into the trees now, and she could tell from the condition of the drive that it was a no-through road. Reappearing into the strengthening sunlight of this late April morning, she saw the village ahead of her. She parked next to a stile and got out, oblivious to the peacefulness of her surroundings, the delicate freshness of the country air.

She glanced at the stile, then at the path that cut straight across the fields to a gate, and beyond that, another field bright with poppies and a dense wood in the distance. She tensed. Almost forgot to breathe. An excitement was building in her. It had been there all morning, playing with her. Now it was strong. And it wasn't pleasurable. She forgot about following Billy. It wasn't about him anymore.

It hadn't really been about him since she snatched the book from him in Goods In the day before. This was all about Julie now: Julie's need. Her *urge* for self-destruction. And that was as good a name for following one's destiny as any other.

Julie's fate lay in her heart, in her loins, in her obsessive-compulsive mind…

…and in a book of walks that led to only one place.

It wasn't so much the place you *deserved* to go to, necessarily. But it was always, in the end, the place you *chose*.

Julie's choice lay over the stile and toward Lord's Wood.


The drive was old and badly maintained. Broken branches from the overhanging trees littered the track. Billy carefully eased the Beetle's tires over them. Potholes and ruts bounced him around in the basic leather seat.

He had nearly missed the little drive on the left of the lane. If he hadn't glanced across at the right moment, he might have driven straight past. He knew instinctively this was the place, although he didn't see the sign until he had guided the Beetle around the first curve, and even then, it was partially hidden in the foliage, the painted letters stripped by age and weathering.


## HOBBEMARKE MANOR


That was all: no indication that it was still operating as a publishing house. And Billy strongly doubted that was the case even before he turned the final bend in the long drive and the building came into view.

He pulled up in a rutted area of gravel in front of the house and switched off the engine.

He got out and slowly approached the main door of the once-imposing building. He knew it was Tudor from his research. Two wings pushed out from either side of the ivied entrance. Three tall and very thin chimneys extended up from the roofs of both wings. It must have been magnificent and awe-inspiring back in the day. Now it was just somehow…threatening.

Every window was boarded over. The door had a rusted aluminum sheet secured across it. The once-sweeping front lawns were knee-high with wild grass and nettles. More weeds pushed through the gravel of the drive and cracked the walls around the door.

The place had obviously not been used for a very long time.

"They said it were the Devil…"

The voice made him spin round. He had assumed he was alone in such a bleak spot as this.

A bent, old stick of a man had emerged from the overgrown rhododendron bushes that clogged the gardens behind the house. He crept toward Billy, one hand outstretched like he was begging for alms. He was tattered and grimy. One shoe had a split all the way down one side. His beard should have been white but was brown with stains. Billy didn't even want to guess what they might be from.

"They said it were the Devil trod 'ere," the man spoke again in his creaky voice.

Billy stared at him. The sentence was the wildest non-sequitur he'd ever heard.

"I don't understand you," he said, wishing the man would go.

"That's why it's called Hobbemarke…d'you see…?"

Billy didn't see. He glanced back at his car, ready to leave again. He was wasting his time here… Or was he? Indecision kept him there a moment longer. He looked into the man's rheumy eyes, hoping to spot any sign of lucidity, and asked the question uppermost on his mind.

"Do you know if a blonde girl called Aura lives near here…? I…

I don't know her surname. Just that I think she lives in Payndom or hereabouts…" It sounded pathetic and desperate.

The man laughed. He obviously thought so, too. The laugh cracked into a cough, and spittle was ejected onto the gravel. The spittle was brown, too.

"You're after a girl, huh? Yep. Course you are. Don' worry. You'll find her all right." He evidently thought that was funny, too. "You'll find her!" He was beginning to turn away, heading back toward the slight path Billy could now make out between the rhododendron bushes. A shortcut back to the village possibly. He might have wondered what the man was after on the grounds of this creepy, old, deserted house, but it suddenly seemed obvious to him: he had been waiting to pass on a message. *Don't worry, you'll find her.*

*He was expected…*

He had come too far and suffered too much despair to be frightened off now.

He walked hurriedly after the man. "Wait, please! You know her?"

The man stopped and turned again. He lifted one crooked hand as if testing the wind direction. He spat again. "Back in the day—an' they were very *old* days—they called it Hobbe after him, ye see… Old Hob. Or old Nick, take yer pick…" He cackled at his own wit. "But I ain't so sure they was meanin' summat else just as bad, cos that ain't His name…they didn't call it Hobbedom, did they…huh?" He cracked out more laughter. "Maybe it weren't the Devil hisself, y'see. You understand? Maybe t'were summat else altogether, just as bad, what made the mark. The house were built on it. Did ye know that? He trod this way an' left His mark. But you kin find out all about Him for yerself: you'll be seein' Him afore too long, iffen you follow the way. An' if you seen the book, that's zactly what you'll be a-doin'." His mouth stretched wide in manic glee. The few teeth he had left were licorice black.

"The book?" Billy was attempting to make sense of the man's crazy words. "The book that was published here?"

"Man is lost…may he each find his way…" The man spat again

with an air of finality. The words were familiar, but in the time it took Billy to remember they were from the preface of the guide book, the man was gone, pushing through the blue and purple blossoms.

Billy struggled through the bushes, but after a while, the path petered out and the branches ripped at his flesh too cruelly. He fought his way back to the drive and climbed into the car, his thoughts racing.

Deluded old fool… or did he *really* know something more?

Billy was wasting time. He felt the urge strong inside him now, a power that made his blood pulse, his head ache. He had the guide book. He was near the village.

He was near the path.

He had to follow its call.

# Chapter Fourteen
# Walk No. 21

Julie climbed slowly over the iron gate.

There seemed no need to rush. She passed the tumble-down cottage without looking at it. Her eyes were fixed on the woods at the far end of the poppy field.

Her thoughts were strange and distracted as she moved through the nodding red poppies. The hatred and bitterness had ebbed, and she felt herself drifting instead into a dreamlike state.

She pictured her boyfriend, who would be at his office right now, bullshitting pensioners into accepting dodgy life insurance. She pictured his stubborn face, the crafty eyes. She had never loved him. She was glad she was walking away from him.

She pictured her mum, all frosty expressions and sarcasm. She had driven her father away with just one of those looks. Was Julie the same? Had she inherited her mother's insecurity and resulting hostility toward all males?

She'd wanted to fuck Billy, though, hadn't she?

Not anymore. No. That was all behind her.

It didn't matter, though, really, did it? None of it.

She had reached the woods now. On the nearest birch, a faded laminated A4 poster had been nailed to the trunk. She barely registered the photocopied picture of a young brunette—or the bold word "MISS-ING" beneath. Cyril Peck had missed it altogether.

She followed the path through the trees.

Where was she going?

It was a distant question in her mind, certainly not a pressing one. It didn't need answering, even if she had been able to. *Just keep going, Julie. You'll get there soon.*

She passed a painted wooden sign nailed to another tree. She barely noticed this either (Cyril had missed it, too). "PAINTBALL ZONE," it announced in lurid, red letters with a wonky arrow pointing down a steep hill to the right. The main path continued straight on, however, and Julie took that one. She wanted to see The Grove (ancient monument included).

No, that wasn't quite right. Julie didn't *want* to see The Grove. She just had no choice in the matter anymore. Her legs took her there while her mind wandered, that was all.

She stepped over a mobile phone, half-buried in the mud. No concern of hers. It was quiet in the woods. She heard no birds. *That sounded like the first line in a novel,* she thought dreamily. *She heard no birds...*

The woods were dark, but some sunlight managed to filter through. The trees were a mixed bunch, and if Julie had taken an interest in nature, she would have appreciated the variety that grew here. But she didn't. Never had. So she didn't enjoy the silver birch, their trunks ghostly in the half-light; she strode right past the bluebells emerging between the roots of ash and elder, all of them dominated by the ever-present oak and the brittle beech. Julie didn't see the woods for the trees at the best of times. Today was not to be the best of times for Julie.

But she did see the figure walking slowly toward her along the path.

She could just make out the long, black robe, the voluminous hood. The figure stopped, as if waiting for her to join it.

The stone dagger in the figure's hand glinted coldly.

It was the glint more than the figure itself that caused Julie to awaken from her dream.

She hesitated on the path, her breath stalling. The figure took a step forward. She couldn't see under the hood. The old, weird dagger was raised.

Julie knew then that her entire life had led up to this moment. Had it been a good one? Had she made the most of it? Had she been good and wise and kind, like you're supposed to be, like the way her grandmother once advised her to live her life when she was just twelve years old sitting in her cramped, old kitchen with a glass of milk and a chocolate cake? Had she? Fuck no. She was a bitch and she knew it.

It all came to this. This was her reward, this dark figure in a dark wood.

She swiveled around, survival instinct brushing away the cobwebs, overcoming the other need that had pushed her here. But turning was no good either. There were two more hooded figures behind her, approaching casually. It seemed they were convinced there was no need for speed. One carried a long staff; the other, wrapped in brambles, clutched a wicked branch laden with innocent red berries and not-so-innocent thorns and flints.

Real fear filled her heart like cold, black treacle. *Would they rape her? Is that what they wanted? Or more than that? The weapons looked ready for use. Was that dried blood on the end of the staff, where the branches were carved into a claw?*

The fear forced her into action. Julie was no wilting flower. She picked up a broken branch about as thick as her forearm and hurled it at the nearest figure, the one with the staff. It struck him in the head, and the hood twitched aside. The figure didn't even flinch, but Julie caught a glimpse of what was beneath the hood, and suddenly she didn't feel as brave anymore. She wanted to shrink down on the path and cover her head, wanted to scream until this nightmare went away, but the figures were closing on her now and...

...and above all, Julie realized she really *wanted to live!*

She ducked to the right, leaving the path and blundering between the trees, leaping through bramble and fern. She didn't dare turn to see if she were being pursued. All she could hear was the pounding of her own blood in her ears and the crackle of the undergrowth as she forced her way through.

She found she was heading downhill, and soon she stumbled through a thick bank of ferns onto another path, the one she had seen earlier, diverting from the main route. Her thoughts were chasing one theme now: if she survived this horror, she would one hundred percent change her ways and live like her Nanna said she should. Oh, she would be so wise, she would be oh so good, and she would be the kindest fuckin' human being *ever* to grace this planet.

She risked a glance back.

And stopped, breath rasping from her exertions.

The bank above her was empty. Trees, fern, and bramble, but no sign of the black figures.

The thought occurred to her that it might all be a stunt. Students playing a game. Then she remembered the brief glimpse of dirty fur beneath the hood, the bifurcated hoof where there should have been a human head. She began to hurry down the path.

She came to a stream, chuckling merrily through the April woodland without a care in the world. Julie paused at the little wooden bridge formed of two planks and looked back again.

Still nothing.

She crossed the bridge, her pace slowing a bit now, a stitch painful in her right side.

Ahead of her, through the trees, she could see a large roped-off section. A couple of corrugated iron huts occupied the interior of the compound, the walls not only battered and rusty, but blotched with different colored explosions of paint. The trees within the compound were similarly discolored. Julie moved toward the huts

Another glance back.

A hooded figure stood on the bridge watching her, staff in hand.

She let out a mew of despair. She whipped her head round to face the paintball compound. It was a good hundred yards ahead through the trees. It looked deserted anyway, disused and neglected. Nobody around to help her.

*Nobody.*

When the figure stepped from behind a pine tree into the path right in front of her, dagger in hand, she knew she would never make the compound—even if there had been someone there to help.

And now, at last, she thought of Billy.

She thought of Billy as the third figure appeared in the dark doorway of one of the huts, twitching the thorn branch in its hand nastily.

She thought of Billy, and she almost loved him again. Or did she hate him *so* much she could no longer tell the difference?

She could call to him, and maybe he would hear… He might have driven back down that drive by now; he might even have started the walk. He might be just up above her on the path she had left…

"Billy…" It was a croak.

She took a deep breath and let out a scream of pure, distilled terror that took Billy's name in vain and shouted it to the world.

But Billy wasn't coming.

She knew that as the figure with the dagger approached her and she saw up close and personal what was under its hood.

*Billy wasn't coming for her. Ever.*

If Billy had read her thoughts, he would have agreed with them. He wasn't coming for Julie. That wasn't part of the plan. He had another blonde in mind entirely.

Billy parked behind the blue Mazda. He wondered distantly if somebody else might be exploring Walk No. 21, but soon forgot the car as he climbed over the wooden stile and leaped down onto the grass beyond. He glanced back once at the silent village behind him and wondered if Aura might be there, safe inside one of the old-fashioned, thatched-roof cottages he could see peering up over the hedge marking the boundary of the field. Maybe he would investigate the village later. Right now, every impulse inside him was pushing him along the path.

He hesitated only long enough to consult the instructions in the book. *After the gate, the path continues onward to the wood.*

He paused on top of the iron gate. The ruined cottage in the middle of the meadow seemed to hold his attention for some reason. He dropped down on the other side and walked through a mass of daisies and dandelions toward it.

Halfway across the meadow, he came to a stream. He hadn't been able to see it from a distance, as it was hidden in a shallow gulley. A small stone bridge spanned the slow water. Billy paused on the bridge, hands on the warm stone and peered down into the ripples and whirlpools. Funny, he didn't remember seeing this stream marked on the map. He pulled out the book again, and there it was. The instructions were clear enough to make him wonder how he had missed it: *After the gate, the path leads to a stream. Cross by the stone bridge and continue onward to the woods.* Maybe he hadn't looked properly before.

He reached the cottage and felt the attraction draw stronger. The skin on the back of his neck tingled, as did his arms. But there was nothing to see inside the ruin apart from broken walls, a towering chimney breast, and sprouting weeds. He watched the drifts of dandelion seeds caught spinning in a shaft of sunlight for a moment. He felt reluctant to move away for some reason..

He stiffened. Had he just caught a hint of Aura's scent—the May blossom fragrance that had so entranced him? He climbed over a pile of masonry into the ruin, nettles brushing against his jeans.

*The aroma seemed stronger.*

"Billy…"

He spun.

He could swear he had heard his name —but oh so faintly, like a whisper from afar, on the fringe of audibility. He strained his ears, desperate to hear it again. It had been Aura's voice. He knew it.

When he felt the touch on the back of his neck, he knew that was hers, too.

He turned around yet again, hope flaring up in him. He desperately scanned the interior of the cottage.

Nothing but nettles, weeds, piles of stone, and shadow. His hand felt the nape of his neck where he had felt the touch (*her* touch!), and he examined what he found there, clinging to his skin. A dandelion seed—a fairy, his mother had called them. He waited, longing for another touch, listening intently.

But he heard nothing more, felt nothing more.

After half an hour, he stepped back over the broken wall and made his way to the path again.

It *had* been her voice…her hand. He was certain of it, though he couldn't explain how. He looked back at the cottage one last time as he walked away.

The dandelion seeds were still drifting in their prison of light.

In the rucksack on his back, the book felt heavy, pressing against his shoulders, as if urging him on.

He entered Lord's Wood, spotted the "MISSING" poster nailed to a tree straight away. The photograph showed a girl in her late twenties, brunette, a little chubby, with glasses. She was smiling, her eyes faded by time and the elements despite the laminate cover. Billy paused long enough to read the date—1989—and then he was past, the poster girl almost forgotten as the urge to advance grew stronger.

*Billy…*

This time the voice was either in his head or so inaudible as to be beyond the range of human ears. He glanced at a signpost pointing to a Paintball Zone along the path that slipped down the wooded hillside to his right.

He kept walking.

The oaks closed around the path, giving way occasionally to arcades of younger pine that were quickly sealed off by more oak and beech. There was not much light. Billy kept going.

He passed a pigeon hanging by its neck from a string attached to a branch.

Billy kept going.

He reached the far edge of Lord's Wood and stepped out into glorious sunlight.

His face warmed by the rays, he knelt for a moment in the grass and removed his rucksack. He didn't really need to consult the book to check that the copse of trees across the grassy plain was The Grove; it was already etched in his mind. Yet he found himself pulling the book out regardless, instinctively falling into a rhythm with the Guide as the main instrument.

The map showed him The Grove and the settlement beyond. After that, the path swung into wild land with no markings or names of any substance. The text told him the path wound past a stream and over the bare hump of heath before flexing around in a wide curve to come up behind the southern fringe of Lord's Wood again.

Billy wondered if he would get that far. *But what else had he come here to do, if not the entire walk?*

He put the book away, slung the rucksack on his back again, and strode through the long grass toward The Grove.

He was struck by the silence. No breeze, no birds. No sign of habitation for miles around. He made The Grove after five minute's steady pace.

*Billy!*

More insistent this time. His imagination again? His scalp prickled.

The book weighed against the small of his back. *What are you waiting for? You can't be afraid of a copse of trees…*

More oaks, twisted in awful shapes. *They don't scare me either.*

His boot nudged something hard beside the path.

He looked down. A mobile phone nestled in a patch of daisies right next to the trail. He recognized it immediately.

He scooped up the blocky cell with a burst of excitement. He stared all around him into the foliage on either side of the path before thumbing the "On" button. It took so long to blink into life that he was sure it was water-damaged and would not work at all. Finally, the outdated menu screen popped up, and his thumb moved to the messages icon.

There they were: every text he had sent her over the last three weeks. He knew if he pressed the voice mail button he would hear his own voice, becoming increasingly forlorn and desperate with each message left.

She had been here then. He had been right…

"Billy."

This time the voice was clear and close. Shivers of anticipation and joy ran through him.

"Aura!!" Again he whirled around on the path, trying to fix on which direction the voice came from. He settled on straight ahead and trotted along the path.

Not more than fifty yards ahead, the trees opened up into a clearing. The sound of creaking reached his ears before he got there. He halted, a thread of fear chasing away the exhilaration. He could see the center of the clearing, ablaze with sunlight. The sound came from the oaks fringing the far side. He began to step cautiously forward…

He was barely surprised when he heard the whistle calling to him. This time, the notes seemed to lull him in some subtle, horrible way; a sedative of fright that sucked at his resolve as if the whistle had picked away at his resistance over time and he was finally giving in to its seductive power. Jubilant and gloating, the three notes beckoned him on into the clearing. And incredibly, he followed the call, his feet moving as if separated from his will. The whistle played over the creaking, a symphony of terror that drew him on instead of repelling him.

Now he could see them.

Shadows hanging from the creaking branches. Nooses fashioned from thick bramble tendrils around their necks as the bodies slowly swung and spun. He could not take his eyes off the revolving forms, as yet still obscured by the gloom beneath the oaks. He took another tentative step forward into the sunlight, automatically shading his eyes with his hand to make out more detail. The whistle stepped up a key, urgent, *expectant*…

"*Billy!!!*"

The voice was a scream this time, echoing around The Grove.

Billy froze.

They could have been dummies or scarecrows dangling in the dark, but the scream had alerted him to the fact that there was no earthly reason why he should find out. The whistle stopped for a second. Then it was back, louder, more insistent. The notes were shorter, *angrier.* Billy rubbed a shaking hand across his eyes. The hanging shadows were gone. *Had they ever been there?*

"*Billy...*" The voice was desolate, imploring. It worked on him even more than the scream. It wanted him to get the hell out of there. Billy backed up, then ran.

He ran like the devil was behind him.

And he didn't stop 'til he reached the far edge of Lord's Wood and could see the ruined cottage two hundred yards away across the sunlit meadow.

Here, he paused at last to catch his breath, his heart pummeling, head aching.

The whistling was gone.

With one or two nervous glances behind him, Billy made his way quickly across the meadow and over the stone bridge to the cottage.

The dandelion fairies were still there, caught in the sunbeam. He waited to hear her voice, to feel the touch of her hand on his skin again.

He sat on the broken wall and waited.

The sun was swinging down to hover above Lord's Wood. Had he really been here that long?

Dusk was beginning to fill the gaps between the trees in the wood until it became one long wall of dark. The sunbeams died in the ruined cottage.

Billy got up slowly and walked to the stile. He didn't pay any attention to the blue Mazda still parked there. He opened the door of his car and sat in the seat for a minute, door still open as if he might hear her call one last time.

When the stars began to peep out of the dark cavalry-blue sky, he closed the door and started the engine.

# Chapter Fifteen
# Ramble On

"Paintball," he said.

"What's that?" Tom looked up from his reports as Billy entered the office.

"This Saturday. Our celebration. Paintball."

"Ooookay." Tom thought about it for a second. He nodded slowly. "Why not? Do you know somewhere that does it?"

Billy nodded and turned to leave.

"Whoah, whoah, whoah," Tom called him back. "You haven't told me where, or how much, or given me any contact details at all."

Billy paused in the doorway without turning back. "You said for me to organize it." He sounded like a zombie, like a dead person playing at being Billy. The manager had often thought Billy was, shall we say, a bit of an individual, but lately, he had become just plain *weird*.

"That's right, I did..." Tom glanced down at the pile of paperwork he had to pore through and sighed. "I suppose we could just leave a skeleton staff of the Saturday-only part-timers to man the shop. About time they proved themselves. We could always leave James behind, too, just in case.... Or not; he would love Paintball, the big kid. Fine," he decided. "Knock yourself out... But Billy?"

The door was already closing on the bookseller. "Make sure it's cheap," the manager said to himself. He scratched his head, then forgot all about the anniversary.


As with so many of his actions lately, Billy had no clear idea why he had just booked the office party to take place at Lord's Wood. Was it just another impulse, like the urge that had pushed him to take the walk, or was it something else, some basic self-preservation in case he needed back-up when he returned to the walk next Saturday?

Because he knew full well he would be going back. And Saturday seemed as good a day as any other; he could even convince himself it had been his decision. He was going back for Aura.

But before all that, he had to deal with the Bristol Rambling Society.

He was shelving in the travel section again. Not because somebody had asked him to, but because he felt the need. Was he guarding the book, which he had returned to its anointed space on the shelf? Did it make him somehow feel closer to Aura? Probably. He no longer rationalized these things; he just got on with it, like an automaton.

One thing did keep revolving in his mind, however, pushing out all other irrelevancies: the voice. *Her* voice. Calling to him. Calling him away from the clearing. But had it really been Aura? And how was that possible? And why warn him away from The Grove? The slowly turning shadows he'd seen dangling from the branches should have done a good job of that already, but he knew if he hadn't heard her scream at that particular moment, he would have stayed, would have approached to see more clearly exactly what was hanging there...

So...what? He was in love with a ghost?

But he'd touched, her, smelt her...kissed her. Her breasts had been very real beneath his hands and tongue. She had been *real*...

So if that was the case, what was he doing *here* then, shelving books? Shouldn't he be back at Payndom looking for her again?

Today was Wednesday. He could wait three days. Saturday seemed important to him. An important day to return. Or was it an important *date?*

That idea confused him, and he was about to look up the actual date on his phone when the Rambling Society made an appearance.

He'd seen them in the shop plenty of times. They were breathless and loud, ebullient hikers who liked to demonstrate their rambunctious embrace of life and nature every time they were in the store. Today, only three of them were present, but it was the noisiest three: Molly was the ringleader, mid-forties, a gray bob, bright red-framed spectacles, and despite her avowed love of walking, saddled with a pear-shaped body; then there was Petunia, thin as a maypole, her clown-red hair sprouting out like a dyed orchid, the most alarming aspect to her being a lack of chin—her lower face sloped away into her neck quite dramatically; rounding off the trio was the only male present today, Maurice, in his perennial straw boater and blue-and-white-striped blazer, his kindly scone-and-cream expression beatific with the simple pleasures of life.

They swept in like a middle-aged gaggle of geese, all high-octave superlatives and received pronunciation as rich as jam tarts. Despite their volume and attention-seeking whirl of motion, Billy barely noticed them as he collected books from the trolley to shelve—until he realized Molly was trawling through the walking guides.

He stiffened. His blood began to thump in his ears. He was about to step around from behind the trolley to intervene when he saw it was already too late: Molly had the book in her hands.

"Ooh, how *extraordinary!*" she trilled, examining the cover. Petunia leaned her stork neck in to see what treasure her friend had unearthed.

"How marvelous," Petunia added, unsure in truth exactly what *was* so extraordinary, or even marvelous about the battered-looking hardback in Molly's hands but feeling compelled to utter some superlative regardless.

"I've never seen this one before," Molly continued to gush. "And yet it looks so old." She flicked open the cover, avidly scanning the index of walks.

"That's not for sale." Billy stretched out a hand to take the book from her. She resisted, squinting up at him through her red glasses.

"I beg your pardon! Of course, it's for sale! I've never heard of anything so ridiculous in all my life. How much is it?" She flipped to the rear flyleaf, then back to the front one, frowning at the lack of a figure. She closed the book with a snap and studied the rear cover.

"There *isn't* a price," she said sternly, looking up at Billy as if had handed his homework in late.

"That's because it's not for sale." He tried again to take the book from her.

"What absolute nonsense!" She pulled the book out of his reach.

Petunia was gawping at Billy like he'd just pulled Maurice's straw hat off and pooped in it. Maurice was still smiling like a vicar at tea time.

"The book is NOT for sale!" Billy's tone was low, almost a growl now. He could feel a panic rising in him. It threatened to sweep all common sense and logic right out the shop door, the ramblers along with it. He was dimly aware he was glaring at them, and his body was beginning to shake.

"Young man," Molly addressed him sternly. "I think you are acting very strangely—and aggressively, if you don't mind me saying so. Now, if you don't summon your manager immediately, I shall be forced to go and find him myself. I've never received such disgraceful customer service in all the years I've been coming here!"

Billy didn't answer. He tried to snatch the book again. Molly promptly tucked it under one arm, where it was sheltered by her formidable bosom. She looked at Billy like he'd just touched her ass.

"Come, Petunia, Maurice; let us remove ourselves from this unpleasant personage and speak to somebody who knows how to serve a member of the public."

She marched away from the Travel section in the direction of the main till, her two geese flapping along behind her.

Billy followed anxiously. They must not buy the book. They *couldn't…*

* * *

Tom was at the main till, trying to impress two young female staff members with his guns, flexing them demonstratively and boasting about how much time he spent down the gym. Molly interrupted his little narcissistic display without any compunction whatsoever.

"Are you the manager?" she demanded in strident fashion, before answering her own question, barely giving Tom a chance to lower his right bicep in the process. "I believe you are. I would like to complain in the strongest terms possible about one of your members of staff."

Tom saw Billy appear behind Molly, and the manager's expression revealed he knew things were going to be bad.

"How can I help exactly?"

"Well, you could start by instructing this young man how to address one of your customers in a polite and courteous manner. He seems to lack the most fundamental basics of customer service! Not only did he refuse to sell us a book that was on the shelf for the express purpose of *being sold,* but he then proceeded to attempt to snatch the volume out of my hands! I mean, I've never seen anything quite like it. Extraordinary behavior." She turned to Petunia for back up. The tall redhead nodded vociferously, her non-chin disappearing further into a nest of wrinkles on her neck with each nod.

Tom looked at Billy. "Why wouldn't you sell her the book?"

Billy glared at him sullenly.

"Billy… I'm asking you a question. It would be better for you if you give me a straight answer. Why wouldn't you sell this lady the book?" He was going into stag mode now, his metaphorical antlers lowered and ready to clash with this bookseller upstart who was daring to challenge his authority.

"There's no price on it," Billy said. It sounded pathetic. "And no barcode either," he added. "Or even an ISBN…"

"Let me see…" Tom reached for the book. Molly handed it over defiantly.

Billy felt irrationally defensive when he saw Tom open the book and search through it for any possible means of identifying a price. He watched closely to see Tom's reaction to the strange guide.

Tom went quiet. He looked almost thoughtful as he flicked from the publication page to the rear flyleaf and finally closed the book. He blinked up at them, as if forgetting where he was, and in what situation he was currently embroiled.

He glanced at Billy, and there was confusion in his eyes.

"Well?" Molly wanted to know.

Tom stared at her blankly. "Sorry?"

"How much is the book!!? Honestly! You don't seem to be possessed of much more nouse than your bookseller!"

"Rather rude, madam, if you don't mind me saying so," Tom snapped back. This attack on his authority and competence had pulled him out of his momentary reverie, however, and conscious of the two young girls watching him expectantly, he turned to the PC mounted on the till to check the title against the stock systems.

"I DO mind you saying so!" Molly's dander was up, good and proper. "If you are not prepared to serve me with some modicum of courtesy, I shall be forced to approach your Area Manager and see if he can shed some light on why I am being surrounded by ignorant imbeciles in this store!"

Petunia nodded chinlessly. Maurice beamed.

This time Tom said nothing. Instead, he reached under the till for some price stickers and pressed a £14.99 label onto the back of the book. He then flicked open a thin booklet on the desk beside the till and zapped one of the random barcode stickers arranged under laminate for the purpose of selling anomalous stock.

"There you go, Madam," he said at last, shoving the book into a plastic bag with the shop's logo emblazoned on it and sliding it over the till toward her. "That will be £14.99 please."

"At last! I am finally allowed to purchase a book from a bookstore!" She handed him the cash with a sarcastic flourish and turned to her cohorts. "Fellow members of the Bristol Rambling Society, we have won a victory here that shall be celebrated by perambulating one of the walks within this volume. And next time we enter this shop…" She faced Tom again, her head tilted back pompously. "…we expect to find every book priced correctly and not to have to undergo a military operation in order to purchase one! Good day!" She swirled around grandiosely, followed by her companions.

Billy watched them go—watched the *book* go—helplessly.

But Tom wouldn't give him the time to mourn it. "A word. My office. Now!" The manager was already striding away from the till, expecting Billy to follow.

Billy glanced at the two girls behind the till, Chloe and Locksy. Chloe widened her eyes in a "You're for it now" expression, and Locksy giggled nervously.

"Sit down," Tom said curtly when Billy arrived.

Billy did so slowly, still thinking about the book.

"Would you mind telling me what the *hell* that was all about?"

Billy shrugged.

"Okay, I'll tell *you* what that was all about, shall I?" Tom sat back and folded his arms.

Billy waited.

"That was all about you being an arsehole, Billy. Pure and simple. I've cut you some slack over the last few weeks for reasons we've already discussed, but when it comes to your bad attitude affecting *customers,* then I really have to sit up straight and take notice. Are you sitting up straight and taking notice of *me,* Billy?"

Billy wasn't. He was slumped in his chair, staring at the wall.

"If you can't be bothered to take your work here seriously, then you know there's only one option, don't you?"

Billy said nothing. He could barely hear Tom. He was wondering if he would ever be able to see Aura without the book. But that was absolutely bonkers. He knew that. He'd already heard her on the path, which meant she was *there…* He didn't need the book to find her again…

"Billy?"

Tom sat forward. "Are you even listening to me?"

Billy nodded slowly, unconvincingly. He had no idea what his manager was saying. It wasn't important.

"Billy, just… just go. Sort yourself out, do something productive today that will convince me to continue employing you…"

Billy rose.

"No, actually, before you go…" Tom waved him to sit again. "Have you done anything else to Julie?"

Billy stared at him, but he might as well have still been staring at the wall. "Julie?" he asked blankly.

"She hasn't come in today. She phoned in sick yesterday but not a peep today. And she's not answering her phone. I just wondered if maybe you two had another row or something."

"I haven't seen her," Billy said distantly.

Tom grimaced and shook his head. "Doesn't matter. By the way…"

Billy waited.

"Have you sorted out the paintball yet? It does actually seem a very good idea…for some reason…" He frowned slightly, and Billy knew without any doubt the manager was now thinking about the book, too. Tom rubbed his forehead as if to clear his thoughts. "Good idea to go there. Yes. Have… have you booked it yet?"

Whatever it was that made Billy nod, it certainly wasn't the truth. Of course, he hadn't booked it.

"So how much?"

Billy stared at him like he had no idea what Tom was talking about. Which was pretty much the case.

Tom sighed. "How much for the paintball? I need to invoice Head Office, budget in a minibus to take us there, that sort of thing."

Billy shrugged, caught out, and not really caring.

"A shrug, Billy? Is that all I get? I could have busted you out of your job for the stunts you've been pulling lately, and all you can offer me in gratitude is a shrug? A shrug does *not* cut it, my friend." He held his hands wide speculatively. "So how much are we talking? Fifty, a hundred?"

"Fifty," he said after a pause, wondering why he nearly added, "s*estertii.*"

Tom nodded. "Do you want me to ring them to check? Because, in all honesty, I'm not at all convinced you've actually booked it…"

"Just bring cash. It'll be fine."

Tom watched him carefully, clearly far from happy about this loose arrangement but strangely unwilling to push it. Billy knew why. He'd held the book, hadn't he? He'd opened the book… The same influence that had worked on him would be playing on Tom's business-like mind now, puppeteering his decisions, steering him in one direction…

It wasn't so much the place you *wanted* to go to, necessarily. Or even deserved. But in the end, it was always the place you *chose…*

He had no clue what that meant, or why he had even thought it, but he knew it to be true.

Tom seemed reluctant to let it go, as if struggling to assert some authority over the confusion in his mind. "Have you booked it for the whole day?"

"It'll be fine," was all Billy said. He got up.

Tom looked worried now. His authority, like his cool, was slipping. "Eleven. You ring them back and tell them we'll be there for eleven in the morning!"

Billy closed the door behind him.

# Chapter Sixteen
# The Caretaker

Billy spent most of the day either on the main till or drifting around the Travel section. He wasn't much use in either location. He shelved automatically, head almost a blank, apart from one maddeningly recurring image: Aura. As he picked up *Lonely Planet Guides to Estonia and Bali*, he was thinking of The Grove, of her voice cutting through the whistle and drowning out the creak of swinging bodies. When he slid a fat book on *Cycle Paths in the South West* next to the *AA Guide to Cornwall*, it was Aura he saw on the covers instead of the attractive female cyclist on the one or the smiling surfer chick on the other. Her features haunted him: her long cheekbones, the shy smile, the enigmatic electric eyes, the hair he could have lost himself in for… for a thousand years…

His reverie was interrupted by Steve.

Steve was Julie's boyfriend. Billy had only met him once before when he insisted on accompanying Julie to the leaving do of a former bookseller. She had spent a large part of the evening rubbing her leg against Billy's under the table. Steve had been oblivious; he was far more interested in arguing about football with Jerry and trying to out-talk everyone else in the bar.

As soon as Steve saw Billy, he hurried over to where the book-seller was leaning against the trolley, eyes far away. Steve was short, his head closely shaved to mask the encroaching baldness. He had what Billy could only describe as a football fan face—aggressive, unimaginative, and cocky. He steamed straight in. "You seen Julie, mate?"

Billy glanced up at him. "Julie?" he repeated vaguely.

"Yeah, you know, skinny, no tits, beaky nose, blonde hair. Works here, for fuck's sake."

Steve looked disheveled and distraught. It looked like he hadn't slept. Contrary to all the evidence, maybe he cared about his girlfriend a whole lot more than he'd ever let on.

Billy wondered if he was being accused of something. Steve was glaring at him with an anxiety that bordered on hostility. Should he feel guilty? He supposed he should, but Julie had practically forced herself on him and had been trying to do so for months. Was that an excuse? He didn't know and didn't care. No, he decided, if Julie had taken herself off somewhere to sulk for a few days, it really wasn't his problem.

"It's my fuckin' motor I'm worried about," Steve elaborated, shattering any notions that he might actually have genuine feelings for his partner. "The bitch took off in it. She hasn't been home since yesterday morning..."

Jerry had heard the conversation from the Sports section. He wandered over, skinny shoulders hunched as he towered over the other two. "She's done a runner?"

Steve rounded on the Liverpudlian. "Do you know anything about it?"

Jerry looked taken aback. "Why would I?"

Steve was working himself up into a lather. He adopted a mock Scouse accent as he faced off against Jerry. "I'm just askin' if you've seen her, mate. Calm down, calm down..."

Jerry didn't like this. He approached Steve and lowered his forehead until it was nearly resting against the bald man's. He had to stoop even more to do it. "You takin' the piss, like?"

Colesley chose that moment to arrive, took in the situation, and decided it was all Billy's fault. "Has Billy been winding you up, Steve?"

Jerry lifted his head, and Steve took a step back, face reddened. "I just wanna know what the fuck's happened to me motor. Has *anyone* seen Julie?" He was addressing Colesley now, mistaking his blandness for calm.

"Tom says she hasn't been in for two days. You mean you haven't heard from her at all?" Colesley affected concern. "She's probably gone shopping or something."

Jerry laughed. "That's the stupidest thing I ever heard." Billy could only agree.

"You think this is fuckin' funny do you, soft lad?" Again Steve assumed a Liverpudlian accent.

"We'll see how soft *you* are when I sling you through that window, son." Jerry was losing it himself now. His long face took on a craggy expression, and his eyes squinted balefully.

"I think you should both calm down," Colesley said, although Billy noted the way he stepped back a few paces, his eyes worried behind the square lenses.

"Don't you fuckin' tell me to calm down!" Steve's voice was rising now. A few customers looked over nervously from the other end of the shop. But his voice evidently hadn't reached as far as Frank, the ever-alert security guard, who was leaning his gut on the main till twenty yards away, chatting to Chloe.

Billy touched Steve's arm. The smaller man shook it off furiously. "Nobody's seen her, Steve. She hasn't been in."

He glared from one to the other of them, spoiling to crack someone's teeth. Then he whirled and stormed out of the shop.

Billy turned back to his shelving but found Colesley's finger in his chest, prodding him.

"That was your fault. If you hadn't been frisking around with his girlfriend, he wouldn't have come in causing a scene like that!" There was open hatred in his piggy little eyes.

Billy calmly removed Colesley's finger with his right hand and picked up some books to shelve as if nothing had happened.

"We'll see what Tom has to say. Your days here are over, Billy no-mates."

Jerry didn't look happy. He had calmed down now, and while he was on reasonably friendly terms with Colesley, he was also a right-minded, if volatile, northern man who didn't like to see unfairness in any form.

"Billy had nothing to do with it, Richard," he pointed out. "Steve came in like a rabid dog, all teeth and froth, looking for someone to bite. He just found Billy first, that's all."

Colesley wasn't going to listen to reason, no matter how poetically presented it might be. Metaphors and analogies were to be confined to the shelves of the Fiction section, not bandied about by the great unwashed, particularly combative lads from Liverpool.

"He's at the heart of all the trouble. He's a waster. A lazy, wom-anizing—"

Billy had a guide to Romania in his hand. Now he held it up men-acingly in front of Colesley. "If it wasn't for the fact you'd probably enjoy sitting on something hard for the rest of the day, I'd be very tempted to shelve this book where no tourist will ever find it, *Dick*."

Billy swung away from the pompous bookseller. He decided it was lunchtime—even though it was actually still a good ten minutes away.

He made it through the rest of the day without any further con-frontations. He chose a slightly different route home, having decided to pick up a bottle of whiskey from the wine store near Arnos Vale cemetery. A bottle of Bowmore single malt was an expensive method of trying to obliterate his ceaseless anxieties over Aura, but he felt he needed something to dampen the incipient madness. It was usually dis-counted at the Arnos Wine store, and he wasn't to be disappointed, even if twenty-seven quid for alcohol still seemed an extravagant way to forget.

Forget?

No chance. But it might burn away the fear.

Because it wasn't just yearning anymore. He was frightened. For her safety, and for his own.

Because he knew he was going back. And this time, no matter what it took, he would find her.

He bought his single malt and headed through the cemetery gates, following the lane that wound uphill through the Victorian burial ground. He tried not to think of The Grove and what he had seen there, as dusk began to close in. Trees on either side rattled their branches in the gentle spring breeze, but the sound was like the clatter of bones to Billy.

On either side of the lane, ancient gravestones were garroted by roots and creepers. A leaning cross had been etched with the words "Jesus Saves." Some vandal had spray-painted an "L" after the "S" on Saves.

Billy heard footsteps approaching him from further up the lane. A gray-haired man with glasses, head down, hands in the pockets of his raincoat. As he got nearer, Billy recognized him. He was a kindly man in his mid-fifties, friendly and effusive. He had known Billy ever since he'd moved into his house on the other side of the cemetery ten years before, and he always stopped for a chat. There was no problem with that. No problem at all. The only problem that Billy could see, and one which caused him to stop in his tracks and freeze like he'd been caught in a sudden snow blitz, was the inescapable reality that the caretaker had died two years before.

The caretaker seemed oblivious to his own apparent disinterment. He ambled closer, with a pleasant greeting on his lips. Then the smile curdled, as did his face, which rapidly assumed a turnip pallor. Clumps of hair slid off his scalp, which Billy could now see was scaled with mold.

He stopped right in Billy's way. "You mustn't go there, Billy," he said, his voice clogged with the mud caking his tongue and the inside of his mouth. "You really mustn't go back."

Billy hurtled past, horror shaking him.

In his terror, he ducked up a side path off the lane and didn't stop running until he was near the top of the hill. The path was narrow and overhung with rattling trees, pressed in on all sides by brambles and graves. But at least he could no longer see the lane and the dead man standing there. Was he still there? *Had he ever been?*

Billy *really* needed that whiskey now.

It was getting darker, and this path seemed to be taking forever to end. He had walked it many times in the past, and he didn't remember it being this long. He reached the top of the steep hillside the ancient cemetery was built on and the path leveled out. The trees pushed closer, as did the graves. He was sure the last time he had been this way many of the trees had been pollarded or felled altogether, but now they seemed thicker than ever. The dusk crept between the stones. He thought he heard an owl, but it could have been a whistle.

His heart pushed against his ribs. He stumbled over a root that snaked out for him like a skeleton's arm reaching from one of the crumbling tombs.

He heard the creaking of branches before he saw the bodies. They were swinging from bramble nooses tied to thick boughs a little way ahead, where the path opened up into a large clearing that had never been there before. The hanged men were almost lost in the twilight. Six of them, swaying, creaking, in the dark. The cemetery path had become Walk No.21. It had led him to The Grove.

The whistle was faint, but growing louder. It sounded ultra-vicious now, the three descending notes dripping with rage. Billy stopped on the path. Ahead of him, the swinging bodies… behind him, the dead caretaker. *"You really mustn't go back…"*

The rising moon peeped through a gap in the trees, and he saw the bodies clearly at last.

Armor breastplates and helmets stained with dark blood glinted in the silver light. Tunics that might have been green but now looked black in the shadows. Sandals on dirty feet, swaying in the evening breeze, more blood dripping from the open toes.

*"You really* MUSTN'T *GO BACK!!"*

But the caretaker's voice was Aura's now, and he took his choice and ran. Ran back down the path to the lane and helter-skelter for the cemetery gates.

He didn't meet the caretaker on the way.

# Chapter Seventeen
## "You Want ta be Murdered?"

He downed three glasses of single malt before he made the call. It had taken three glasses to blur the image of the hanged Romans in his mind. But he knew they were still there. In his mind, if not the cemetery.

He found the number easily enough. *Maybe too easily? ("You mustn't go back!")* It was right there on a website about Payndom he'd never seen before in his searches. Not much information about the town, but the pub was listed, and it seemed the obvious choice.

He waited patiently for an answer. Just when it seemed nobody intended to, he heard the click of an open line and a guttural voice said, "Who?"

Billy faltered. The male voice was almost animalistic, and the choice of greeting hostile and ignorant. But he would not be deterred now.

"I need to book a room…" He waited again, listening to the hoarse breathing on the other end.

Then, "Who…?" again, but this time more brutal sounding, with an unpleasant gloating mixed into that one simple word.

"Billy…" Why did he have the horrible suspicion that the man on the other end of the phone already knew who he was? He pushed on regardless. "I need a room for Friday night..."

Another pause. Then the growling voice again, almost indistinct, but Billy was sure he heard the words, "Do you want ta be murdered?," and his body iced. His neck hairs were up and boogying, his eyes staring wide at nothing as he squeezed his mobile phone.

"What... did you say?" he forced himself to ask.

"Your room ready for the Billy." The phone went dead.

# Chapter Eighteen
# A Different Path...?

There were five of them in the red Volvo Estate.

There should have been more in other cars, and Molly was not happy about those who had dropped out. So what if it was a Thursday morning? That was their weekly Ramble Day, and everyone who belonged to the group had signed up for it. The majority of the Bristol Rambling Society (membership twelve) were either retired, self-employed, or working part-time, and Thursday had always seemed like the perfect day for them all. The weekends suffered from too many familial demands, and Friday was market day in Wells, so that was no good. Thursday was the day, and they all knew it. So where were the rest? Molly had received a couple of apologetic phone calls and one text, but the others hadn't even bothered replying to her messages and emails. As if this was just an ordinary Rambling Day!

Molly sat in the front passenger seat, cradling the book on her lap. She felt more excited about this walk than any she could remember. She had pored over it the night before, and all the details of the route were etched in her mind, yet she couldn't resist continually turning to the bookmarked page to re-read the old-fashioned text over and over until the words, as well as the map, had taken firm root in her brain.

Beside her, Derek drove carefully and patiently. He was a big man in his mid-fifties, with a face that had once been handsome but was now softening around the edges, his hair freshly dyed dark brown. He wore a Barbour jacket with a checkered farmer's shirt and fancied himself a bit of a landowner as well as a lady's man. Nobody was cruel enough to point out to him the only land he owned was the tiny square of garden in his suburban semi in Yate, or remind him the last lady he'd successfully wooed had been five years before—and hadn't that ended disastrously? Molly remembered the shame. She had been half his age, admittedly, and half his intellect, too, which is why she had fallen for his lines. She was forced to leave the Ramblers Society after she complained about Derek fondling her inappropriately in Tesco's. Nobody had believed her. They needed Derek too much for that. Or to be precise, they needed his Volvo. Derek was always willing to sacrifice his Thursdays to drive the group around the countryside, and he never gave up trying to woo the ladies either.

But right now Molly didn't even hear his saucy double entendres. She was focusing on the road ahead and waiting for the Payndom sign to appear. She knew it must be coming up soon.

When she saw the lane turning off the A road twelve miles from Weston, she hooted with excitement. "There it is!" She turned round to beam at Petunia, Maurice, and Lucy in the back. She felt elated beyond measure. She really could not wait to get started on the walk. If the others found her enthusiasm for this new walk strangely out of proportion, they did not mention it. They, too, were oddly compelled by the idea of the ramble ahead—or was it just Molly's infectiousness wearing off on them?

"Funny little place," Derek said as they emerged from the tunnel of leaves and saw Payndom ahead of them. He was squinting through the windscreen at the collection of black-and-white buildings, with their Tudor beams and tilting foundations, the sunshine half-blinding him.

"Park just over there by that stile," Molly chirped. "That's the first stage of the Walk." Walk No. 21. The words were recycling continually in her mind. *Walk No. 21… Walk No. 21…*

Derek parked the Volvo and jammed on the hand brake. Molly was first out, almost clapping her hands in eagerness. Maurice was last, re-adjusting his straw boater after accidentally knocking his head on the ceiling of the Volvo as he climbed out. Lucy and Petunia gathered around Molly, Lucy stepping quickly away from Derek as the driver's hand appeared from nowhere to slip down from the small of her back toward the blonde girl's rather plump rear.

Lucy was slightly overweight but in a voluptuous, orchard-girl sort of way, her rosy apple cheeks and summer-blue eyes a perfectly appealing substitute for model beauty. Undeterred, Derek stole after her, leaning in to whisper something about Molly being more excited than she ever was on her wedding day. Lucy pretended not to hear. She moved away again, brushing Derek away like a wasp at a picnic.

Molly stood by the stile, looking at the field beyond. She frowned in puzzlement, some of the excitement drained from her face.

"What's up, Molly, my sweetheart?" Petunia asked, noticing her friend's expression.

Molly frowned, still staring past the stile. "There should be a gate at the end of this field, then another meadow, and …" She was straining her eyes against the sun, but she couldn't make out what she was looking for.

"And what, Moll?" Derek said, putting his arm around her instead. Molly was too bewildered to shrug him off.

"Well, where's Lord's Wood gone, for a start?"

They were all peering at the path ahead of them now. It wandered across the field beyond the stile before climbing fairly steeply toward a ridge after a half-mile or so. There was no sign of any wood for miles around, just bleak moorland to the north and east. To the west, a range of hills pushed up against the sky, while to the south lay Payndom.

Molly flicked open the book even though she had memorized the route perfectly well. "There, you see." Her stubby finger pointed at the page. They gathered round to examine the circular path sketched on the page. "Lord's Wood should be over there…" She moved her finger to gesture in the direction of the ridge stretching across the eastern horizon. "There's no mention here of a ridge or an ascent of any kind."

"Oh, Molly, it's probably because the book is so old," Lucy chided her good-humoredly. "The landscape is bound to have changed since this book was published."

Molly didn't look convinced. "I agree. A wood could be felled, yes…but…where did this ridge come from, this moor? They're not described in the text."

"You're such a perfectionist, Moll," Derek laughed, squeezing her tightly with an affectation of fondness.

"Are you sure this is the start point of the walk?" Petunia said, and Molly glanced at her as if she were mad.

"Of course, it is. Here, if you don't believe me!" She held out the book for her friend to see. Petunia was a little stung by the sharpness in Molly's tone, but she glanced at the map to appease the gray-haired rambler.

"You see!" Molly pulled the book back rather forcibly and blinked at the path again, nudging her red-rimmed glasses up her nose to focus better.

"It's probably just a shorthand text, missing out extraneous detail," Lucy said brightly. Again Molly looked unconvinced, but she decided they had dithered long enough by the roadside, and without another word, placed the book reverentially in her bright red rucksack and began to swing her left leg over the stile.

"Would you like a hand, Moll?" Derek moved forward eagerly, both hands more than ready to help propel Molly's box-like backside over the stile, but he was too late. Molly was over and already striding purposefully along the path, determined to be neither delayed nor groped any further.

Derek followed, trying to be sprightly, but succeeded only in catching one walking boot on the stile on the way over and nearly spilling headfirst into the daisies. He stumbled to regain his balance and caught up with the leader.

Petunia, Maurice, and Lucy were soon over the stile, too, and in hot pursuit.

Molly didn't let up her stride to allow them to keep up. She was determined to get to the top of the ridge so she could settle the puzzle in her mind. The text had clearly stated there was a ruined cottage in the meadow beyond the first field. If she found that, she would feel like things were definitely going to plan again.

But when, after a quarter of an hour's steady climb, Molly reached the top of the ridge and paused to catch her breath and take in the view, she was in for a disappointment.

Scrubby moorland fell below her gradually before rising again to a clutch of sparse shrubbery on a further ridge. No sign of a tumble-down cottage or wood of any description. She squinted at the bushes capping the further rise and could make out what looked like spindly stalks standing out against the horizon. She pulled out the book again. And nearly dropped it. Behind her, the gasps of ragged breath from the rest of her party as they puffed up the last of the incline went completely unregistered. Molly flicked back a few pages, convinced she must be looking at the wrong page, then back. No, Walk No. 21 it was, only the text had changed.

And so had the map.

She sat down on the grass, feeling a little dizzy. Was she going mad? Words on a page could not *change*! That was insane. A more plausible explanation would be that she had been looking at the wrong walk all along, and she seized on that idea with some alacrity. But after a peremptory examination of each path listed in the book (and there were a lot!), it soon became clear that none of them matched the description she had seen (*thought* she'd seen) earlier. So she was either losing her mind or … or…

*But she'd seen Payndom marked on the map.*

It was inconceivable there would be another village with the same strange name connected to a walk in the book.

She took off her glasses and rubbed her eyes, then replaced them to examine the text and map again.

There was no mistaking it; Walk No. 21 had changed. No mention of a cottage in the text or corresponding symbol on the map. No Lord's Wood. But one thing had stayed the same…and for some reason, Molly felt a disquieting sense of dread when she spotted it halfway along the circular route.

The Grove was still there.

*For the Pathes may change for those who walke them…*

The words tripped across her mind. Where had she read them? It felt as if a cold finger touched the small of her back. The preface, of course.

By this time, her fellow ramblers had reached the top of the ridge. Lucy looked more rosy-cheeked than ever, her white teeth shining in the sunlight, eyes shining, too. She was enjoying herself. And why not? It was an adventure, wasn't it? But suddenly Molly couldn't share the younger girl's enthusiasm anymore. Petunia noticed her troubled look and sat down on the grass next to her, thin face flushed, small bosom heaving flatly.

"Are you all right, Molly, love?"

Molly decided to keep the strange situation to herself. It would not help the Ramblers' morale to find out their leader was losing her marbles.

"Yes, yes. Splendid view, Petunia…" She affected serenity and kept her eyes shaded by one hand as she surveyed the bleak landscape.

"I don't see any wood, Moll, my lover," Derek stated bluffly, just beating Maurice to the top. Maurice had his usual delighted grin plastered across his face, one hand holding onto his straw boater as if afraid it would blow off, despite there being no wind.

"Never mind," Molly said firmly, more to herself than the others. "The map says, and I quote: '*Follow the path for but half a mile to a second ridge, where you will find a small lake, known locally as the Wailing Pool.*'"

"Wailing Pool? Well, that sounds a bit creepy, Moll, I must say." Derek raised his eyebrows dramatically. "I've heard of the Wailing Wall, but never a pool."

Petunia peered over Molly's shoulder at the tiny sketch of a lake marked on the route. "Wailing Pool" was annotated in archaic handwriting next to it. Beyond that, the path wound on through marshland—the map marked with wisps of grass to denote swampy land—before arriving at The Grove.

"I'm sure you said earlier Lord's Wood was on the map," Petunia pointed out. "It's definitely not on here."

Molly stood up abruptly. "Come on, Ramblers!" Her enforced jollity sounded hollow, especially to herself. "We have some rambling to do!" She had replaced the book in the rucksack, and after settling it on her shoulders, set off down the slope. After a while, the others followed.

It was noon, and the sun was becoming warmer. Molly was sweating freely now, the bag on her shoulders causing her blouse to cling to her skin. She didn't mind the discomfort. She didn't even mind Petunia's insinuations that she had mixed up the walks. No... What bothered her most was that with each step she took, The Grove was getting closer. On the map, and in her mind.

By the time she had climbed up the second ridge and stood next to the long, narrow pool at the top, the worry had become a distinct fear.

Because now she could see it.

She walked around the pool to the far lip of the flat ridge and scanned the horizon, drawn to get a better view. Here, the path dropped slightly down again to a stretch of boggy marshland in the vale below, and beyond that, she saw the clutch of trees.

Derek was the first to join her at the top. "I can't hear much wailing going on. Anybody fancy a swim?" He turned to offer Lucy a hand up the last steep section of path, but she waved him away.

"We could always skinny dip," he ventured on hopefully. Petunia and Lucy ignored him. Maurice grinned, though whether at Derek's proposition or simply because he liked to grin was up for debate.

"When do we stop for a picnic?" Lucy wanted to know.

"What about right here?" Petunia was admiring the pool, fingering the velvety head of one of the bulrushes—the spindly stalks Molly had seen from the first ridge.

"Marvelous idea!" Lucy was already shrugging off her rucksack and sitting down on the edge of the plateau near Molly, leaving no room for argument.

Out of politeness, Petunia turned to their leader before removing her own. "Molly?"

Molly blinked and turned to her friend as if waking from a daydream.

"Shall we? Have a picnic here by the little lake? It's simply too beautiful. And you can see for miles."

"Picnic?" Molly repeated the word without taking it in.

"Are you sure you're all right, Molly, dear?" Petunia was giving her an anxious look.

Molly snapped out of it. She was the leader of the pack and had a responsibility toward her fellow Ramblers. "Yes, darling. Of course, I am! A picnic sounds simply splendid!"

Yet she continued to stand with her rucksack firmly on her back for several more minutes, staring across the marshland to the distant Grove. It was only when Petunia began trying to remove the pack herself that Molly responded with a forced smile and shrugged it off her shoulders.

By this time, Derek was already on his second salmon and cucumber sandwich.

Not one of the Ramblers noticed the ripple stir the surface of the water as they sat with their backs to it on the edge of the ridge. Not one of them noticed the gray hand that broke through like a fish after a fly, fingers questing, then disappearing back beneath the dark water.

Molly poured a cup of coffee from her flask and tried not to think about the book, the map, and The Grove.

# Chapter Nineteen
# The Helmet

There was only one reason Billy came to work Thursday morning. There was only one reason he'd turned up for the last two and a half weeks, and it had nothing to do with paying the rent on his flat.

He knew deep down she wouldn't show in the bookshop, but that didn't stop him hoping. But he was also now beginning to realize that seeing Aura again depended on a positive action from him. It was becoming all too clear what he had to do. Returning to Somerset, to Payndom and the path that haunted him seemed the only option left. He'd heard her voice there, for God's sake, and hanging Romans, bodiless Whistlers, and blood-chilling greetings from Innkeepers was not going to deter him any longer.

As soon as he arrived, he headed straight for Goods In. The book was gone, so there was no point guarding that in the Travel section anymore (and, of course, that was exactly what he'd been doing). But he could at least try to find something else about his destination. He could plan his next step carefully...

Tom caught him midway across the shop. He looked worried. "Are you sure it's all booked?"

Billy gave him his now-patented one thousand-yard stare in response.

Tom frowned in irritation. "The paintball!"

"I told you. Just—"

"Yeah, I know: just turn up. Well, you'd better be right. I've organized a minibus and everything."

Billy nodded and left him standing in the center of the shop looking confused.

To his dismay, James was already in Goods In, unpacking a box.

"Wahey, it's the Lost Boy," he greeted Billy jovially, eyes twinkling from behind his round lenses.

It was Billy's turn to frown.

"You always look like you're one needle short of a fix these days, sunshine," James elaborated. "And what you done with Crazy Julie? You sure you haven't stashed her away in a basement somewhere, draining what little blood that skinny body's got left in it?" He hooted at his own wit. For an Assistant Manager, he was surprisingly uncouth and insensitive, but he meant well, so Billy nodded politely as he sat at the desk in front of the PC, wishing James would go.

"No, seriously, mate," James persisted, straitening up from his task, an earnest expression replacing the cheeky grin. "I think you must've twisted her melon out of shape for her to do a bunk like that with her boyfriend's motor. Even though he *is* a charmless jerk."

Billy remained facing the PC as he entered Payndom, Walks in Somerset, Hobbemarke, and every variation he could think of into a search engine, wondering if he could unearth more hits this time and also if James would ever shut the fuck up. "I think it's precisely because he *is* a jerk that she's gone," Billy said stiffly after a period of silence. "Why do I have to come into it?"

"C'mon, you know she had the serious hots for you…"

Luckily, at that moment, Tom's voice came over the Tannoy system, summoning James to the manager's office.

"What the fuck does that pillock want now?" James sauntered toward the door, giving it his best hip-hop swagger, then paused and swung his chubby head back to Billy. "Bit of a hit with the ladies, ain't you,

Billy Big Balls?" He winked amiably and then gestured at the half-unpacked box he'd been working on. "Finish that lot off, could you, mate. I'll go and see what Tom Dumb wants."

Billy returned his attention to the PC. Nothing new on Payndom. He couldn't even find the entry with the pub details he'd found yesterday. The other variations met with little relevant success, too, apart from the same black-and-white photo of Hobbemarke House. He tried several more times with the same dissatisfying results. He was about to try one last time when he heard the Whistling.

He stiffened on his chair, hand frozen in mid-air about to push the "Enter" button on his search.

The skin on his back crawled. He felt a cool breath on the nape of his neck. The whistle was close by, calling malevolently…

He got off the stool and scanned the dingy unpacking room.

The sound seemed to be coming from beyond the fire doors. He stepped slowly toward them, and there was no mistaking it; the whistle grew louder as he approached.

He hesitated for only a minute, then popped the fire door bar. The whistle was pulling him. He couldn't resist. Ever since he'd first heard it, he'd been lost. Lost Boy. James was right. And there was no cry from an invisible Aura to stop him this time. He pushed the doors open…

It was louder now, more mocking than ever, tuneless evil.

He stepped out into the bleak concrete service corridor that was used by all the stores on this side of the Galleries complex and followed the malignant lure down the flight of steps to the basement. This was where all the rubbish skips were stored, and the area was completely deserted. A single fluorescent bulb flickered above his head. The whistle appeared to be emanating from behind a particularly large skip in a far corner, where the shadows were thickest.

He hesitated again. He sensed he was being deliberately enticed down here, but apart from the fact he seemed to have no free will in the matter anymore, the whistle was becoming inseparable in his mind from thoughts of Aura now. If he was ever going to find her, it seemed he would have to face whatever was making this sound first—however horrible it might be.

*And how horrible could it be?*

*Coward. Just do it. Find the whistler, find the girl. Do it!*

He stepped toward the skip and the shadows surrounding it.

There was nothing lurking in the corner. The whistling lowered a key, reeling him in. He found himself standing next to the skip in a kind of dream, and if his hold on logic and reality had been slipping quite a lot of late, it was about to drop away altogether as he noticed something nestled on top of a stack of flattened cardboard boxes and general paper waste inside the skip.

A battered, blood-encrusted Roman helmet. The metal was buckled; rust vied with the dried blood spots. The once-proud blue plume on the crest was filthy and tattered. Before he could stop himself, he was reaching out for it.

And placing it on his head.

The whistling stopped.

And the basement storeroom was gone. The skip was gone.

Billy was gone, too.

# Chapter Twenty
# Ramblers vs. Druids

Molly finished her coffee and screwed the cap back on her thermos. Petunia was beside her, munching on the last of her sardine and cucumber sandwiches and enjoying the view despite the fact a midday mist had appeared on the marshland below, hiding The Grove from sight. Derek was sitting next to Lucy, leaning against her, seemingly oblivious to the way she shuffled her buttocks sideways along the grass away from him. They watched the mist curl toward them over the tussocky bog. Maurice was standing up by the water's edge behind them, stretching, watching the sunlight play on the surface of the pond.

"Absolutely magnificent day!" Molly exclaimed loudly and brightly to the group. "A real boon to us on our adventure! Those cucumber and salmon sandwiches of yours were just divine, too, Petunia, dear!" She knew she had been uncharacteristically quiet for the last quarter of an hour and didn't want her friends to suspect just how perturbed by events she actually was. So she decided louder and brighter was the way to go. "Perfect weather for a picnic. Don't you all think so?"

Petunia finished her sandwich. "Gorgeous," she agreed, but she regarded Molly doubtfully. An intelligent and classy lady, with hidden depths belied by her "Tea-and-scones" exterior, Petunia was going to be the hardest to convince of all. And if she thought about it sensibly, the only person Molly really needed to convince that everything was all right was herself. Was she making far too much of it all? Molly gazed at the mist rolling with increased vigor across the swamp, making her enthusiastic statements regarding the weather sound rather hasty and foolish.

"Derek, *please!*" Derek removed his hand from under Lucy's ample buttock with an air of wounded innocence. For once, Molly was glad of the distraction from her thoughts.

"Do behave, Derek," she scolded him lightly. "Or we shall be forced to cool your ardors in the pool."

"I don't think even ducking him in there would cool Derek's ardors," Petunia said.

"Ladies, I am most misunderstood!" Derek swiveled round to appeal to Maurice for help, but his fellow male Rambler still had his back to them, gazing happily at the sun twinkling on the water.

When Maurice didn't answer, Derek turned back to the women with a sheepish grin. "I can't help myself. You are all so dashed attractive!"

Petunia narrowed her eyes at him scornfully. "Derek, you are a menace. A menace to all womankind."

"We should put you in a home for frisky, elderly perverts," Molly chided him with a smile. Again, her voice was a little too loud, her smile a little too wide. She shifted her position on the edge of the ridge. The fog was closer.


Maurice yawned and then froze mid-stretch.

Something was stirring in the murky water below, a few feet out from the edge. An object broke the surface. It looked like dark, sodden cloth, rising slowly to reveal itself to be a hooded head. Maurice caught a glimpse of black fur beneath the folds of the cowl, which was draped with a wreath of pond scum and weed.

Maurice continued to stare in astonishment as the figure hove out of the water, wading ashore. It carried a long staff in one furry hand. Maurice's gapey grin was still on his face when the carved claw dug deep into the soft crown of his boater and the scalp beneath it.

With one flick of its arms, the figure hoisted Maurice into the lake like a macabre angler tossing back a big fish.

The others heard the loud splash and whipped around.

The Black Druid was standing on the bank, forcing Maurice under the water with the staff.

They sat staring for long, precious seconds. Incomprehension rooted them. They might have expected wasps or flies to interrupt their picnic, but never this…

Molly got up as if in a dream, started to move toward the figure. Derek followed hesitantly. Lucy shrank into herself. Petunia screamed, a long wail full of horror. *The Wailing Pool,* Molly thought dumbly. The wails were from those who came here…

Maurice was still alive under the water. The wooden talons nailed the boater into his head, holding him down. His quaint hiking boots thrashed above the surface. The druid pushed harder. Maurice stopped kicking. The druid gave one final shove, twisted the claw free of its purchase, then swung to face Molly.

Molly's turn to freeze. Another robed figure was rearing out of the scummy water. This one clutched a jagged stone knife. It waded ashore, water pouring out of the hood. Molly saw a face inside, long, goatish, patches of decomposing flesh and filthy fur clinging to the bone, black rips where eyes should be.

Petunia screamed some more, but now she was running. Down the short slope, away from the pond toward the marshland, toward the mist that reached for her. Derek hovered behind Molly for a second, his mouth working but with nothing emerging for once. Then a light came on in his brain, and he hightailed it after Petunia, leaving Lucy curled up, sobbing on the ridge.

"Is this some kind of macabre passion play?" Molly's incredulous question was aloud, but it was really herself she was asking. Maurice had indeed disappeared into the rank depths of the pond, thrust there by a murderous figure in black, but she couldn't give up her devout faith in the intrinsic splendidness of things that easily.

But when the figure with the knife reached the shore, Molly realized she just might have to. It paused, the goatish face inside the cowl regarding her with rapacious glee.

Molly's crazed thoughts centered on the guide book in those helter-skelter moments: on the path (Walk No. 21), on the irresistible urge that had compelled her to come here as she struggled to understand the horrible trick of it all, and finally grasped it. She saw it in the eye holes of the rotting goat face. She saw the twisted truth that squats at the sphincter of the world and knew Walk No. 21 was special in a way she could never have anticipated. A destiny awaited them all, so malign, so obscene in its cruelty that Molly's soul withered to contemplate it. Her bladder voided its contents in the moment of seeing. She sensed fate leering from the fabric of the inevitable, laughing like an evil clown, and saw the nature of desire, no matter how innocent that desire may be. She had so badly wanted this path to lead to excitement, discovery, and revelation, and it hadn't let her down...

Lucy's sobs snapped her out of her trance. Her maternal urges had never been satisfied by having her own offspring, but Lucy was young and kind and always looked to Molly to lead the way. She wasn't going to give up on her now. Molly ignored the dampness staining her crotch and hurried over to the normally vivacious blonde. She slipped her arms under Lucy's and hauled her bodily to her feet.

"We need to go, Lucy, dear. We need to go right *now*!" She slung her left arm around the younger woman, helping her down the path to the marsh. Ahead of her, she saw Petunia and Derek disappear into the mist that had so rapidly developed into a thick fog.

Lucy continued to sob, though she allowed herself to be guided forward. Molly risked a look back. The figure with the knife stood amongst their abandoned rucksacks on the ridge, outlined against the sky. Was it letting them escape?

Or herding them on... Even as Molly looked back, the figure slowly began to stride down the path after them.

"Come on, dear. We'll be all right." Molly knew it was a lie. They weren't going to be all right.

The fog took them.

Molly stepped into gurgling bogs several times, once almost spilling headfirst into the swamp. If it hadn't been for Lucy clutching her so tightly, she would have gone in.

The Grove couldn't be much further. Maybe they could hide in the trees. *Play Hide and Seek with the Devil.* A more positive idea occurred to her, one she would have naturally thought of immediately if she had chosen to succumb to the twenty-first century disease of possessing a mobile like seemingly everyone else. "Lucy," she hissed. "Do you have your phone on you, my lovely?"

Lucy stifled another sob, but Molly could feel her rummaging in the pocket of her anorak.

Molly glanced down, saw the slim, white iPhone 5 in Lucy's hands, just as a figure rose with a sucking squelch from the bog beside the path to confront them. Black robes festooned with bramble, hooded, holding a branch armed with flint shards and evil-looking thorns. The branch slashed out across Lucy's face and chest. Lucy shrieked, dropped the phone into the marsh. The branch lashed out again, demolishing her cute face, leaving runnels of gouged flesh, tearing out a hank of soft, blonde hair from her scalp. The branch ripped at her chest again, rupturing the material of her anorak, shredding the pretty red top beneath, exposing her full breasts that heaved against her bra.

Molly saw all this happen and her brain froze. She stumbled backward, felt a bog hole suck at her boot. She regained her balance and her state of mind at the same time and seized the branch from the figure, wresting it with surprising strength from the druid. The druid released it, momentarily caught off guard.

Lucy subsided on the path. Molly stepped over her to face the druid, clutching the branch above her head. She lashed out at the cowl, the thorns and flints catching the hood, tugging it aside.

Molly should have pressed home her advantage, struck out with the branch again, but the face revealed bereft her of any ability to act further.

She watched dumbly as the figure reached inside its robe and pulled out a new weapon. A sickle with a long wooden shaft, the type used to collect holly by kindly old druids in white gowns like the ones Molly had once seen in *Asterix* books.

This one was in black. And it was a million miles away from Goscinny and Uderzo.

The sickle arced down, and the branch in Molly's hand fell. Molly's hand fell with it, severed at the wrist.

The sickle rose again. Molly clutched at the stump, feeling her life fluids pump out over the path, over the marsh grass as she wove on the point of collapse.

Then a figure was smashing into the druid from behind, slamming it into the swampy waters. The druid sank into the bog. Fog closed over the gurgles. "Molly!" Petunia seized Molly in her arms, hauled her back along the path toward The Grove, still obscured in the mist. Blood saturated Petunia's jacket now, but she ignored it.

Molly reeled on the brink of unconsciousness. The fog parted at last, and the oaks were just ahead, their trunks ghostly white as the mist itself.

Molly had wanted to go to The Grove. All along that had seemed the most sacredly exciting symbol on the map. A few minutes before, she had even planned on hiding there with Lucy. But now, as her blood ebbed from her wrist, she knew it was the last place they should go.

She tried to tell Petunia, but her Rambler friend was already hauling her into the trees.

Molly sank to her knees. Petunia released her. They could hear Derek screaming in agony somewhere ahead of them in the fogbound copse.

*It all ends here.*

A figure stepped out of the mist.. It held out the sickle tormentingly, its robes slick with slime from the bog. Its other hand clutched Lucy's severed head, dangling by her long, blonde hair, as the creature moved steadily into The Grove.

Beside it, another figure, dagger in hand. The eyeholes in the bony face locked on them eagerly.

"Go!" Molly gasped at her friend. "Hide!"

"I won't leave you!"

"I'm dead already, my dear. Please... Save yourself..." She collapsed forward onto the path, consciousness leaving her.

Petunia hesitated only long enough to see the mess the sickle was making of Molly's head. And then she was screaming again as she blundered away into the trees, stumbling, colliding with trunks, ripping her trousers on brambles. The laces on her right boot came undone. She lost the boot after five more yards.

She knew they were behind her.

Ahead of her, she heard Derek wail, as if he was losing his soul as well as his mind.

She couldn't go back. She couldn't go on. Then *what?! Where...?*

She panted onward regardless. Maybe if she found Derek they could help each other.

She found Derek in the clearing.

He was hanging from a noose of brambles strung around a thick branch on the edge of the open space. Petunia could see the thorns lacerating the saggy skin of his neck. One of his legs had been sawn off. Blood dribbled from the stump. He wriggled a few more times and was still.

Petunia staggered up to his dangling corpse. Her hands went out to him as if forgiving him all those surreptitious gropes. She opened her mouth, but nothing emerged. She had no more screams left.

The mist closed in on her.

As did the druids.

# Chapter Twenty-One
# Goth Chicks and Blood Stains

James was leaving Goods In when he spotted the queue building up at the main till.

He swung in beside Richard Colesley and called for the next customer to move forward. A biker with belligerent eyes and a belly to match wanted a diet and exercise book. James bagged it and took the fellow's money. "Good luck with that one," he quipped good-naturedly, handing it over. The biker frowned and left without a word, like an extra in a TV show not paid to speak.

Colesley was unenthusiastically serving a plump Goth chick. He was examining the dark fantasy novel the girl handed to him with evident distaste. When she asked him politely if he could recommend anything in a similar vein, the bookseller smirked as if she were cracking a joke. "Absolutely not," he laughed contemptuously. James bristled. He knew Colesley was a condescending prick, but being an affable sort, had never really called him up on it.

"I think you should show the young lady the Horror and Sci-Fi section, Richard, don't you?"

Colesley glanced at him, suspecting a jibe, but for once James wasn't smiling. Colesley sighed dramatically, waving a hand in the direction of the relevant section, which was hidden away near the toilets.

"No, I mean actually move your ass and show her." It took a lot to rile the mild-mannered ex-hooligan, but Colesley's arrogance had managed it effortlessly. The bookseller glared at him resentfully and was about to argue when the Goth chick interrupted.

"It's all right, really. No trouble. I can find it."

But rather than heading for the section Colesley had indicated, she hurried out of the main doors instead.

"Well done, Dick." James was furious. "You just lost us a valuable punter. And if you can't bear to recommend something you clearly feel is beneath you to a paying customer, I really have to wonder if you're in the right job."

Colesley's eyes narrowed venomously behind his glasses. "Just because you're the assistant manager doesn't give you the right to talk to me like that."

"I think you'll find it does. But if you don't like it, take it up with Tom." Which reminded James of his Tannoy summons.

James swung out from the till and headed for the manager's office, fuming.

Tom judged his mood as soon as his second-in-command entered. "What's bitten you?"

James sat on a swivel stool, face flushed. "That pompous twat Colesley."

"Richard? A valuable member of staff."

"You have got to be kidding. But then you probably just can't see it. The guy is so far up your ass, Tom, that you can't see *him* either. Can you believe he's just made a customer walk out because he didn't want to dirty himself walking into the Horror section? And that's not the first time his behavior's caused offense. Just last week he nearly got a smack in the mouth from Sci-Fi Simon. Simon's just had a fantasy novel published. Colesley dismissed it as facile crap. He's just jealous of Simon's achievement—frustrated writer syndrome and all that. But if that was me, I would have stuck one on him right there on the main till."

Tom nodded along distractedly. He didn't want to hear all this. Right now he didn't care about Colesley or Sci-Fi Simon (who was, as per usual, following managerial edicts, forced to work in the Cookery section despite his great knowledge of all things science fictional.)

"It's not Colesley I called you here to discuss."

"No? Well, it should be."

"Calm down, James. Forget Richard. It's Billy we should be showing the door to."

"Billy?" James looked confused. "What's he done now?"

Tom rubbed his forehead. He'd been building up to mentioning this to James for a while now, especially after the Julie incident, but suddenly it didn't really seem important anymore. The title of that damned book kept droning through his thoughts. *101 Walkes to Hell... 101 Walkes to Hell... 101 Walkes...*

To Hell. He shuffled a personal development plan on the desk in front of him in irritation. It was Billy's.

"Clarke's found out about Billy and Julie's little indiscretion." Clarke was the Area Manager for the book chain. Once a month he visited the store and sat on everyone. Tom always received the biggest squashing, naturally.

James leaned forward on his stool, hands on knees. "How?" Tom had told James in confidence. "Hope you don't think it was me?"

"No..." Tom sighed again. "It could have been Julie's boyfriend. He's been in the shop causing trouble. He may have suspicions of Billy and could have taken them above my head."

James frowned. "Seems unlikely." He shook his head as another thought occurred to him. "My guess is Colesley. For a start, he fancies Julie himself and doesn't like the attention she gives Billy. For another, he's a dick."

"I said forget about Colesley. Doesn't matter who told Clarke. Fact is, he knows. He's coming down on Monday to throw me around a bit. Give me a metaphorical black eye and squeeze my nuts. He wants Billy out."

James considered this. "And Julie?"

Tom shrugged. "Moot point. Looks like she's legged it anyway."

Tom's attention drifted away from the usually jovial face of his assistant manager. The words were still tripping through his head.

"One hundred and one ways to hell."

"What?" James blinked at his boss, confused.

Tom slammed a fist down on the table. "Nothing! Just needed to fill you in, James. Billy's history: I'll tell him tomorrow. Up to him if he comes with us to the paintball party, though..."

"I'd forgotten all about that particular joy."

Tom shook himself mentally. "It'll be good for morale." He didn't sound convincing, even to himself. "We *have* to go."

"Do we? Would have been cheaper, easier, and probably loads more fun to just go to the boozer for a party."

Tom stood up. "It'll be good..." he repeated.

James picked up on his boss's distracted frame of mind.

"You all right, Gov?"

Tom usually smiled at his second-in-command's use of the police term. It was a mark of friendship between them. He didn't now.

"As you were, James. This shop doesn't run itself."

Tom waited for James to leave before getting up. He approached the door to the shop floor through which James had just sauntered and hesitated. He breathed in deeply, trying to calm his thoughts. But the refrain was still dancing in his head. It wasn't going to be silenced easily. He straightened his back and opened the door, the gentle classical music playing out on the shop floor immediately promising peace but not drowning out the rhythm in his mind. He ventured out, dodging a mother with a pram who was looking at him with a request for help already on the tip of her tongue, cut straight through Children's and round the corner to Travel.

He spotted the book straight away.

It stood out from its fellows as if demanding his attention on the shelf.

He pushed between an Asian couple who were searching through the Indonesian books and reached out gingerly to pluck it from the shelves.

He turned it in his hands, almost reverently. And nearly dropped it.

The front cover was saturated in blood.

# Chapter Twenty-Two
# Centurion

Billy knew he was still in the storage room with the skip right next to him. Of course, he was. But right now he couldn't see the concrete walls and the stacks of flattened cardboard boxes that filled the receptacles.

Right now all he could see was trees and grass…and blood.

His world had changed as soon as he put on the old, battered helmet.

Except it wasn't old and battered anymore. He knew without having to look that the blue plume would be firm and proud, the metal undented and rust-free.

Although there would probably still be blood on it.

Blood was seeping between his hands.

Blood was soaking into the grass beneath his body.

He was lying on his side in the bushes at the edge of the clearing, and the one thing he was conscious of was that, despite all the blood, he felt no pain.

He could see his men—and he understood instinctively they were *his* men—surrounding the blonde girl on the stone. He had been stabbed and left to die while the rabid legionaries raped the girl.

Sciro was molesting her as she lay in a faint. Billy tried to raise his head some more, and the dizziness swept through him, yet still no pain. He wanted to rise, to help her, to stop the monsters his men had become from doing what they so badly wanted to do to…

Her.

His vision cleared. Sciro was ripping away the fleece that covered her body and kneeling to flick his tongue between her legs. Billy's gaze took all that in, and her face, too.

A thousand years and more.

He knew her at last. He'd always known her.

Aura.

The shock immobilized him even more than the stab wound.

A grunt left his lips. He levered a hand under his body, trying to gain enough strength to push himself up, and as he did so, he heard the whistling.

And for the first time, Billy saw the Whistler.

Three black-robed figures stood at the far side of the clearing.

One clutched a vicious staff, the other a stone knife. The third, the Whistler, held out a bushy branch spiked with thorns and flint blades. Coils of bramble festooned the tall body. The eerie warbling was emerging from the dark hood, the features as yet unseen.

Billy's nightmare was flesh now, his invisible tormentor of the past month revealed at last. His trembling hand inched toward the sword in its scabbard. He instinctively knew this was evil of a far worse kind than the base brutality demonstrated by his legionaries. But then he had known it the first time he heard the whistle in the unpacking room that evening at the end of March. First time? No. He realized *this* was the first time. Over a thousand years before he heard the sound in a bookshop in Bristol, Billy had lived as another, leading his men on a mission into darkness. And the Whistler had come for him.

The three figures began to move. They were approaching the stone slab where Sciro was still too busy exploring Aura to notice the new arrivals on the scene. He was tasting her womanhood and grunting with bestial pleasure. His hands moved up her now-naked body and viciously squeezed her breasts. The whistling obviously only registered on a sub-liminal level at first, so great was his lust. Billy struggled to rise, but again dizziness held him down. He could now see Sciro was finally picking up on the trembling notes; the brutish Roman withdrew his head reluctantly from between Aura's sleek thighs, fury at the interruption knotting his brows.

The rest of the troop was rooted in bewilderment. Bellari finally realized he should do something and stepped forward to counter the latecomers, his huge frame tensing in preparation for battle. Martus drew back behind his fellow soldiers.

Sciro left Aura and fell in beside Bellari, sword in hand.

The whistling stopped.

Sciro took his cue, swinging his blade at the Whistler's hooded head.

Whistler caught it in one misshapen hand, wrenching it away from the Roman like a parent confiscating a dangerous toy. The branch in its other hand whipped across Sciro's face and throat. Sciro screamed and fell back. Bellari roared and came in with bare hands, attempting to lift the Whistler from the ground in a savage bear hug. The druid's boots remained firmly planted. Bellari strained, squeezing hard. The Whistler dropped the branch and closed both gray hands around the Roman's head, squeezing back.

Billy heard the crack from where he lay amongst the bushes. Blood ejaculated over the druid's hood, spattering the wreath of bramble.

Whistler pushed the dead Roman away from him.

The three remaining legionaries dropped all pretension of combat. Martus broke first, his sandals stamping next to Billy's head as he fled back the way they had come. The druid with the staff leveled it like a javelin, and his aim was true: the whittled prongs at the end slammed into the legionary's back, halting his flight. Martus dropped into the nettles, writhing, the staff standing up from between his shoulder blades. The druid moved slowly to retrieve it. The weapon was withdrawn, then used to dig away at the back of Martus's head until nuggets of brain were uncovered from the broken skull.

That left two still standing: Pachellus and Cartelli.

The druid with the dagger closed on Cartelli. The stone blade punched through his forehead and exited from the back of his head. Blood, brains, and cranial fragments exploded outward, showering Billy where he lay.

Pachellus whimpered like a baby, hacking wildly around him with his sword, turning in faltering circles. Billy saw his blade drive forward into the robe of Cartelli's killer. The figure rocked back a step, a rent in the material releasing a black trickle of ooze. The druid seemed indifferent to the sticky flow, which soon staunched itself. The dagger in its hand caressed Pachellus's throat almost fondly. Blood pumped over the dark robe, making it darker. So much red.

Billy was sure it was all over. The mission, his squad, all done. But there was Sciro, still alive, if not kicking, stumbling along on all fours, blind after the branch had destroyed his face. Whistler casually scooped him up by his legs and swung him against an oak, Sciro's head crunching against the trunk. The druid swung the legionary again until Sciro's head was a wet, broken bag of mashed bone.

The bodies were dragged into a pile at the center of the clearing. Billy, hidden in the bushes, hovered on the brink of unconsciousness. Whistler uncoiled the brambles from around his robe and fashioned them into vicious nooses around each Roman's neck. Soon, the five legionaries were swinging from the branches.

That left Billy, the centurion. The glorious leader of the pack. *But it's not me! I'm not this man. I'm Billy, the lazy bookseller. I don't belong here. This isn't ME!!*

But it was. He had known that the first time he looked in Aura's eyes. This was how he'd known her before. And this was where it was always going to end.

Light was beginning to filter through the trees. A dim part of his mind accepted that dawn was breaking. The three blood-drenched druids strode toward where he lay.

# Chapter Twenty-Three
# Love in the Fourth Century

"No..."

Her voice was soft and not commanding, yet it stopped the druids in their tracks.

She was sitting up on the slab now, her beautiful body smeared from Sciro's pawing. Her eyes locked on Billy's.

He felt something he had never experienced before. It flooded him: a light, a warmth. He lifted a hand toward her, the dizziness receding temporarily.

She slipped off the stone and approached, eyes still on his. She knelt beside him, and her soft hand touched his cheek.

"Not this one..." she breathed.

The druid with the dagger moved toward Billy again, the weapon held out threateningly. Billy saw the goat skull within the hood, bits of flesh clinging to the bone. It spoke, and the voice was a deep scratch across Billy's mind. "None must live."

Aura turned her eyes on the druid determinedly. "Not this one! He was for saving me. I will stand by *him*, too."

"None must live," the abhorrent voice repeated. "The rite will not be broken. Dawn rises. He who Treads in Dark Places will have blood and a bride. The soil has thirst. Let it drink so He may come."

Aura looked back at Billy. Her hand strayed to his chest, down to the wound that still pumped away Billy's lifeblood. She caressed the wound, and her eyes were filled with something he had never seen before. "This one lives," she said firmly, and all hell was let loose.

Billy saw the javelin suddenly sprout from Goat-face's chest. The druid staggered under the impact. Shouts and bellicose roars filled the clearing. Billy's faltering eyesight took in a flurry of tunics and breastplates, helmets and swords. Sandals crashed past Billy as legionaries stormed The Grove. A century had arrived, almost in time. Almost? Billy had the suspicion that he was a pawn in a game that had been played and nothing had gone against Roman planning. The expendables had done their job. The scum squad nobody wanted to lead. Well, *he* had led them… into a trap that was not of druid making after all.

Bait. Just bait, to lure out the cult. That's all they'd ever been.

Blackness summoned him down, but he fought it. He struggled to focus on the carnage that was taking place in the clearing.

Aura was still crouched next to him, her hand pressed against his wound. Blood seeped through her long fingers as she watched the battle.

The druid with the staff was down now. Three Romans slammed and hacked at him with their swords, the superstitious terror driving their fury intensified when the large hoof-head was revealed. Their blows struck oil, or rather the thick, black sludge the druid used for blood, and soon the body was falling asunder under the repeated blows. The flurry of blades shredded robe and the black-furred flesh beneath.

As Billy watched, a Roman soldier was held aloft by Whistler and flung across the clearing to smash against an oak in a welter of blood. Ten more took his place, stabbing, thrusting.

Goat Face was bristling with javelins. Sword cuts uncovered the skeletal rot beneath the robe. The druid fought back with his primitive dagger, separating Roman heads from their bodies, opening up tunics and guts, gouging eyes and removing arms. But the force of the attack was telling. Goat Face staggered back, a legionary clutched to him like a doll. He bit out the Roman's neck with his long incisors and dropped the body. More swords rose and chopped. Goat Face was a hacked mess of dirty bone and ripped cloth. The bony head tilted upward, and the ripped eyeholes focused on Billy from across the clearing.

Billy heard the words as if whispered in his own ears.

*"When the stars realign, our brood shall return…And a God shall walk among you…"*

The head was hacked free. It rolled into the nettles.

For a moment, there was silence after the fury of the battle. Only the ragged panting of the legionaries broke the peace.

Then another voice, one Billy recognized from the camp at Aquae Sulis, a centurion of far higher standing than he: "The girl, too…"

# Chapter Twenty-Four
# Dawn

Billy heard the words and felt Aura shrink against him. She turned her eyes to his again. Now fear was in them, along with the other emotion that he could not explain, only that he knew he felt it, too. Her gaze fell inside him, right down to the roots of him. It lit a fire of need and want and answered every question he'd ever asked about the world and his place in it.

In a bizarre twist, the tables had turned; now, it was his turn to save her again. He would not, could not let anything happen to her.

The centurion had other ideas. "Kill the witch!"

Two legionaries promptly moved forward, swords lifted.

Billy forced himself into a sitting position. The clearing swung around him. His vision went black, then kicked back in seconds later. Aura's face swam into focus. But something was wrong. The passion in her eyes was dying. Blood lathered her gorgeous cheekbones. Her eyes still stared into his, but the light was fading. Her head fell against his chest as the Romans continued to stab.

He stared into those bluebell eyes, and there was a roar, an unending scream, echoing in the clearing.

Eventually, it dawned on him that it was his.

# Chapter Twenty-Five
# Thousand Year Stare

"What the fuck are you doing?"

Billy didn't hear the voice at first. It wasn't until James stepped closer and tapped him on the shoulder that he realized he was no longer in The Grove but back in the storage room of the Galleries.

James's face was a mixture of incredulity and amusement. "You really are losing it, son. Big time. What the fuck is going on in your nut? I'm sure you've got a *really* good reason for standing down here with a kid's plastic helmet on your head, but right now I'll be fucked sideways if I can think of one."

Billy reached up and removed the Roman helmet. Except it was no longer a real helmet fashioned from metal and bronze. As James had pointed out, it was made from plastic and had clearly been discarded from the Galleries toy shop, which happened to use the same storage room.

James folded his arms. "Well?"

Billy looked at the toy helmet in his hands, then up at James.

"Mate, you don't look the business. Might be a good idea if you take the rest of the day off. You are sporting one hell of a thousand-yard stare…"

*Didn't he mean thousand-year stare?* Billy handed the toy to a bemused

James before heading back up the steps to the wide-open fire escape doors. He walked out of the shop without saying goodbye to any of his colleagues.

He wouldn't be going back.

Billy didn't sleep well that night for three reasons.

The first was due to lying in bed for hours pondering the significance of his "vision." That he had some link to the centurion appeared to be the only conclusion he could deduce from it all, which also explained his connection with Aura and why he felt so strongly that he had met her before. But what the hell could it mean? What possible link could he have with some Roman dead for over a thousand years? And where, exactly, did the Aura he knew today fit in with the blonde from The Grove? None of it made sense; none of it was logical. Yet of one thing he was certain: he knew instinctively the events in his vision were real (so real he had felt the cold damp air of The Grove, smelled the blood in the grass…), which meant he had already seen Aura die once. If, by returning to The Grove, he could somehow prevent it from happening again… That was the only thing that *did* make sense to him, the only thing he could cling to. The vision had taken place in The Grove. Over a thousand years ago, Aura had died there. This time, he would save her.

The second cause of his sleeplessness came later when his mobile activated itself even though he was sure he had switched it off before going to bed.

He had actually drifted off briefly, though only to find dreams chasing him through The Grove. Dreams full of blood and swords. So when the LG notification sound cut through the terror, he was only too relieved to wake to find his mobile screen switched on, even though he had no idea how that was possible.

The cell was on the bedside table right next to his head. The Smartphone had somehow chosen to play a YouTube video Billy had certainly never searched for—he could see the logo at the top. The video showed The Grove, and the seven-inch screen revealed Aura lying naked on the sacrificial stone… And she was alive. The Romans were hanging from the branches, and the camera panned to close-ups of the bramble nooses cutting into their throats as they swung, blood still oozing from the thorns. By this time, Billy was wide awake and sitting up in bed.

Still dreaming? He didn't need to pinch himself or perform any clichés because he could feel the cold of the night drying the sweat on his naked body, and he could feel the hair standing stiff on his nape as he watched the camera focus on Aura again, and now she was talking, and he could hear her voice emanating from the tinny phone speakers. The mobile was warm in his hand as he picked it up and held it close.

She wriggled sexily on the stone as she spoke, and the incongruity of the ancient Aura sounding all matter-of-fact and informative, like a modern documentary narrator, was just another crazy element of the general slide into insanity that Billy's life had become. And wouldn't that explain *everything*? If he was mad, there would be an end to it all, almost too easy a resolution. But he knew he wasn't. He knew he was faced with a real and terrifying challenge he would never be able to run from by hiding in an asylum. So he listened to the Aura he had kissed in Tortworth Court speak with the lips of the Aura who had died when Romans ruled the land from the screen of his cell phone, and if that was crazy, then what exactly was sanity? He no longer knew.

"He walks in The Grove but once a millennia or more, when the stars wheel to their aligned positions and His wild offspring call, seeking the blood of man and a bewitching bride." The video buffered, and Billy was left staring at a close up of Aura's face in "Pause" mode, her lips open, eyes strangely calm. That this was a message for him sent by Aura he had no doubt. He began to feel strangely calm, too. If this bizarre video was her attempt at warning him away from The Grove, it wouldn't work. She was his and had been for over a thousand years. No matter how she tried to save him from danger, he would disregard her efforts.

The video clip unfroze. "The bride is of the nymph people, and she will be borne to The Grove and there offered to the lusty by His Darke Children. Sacrifice of lecherous man shall awaken Him, and Weird Call shall summon Him. From out of the darkest bower shall He step to take her for Himself. There will always be men happy to go to their doom for the beauty of a Nymph."

The clip buffered again. When it stabilized, The Grove was gone, and Aura was speaking to him from the table on the terrace at Tortworth Court.

"Don't come, Billy. Please. Don't come for me."

Then a close up of her beautiful, anxious face, the calmness of the documentary narrator abandoned. Her words spanned the void of years, mingling the archaic with the modern dialect he knew, and the country burr made him ache for her. "They wanted me to lure you, Billy, as I did before…more than a millennia ago. But you were not like the other lusty men, and you would save me. For that and more, I gave to you my heart. I loved you then, I love you now. Do not come for me. Do not heed the whistle…"

The cell went dark.

Billy thumbed it back to life, and it reverted to the menu screen as it should. And no matter how many times over the next half hour he searched YouTube for entries on The Grove or ancient sacrifice in the vicinity of Payndom, his efforts were always disappointed.

Eventually, with the alarm clock beside his bed indicating 3:10, he dropped the cell back on the table and lay back.

Sleep, of course, would not come. But the third reason that made it impossible was that Aura came instead.

He first became aware someone was in the room when a shadow blocked out the moonlight filtering through his thin curtains. He turned over onto his back and raised his head from the pillow. The shadow stood at the foot of his bed.

For one frigid moment, he was terrified. Then the scent reached his nostrils, and he knew it was her.

The shadow moved closer, away from the window, and now he could make out details in the darkness. Her face was still dim, but a moonbeam slipping between the curtains fell across her chest. He could see she was wearing a long, semi-transparent nightdress. The silver ray picked out her cleavage, revealed the dark patches of her nipples thrusting against lace, a darker patch between her thighs.

He sat up in bed, body aroused despite the impossibility of the situation.

"Aura…?" His short hairs stiffened, too, supernatural fear and desire mingled intoxicatingly.

Instead of answering, she drew closer. He could see her teeth glisten as her lips parted. He reached out to turn on the bedside lamp, but she stopped him, her hand resting gently against his arm. The touch was cool. The blossom scent intoxicated him. He stumbled to express his delight, his confusion, blundering after explanations that hardly seemed to matter in the moment. "How are you here? Where were you—" But words were needless, there was no reason in any of it…just Aura. Aura: here, now. She stooped to kiss him softly, and her nightdress fell open. His arms welcomed her, as did his lips.

Her lips tasted of cool streams, her tongue a warm trickle of fire. Every sense in his body ignited. She broke the embrace, pushed him back on the bed, and slipped out of the nightdress. His eyes were adjusted sufficiently to the darkness now. He stared at her lithe body, the pert nipples swollen against their aureole discs, the small tuft of hair above her private parts. Her eyes held his, blue as polar skies, her hair a fall of dusky gold. She knelt on the bed, lowered her head to kiss his chest, licking his right, then his left nipple, her tongue trailing down to his belly button, teasing around his thighs.

Billy's arms shivered with goose pimples as he stroked the cool velvet of her shoulders. His hands moved into her hair as she dipped her head between his legs, taking him in her mouth. He groaned, back arching as her lips closed around his tip, then released him to allow her tongue to slide down his shaft and back up. She took him in again, down to his hilt, her mouth a warm, gorgeous sheath into which he gently began to thrust.

When he felt he could take no more without exploding, her gorgeous mouth drew away. She lifted her lips to his and he tasted himself on her lingering kiss. He slid his mouth over her sleek cheekbones, wanting to devour her beauty, so intense was his desire, not caring now how she came to be here, only exulting in the fact that she was.

Her eyes locked on his, a dawn flash of blue mystery, of teasing ambiguity. Then she was moving up the bed on her hands and knees and offering him her small, perfect breasts to kiss, to lick, to fondle. He pressed his face against them, tongue toying with the bud of her right nipple, sucking as if he had found the source of all beauty, love, and delight, the answer to life's eternal secret. His hands caressed her sleek thighs, clasped her peach buttocks. This time it was his turn to move, sliding down the bed until his head was level with her gorgeous pussy. A light scent of heather and perspiration greeted him. Her thighs eased gently around his head, and his tongue flicked at the sensitive areas around her lips before teasing the hard bud of her clitoris and finally probing inside.

She uttered no sound, but her juices flowed onto his chin as he licked and kissed. The taste of her had him shuddering for more. His entire body rippled with ecstasy now. He gently pushed her over on her back, exploring her wet cleft with two fingers of his right hand, his other molding her breasts, squeezing gently, then harder, his passions driving him on.

She lifted her legs to allow him in, his first thrust gentle, sensitive, the second sliding further, the third deep, deep into her. He let out a sigh of ultimate pleasure, his eyes finding hers again. Still, no sound from her, though her lips were parted sensuously, her eyes…

Her eyes were full of derision and scorn.

And evil. Mocking, taunting evil.

He froze mid-thrust.

Her flesh was changing. No longer creamy white in the dim moonlight but blotchy gray. Warts and lumps pushed out from the skin, the breasts sagged inward, became scarred pectoral muscles; the neck fell into creased folds like elephant skin. The nose was gone, replaced by a blank expanse of leper's flesh; ears dropped to the bed sheet to leave ragged holes while the long, blonde hair slithered to the bedsheets. Once-gorgeous eyes were ruptured by bramble tendrils that quested out from the sockets, then twined around the head, wrapping it like a cocoon. Only the mouth was left uncovered to pout lewdly, as if about to blow a kiss.

Billy flung himself across the bed from her—it—huddling back against the far wall. The vagina he had so lovingly kissed and thrust inside had healed over and a limp tube dangled, fringed with warts.

The brambly head pursed its mouth at him and whistled.

*This is when you wake up, Billy! This would be EXACTLY the right time to wake up because this is the mother and father of all nightmares.*

Except it wasn't a nightmare. Like the YouTube video popping onto the screen of his phone earlier, he knew this was all too real. He could feel the cold wall behind his naked back, could still taste the husky heather flavor of her on his lips, and smell the blossom scent hanging in the air.

He closed his eyes, willing the thing on the bed to be gone when he opened them.

The whistle rose in key, jubilant in its evil.

He opened his eyes.

The Whistler was still there, obscene and naked on the bed.

Billy ran to the bedroom door, wrestled with the knob. The door would not budge. He darted a look over his shoulder to find the Whistler had risen, approaching him, bramble-bound arms reaching out for another embrace. The whistle was full of lechery and warped hunger now, the gray lips pursed obscenely.

The knob turned in his hand. Billy yanked the door wide as a cold, horribly moist finger prodded his shoulder.

He hurled himself along the landing and down the stairs, then raced for the front door, not caring he was naked. He twisted the latch, and the door opened easily. He threw himself out onto the street beyond, risking another look back when he was safely through.

The hallway was empty. The whistle had fallen silent.

He hesitated, his whole body shuddering from the cold and the horror.

The sweat began to freeze on his skin, and still, he waited. No movement, no sound from inside the house.

He considered hammering on the door of his neighbor's house. He didn't care right now that he had never got along with the couple in there, he didn't care he had no clothes. His mind reeled with terror, and his body flinched with absolute abhorrence. He had been utterly defiled in every sense.

He waited on the front step, shivering badly, intermittent sobs heaving up from deep inside himself.

He stayed that way for a good twenty minutes until the shudders subsided and a cold anger began to replace the horror and build inside him.

They had used Aura's image in the most heinous, twisted way imaginable. Of course, it had not been her in the flesh. They had climbed inside his mind and fucked it. They had defecated on his most-private, innermost fantasies and cherished thoughts. But this time they had most definitely gone too far.

Steeled by his mounting fury, Billy strode back inside the house. He went to the kitchen and drew out a long carving knife from a drawer.

If the Whistler was still in the bedroom, it was about to lose a few more parts.

The stairs were dark, darker than the bedroom had been.

Billy flicked at the light switch.

Nothing.

The darkness seemed to become even more intense. He could barely see the cold, liquid gleam of the blade in his hand. He moved resolutely up the first few carpeted steps, heart a fist in his chest. His ears strained for the slightest sound.

He reached the top of the stairs, moved to the half-open bedroom door.

He could see, hear, nothing beyond it.

He paused in front of the door a second, two…then kicked it wide and sprang inside, brandishing the knife.

At the same time, he hit the bedroom light switch with his left hand.

The switch clicked dully, but absolute blackness prevailed. The moonlight no longer filtered through the curtains. Somebody had switched out the stars.

He froze just inside the room, his breath hoarse and gasping. It sounded like he was breathing through an aqualung.

He scanned the dark, knife cutting the air in front of him defensively, his left hand flicking the light switch on and off repeatedly with the same result.

Finally, an explosion of light.

He was standing in an empty room.

The bed covers lay on the floor where he had kicked them off as he fucked the obscenity that had taken on the form of Aura. There was nothing else to indicate he had ever received his nocturnal visitor.

Nothing but a lingering scent of blossom…blossom that had begun to decay.

# Part Three
# The Grove

# Chapter Twenty-Six
# The Pandemonium Inn

Billy set off early the next morning, the door of his house closing behind him with a finality that resonated through the layers of exhaustion and dread that weighed on him.

He sat in the car for a long moment before turning the keys. If he was deliberating whether to give up his crazy mission, then it would have been difficult to tell from the grim set of his features in the rearview mirror.

The Beetle started up first time, and he pulled away from the curb with a defiant *blatt* from the twin exhausts.

He was on the A37 in no time. It was an overcast day, this last day in April. And if he realized the significance of the date, it would not have made him deviate from his course now. Beltane didn't mean jack all to a bookseller going to an almost-certain death in search of his lost girl.

Yet the dread was there all right; it coiled and snaked in his belly, wrapping tight around his heart, questing amongst his thoughts. And it grew stronger with each mile he drove.

He tried to push the horrors of the night before from his mind.

It wasn't easy; he had cleaned and rinsed his mouth several times since and showered until his flesh was raw and crimson, but the one thing he couldn't scrub was his mind.

They wanted him to come. That was obvious. They had called him (*"Do not heed the whistle"*), and he was driving 65 miles per hour into their trap (he would have gone faster if the old bug could have managed it). Of course, he was coming… (*"There will always be men happy to go to their doom for the beauty of a Nymph."*) Was there a choice?

Ever since Aura had walked into his bookshop and picked up the guide, there had no longer been a choice. His fate had been sealed by her beauty, even more so than the lure of the book and the whistle. She had done her job so well. *Too* well. What the Whistler and his two monstrous allies had failed to appreciate was the more than one thousand-year bond that somehow still existed between them. Between the wood nymph and the Roman. Between Aura and himself. "*I loved you then, I love you now.*"

She had tried to warn him off, and they hadn't anticipated that, had they? He recalled her haunting voice at the ruined cottage and in The Grove, a call to him that was on the verge of the imagination, disembodied and faint like a memory echo; the dead caretaker in the cemetery, that had been her, too, sending a friendly face from the past, which they had countered with mounting fury, curdling the vision with decay and inflicting the dead Romans on him instead, as if promising their fate to him; then there was her YouTube video, to which they again reacted with hellish spite. But here he was, sitting in his 1974 Beetle driving toward them with a big Fuck You in his heart, coming for the girl. *His girl.*

Twelve miles to Wells. His destination waited for him, drew him on. But this time things would be different: no matter how often Aura tried to warn him off, he was going all the way. All the way along the path if needs be until he found her…all the way…to Hell?

Billy had never loved anyone before. An orphan at the age of seven, he couldn't even remember the parents who died in a train crash. Two dim faces staring down at him, shadows with smiles. That wasn't a lot to instill a lasting fondness. Then there was the stream of non-friends at school and beyond. He was a loner, and damn good at it. Friends cost. They used up your time and your trust, and Billy had been in short supply of both. Girls? A few. He had tried to feel for them, and he guessed they had done the same, but always with the same result. Fumbles in the dark, both physical and mental, were the only legacy they had left him. Until Aura.

Aura had turned his world not only upside down, but inside out and back to front. Aura was the one he'd been waiting for all his life. And if he believed his vision, a whole lot longer than that.

The turnoff for Weston came and went. The Beetle's engine buzzed along like a happy bee, its sound totally incongruous with Billy's state of mind. Not far to Payndom now. Payndom... Pandemonium Inn. Why should he be surprised at the obvious connection? Though what it meant eluded him. In his mind, he saw the old man at Hobbemarke Manor laughing again amongst the rhododendron bushes: *"Maybe it weren't the Devil hisself.... I ain't so sure they was meanin' summat else just as bad, cos that ain't His name..."* And most alarming of all: *"You'll be seein' Him afore too long, iffen you follow the way."*

And here he was, approaching the lane to Payndom, all ready to follow the way...

He had no idea what he was going to do, apart from exploring the path for as long as it took until he found Aura. His room was booked at the Inn, and he was not going to leave without her.

There was the lane. He cruised down through the leafy tunnel, past the muddy drive up to Hobbemarke Manor, and out again into the dull gray April morning.

Instead of parking at the stile, he carried on up the main street, past all the queerly old-fashioned, Tudor-style buildings until he came to the inn. He parked alongside it and climbed out.

If he had expected the sign to creak menacingly in the wind, he was going to be disappointed, although the design on the old, partially rotten wood certainly didn't offer anything in the way of encourage-ment. It depicted The Grove in faded paint, and the bodies of six indistinct shadows swinging from the branches. He felt no shock at this reality-sync with his vision in the Gallery's storage room, the cemetery, and, of course, The Grove; things had already crossed the Weird border way too many times for that. *Very welcoming*, he thought grimly. They should have just gone right ahead and called the inn The Hanging Romans.

The building was as old as all the other buildings seemed to be in the village. Lopsided with antiquity, it was listing as well as listed. Great, crumbling, black timbers crisscrossed the pale stone. The walls bulged out like cake that had risen too much. The windows were squeezed by the battered masonry, the mullions cracked and flaking. *Spend a night or two at our quaint historical inn, m'lud? Don't mind if I do, sir... ("You wanna get murdered?")*

Was he cracking up right when he needed every sense to be at its keenest? He had a job to do, remember? Save the girl. He took a deep breath. It smelled of dust and stale beer. And he hadn't even entered the building yet.

He considered wandering around the village but discarded the idea. There was no sound either, from the pub or the rest of the huddle of houses along the main street. He was more drawn to the path. He had felt Aura's touch there once, in the ruined cottage. Maybe she would make a more physical appearance this time.

He walked back to the stile. He climbed over it, only mildly surprised to find a railway track cutting through the field beyond. The path crossed the gully in which the disused track lay and continued up the further bank. He could tell the line was disused from the rust on the rails and the weeds that grew between the ties.

It hadn't been there before, obviously. Again, was he surprised?

He descended the bank and stepped across the silent rails, then up the other side. The iron gate was still there, and beyond it, so was the cottage.

He was up and over the gate without a pause and making for the cottage through a field of tall sunflowers that hadn't been there before either.

Lord's Wood remained, dark and menacing as ever, marching across the horizon. And The Grove beyond that, no doubt.

He strained his ears as he approached the tumble-down cottage, hoping to hear her voice whisper his name, whether in his ears or mind. Nothing. He widened his nostrils in anticipation of a scent of blossom that did not arrive. There was no sunbeam today, falling amongst the nettles and broken stones. No dandelion seeds dancing in the rays.

He sat on the collapsed wall and waited.

The sun was past the noon position in the sky, which meant he had been waiting for some hours. He hadn't bothered to check the time on his mobile—had he even brought it? He wasn't sure, and he didn't check his jacket pocket now. It didn't matter. He had a strong suspicion that modern technology would not be able to help him today. Not even a YouTube video.

Nobody walked the path this afternoon. No sounds came from the distant village. He spotted no birds flying over Lord's Wood, and certainly, none flew over the cottage.

He shifted his position on the wall, and as he did, a piece of masonry fell from the tottering stack that had once been the hearth.

He watched it drop from halfway up the pile of stone, making a grinding sound before it popped out, almost as if it had been pushed rather than simply falling from its place.

He stood up. The stone rolled into the nettles at his feet. He stooped to gingerly fish it out from the stingers, clasping it finally in both hands, turning it over and over until he found the reason for its displacement.

Something had been scratched on one surface of the hunk of masonry, presumably with a smaller stone used as a marker. It was a crude sketch of what Billy thought at first was a broom or a trident, and then with a flash of remembered horror, realized it was a staff like the one carried by the druid in his vision.

He pondered the significance, even as he explored the cottage inside and out in search of whoever might have pushed it. Failing to find a trace of anybody, he scrutinized the stone again, determined to interpret its meaning. If he expected Aura's voice to guide him, he was not going to be so lucky this time.

One end of the sketched staff was a jagged mess of lines, indicating the carved prongs of the "claw." The other was the handle, and halfway down the shaft, there was a little scratched squiggle that could have denoted a string tied to the weapon or a thin band of material. He clutched the stone, desperate to decipher it, convinced it was some message for him. But from Aura…or his tormentors? He did not know.

He waited for what could have been another hour or so before finally turning his back on the cottage and making his way through the Sunflowers and across the railway track to the village.

He had a room booked, and a veiled threat from the landlord. Maybe he could find out more inside the Pandemonium Inn…

He stopped at his car, unlocked it, and placed the stone on the passenger seat. The meaning of the crudely scratched picture would come to him, he was sure.

He locked the Beetle securely and, without looking up at the sign again, went to the entrance and pushed the black oak door.


The pub stank of worse than dust and ale.

It stank of disease, and rank body odor.

It was very dark in the ancient saloon, and at first, Billy wasn't sure where the stink was emanating from. Then he saw the man sitting at a table in one gloomy corner, completely naked except for a black leather goat mask.

That made him turn right around and try to leave again, but there was already somebody in the doorway blocking his exit. This man had obviously followed him inside the pub, and he was naked, too, his body bloated and greasy. He also wore a goat mask, and his penis was not only erect but sheathed in blood.

# Chapter Twenty-Seven
# The Darkest Bower

"Don't mind the blacksmith, he be all cock and no manners…"

The voice came from the landlord, who was watching Billy from behind the bar. The man was tall, skeletal, with one eye stitched shut. He, too, was naked, at least from what Billy could see of him behind the counter. The man had a concave chest and a goatee. He looked at Billy steadily with his one eye.

"A drink for the Billy…" He slid a pint of ale across the bar top. "For the sacrificial Billy…" More naked villagers were filing into the pub now, blocking off Billy's retreat. Some of them wore goat masks, most of those without were disfigured. Women were among them, young, old, nubile, withered. They clustered around Billy and began to bleat like goats.

Billy stared around the dark saloon, panic rising. There was a corridor and a flight of stairs to the right of the bar. There might be a back exit down the corridor. The nightmarish bleating rose in volume.

"Drink it." The landlord sidled along the bar nearer to Billy. "You'll find her quicker if you do." He threw something down on the bar in front of Billy. Room keys. "*Ya want ta be murdered?*" So he hadn't misheard the landlord over the telephone. He had walked blindly into this death trap all of his own accord.

"Your room be upstairs. You'll find it in the Darkest Bower." The man's voice was full of horrible eagerness.

On impulse, Billy reached out for the pint, then threw the contents in the landlord's face. He lunged down the dim corridor only to find more figures emerging from the gloom at the end. Which left the stairs. Billy sprinted up them two at a time. He could hear the bleating following behind him, exultant, vile.

He came to a landing with two doors. The first was locked when he tried it. The second opened easily onto darkness. He threw himself inside and slammed the door shut, groping for a key to lock it. No key. No bolt either.

He backed away as the door opened. The crowd of villagers was framed in the doorway, the landlord at their head.

Billy continued to back away into the room. When his foot crunched on what sounded and felt like a pine cone, he felt a stab of unease. He turned to face the room, straining his eyes to see in the thickest blackness he had ever experienced. A cold wind slipped down the back of his neck. His groping hands touched a branch. More cones and twigs snapped beneath his stumbling feet. *"Your room is upstairs. You'll find it in the Darkest Bower."*

Turning back again, he could still see the doorway, a paler patch against the black, but it was receding fast, as if Billy were moving at a great pace in the opposite direction. But Billy was standing dead still.

Somewhere off in the distance he heard branches cracking.

A great thud of monstrously heavy feet shook the ground.

Trees snapped and were smashed aside. Whatever was out there in the darkness was approaching steadily…

The receding doorway suddenly took on a more appealing aspect, even if retreating meant he would have to face the bestial pub clientele again. The darkness around him appeared somehow sentient, as if whatever was approaching him were part of it, as if the darkest heart of the woods had taken on form and was hunting him down. But that was crazy; he was just in a room at the inn, that's all. He wasn't outside, wasn't in the woods. This was all in his mind. Had to be… The ground shook more substantially. The heavy footfalls were nearer. The sound of a heavy body crashing through the undergrowth grew louder.

Billy began to run toward the doorway. Nightmare logic took over. With every step he moved forward, the doorway receded further.

His breath tore through his lungs as he ran. Branches snatched at his jacket and hair. The shaking ground threatened to topple him.

Was the doorway closer now? The gray, rectangular patch seemed to have grown slightly.

He stumbled over a tree root and was flying. He hit the earth hard enough to wind him. Behind him, the crashing paused. Billy lay still for a handful of seconds waiting for his breath to return, ears strained to hear what might be coming for him out of the dark.

His entire body prickled with primitive fear. Whatever lurked out there in the heart of the woods was not meant to be seen by human eyes. He sensed a great presence watching him. His own breathing echoed amongst the invisible trees.

Then the massive tread began again, and terror forced Billy to his feet.

The doorway was closer, but the gray rectangle was diminishing in width. The door was closing!

Billy pushed himself to his limit, scrambling over fallen branches and through briar patches, his jeans tearing, his cheeks and hands lacerated by thorns.

The sliver of gray was almost gone now.

Ten feet away, bushes smacking him in the face as he forced his way through, twigs blinding him.

And then his scrabbling hands found a smooth wooden surface and a door handle, and he was forcing his weight against the crack of gray, forcing it slowly wider.

The door flew open, and he fell out into the pub landing.

There was nobody on the other side.

The pub was silent.

Billy stood for a moment, gasping like an old man, the walls and wooden floorboards threatening to swap places, to spin him into blackness almost as deep as the one he'd just fled from.

He fell back against the wall until the dizziness faded and his breathing took on a normal rate. He listened again. Still nothing. He crept to the open doorway and peered inside. He saw a small room with a basic bed and a lopsided wardrobe, nothing more.

Carefully, he made his way to the top of the stairs and peered over the banister. The ground floor hallway was deserted.

Billy considered his position. Maybe they had abandoned him, sure of his fate at the hands of whatever crashed toward him in the Darkest Bower... Or maybe they were all just playing with him, and this was another element in a sick game of Hide-and-Seek. He could hide up here until the goat mask-wearing villagers decided to come seek him, or he could go down and front it out, try to do something constructive toward finding Aura.

He began descending the stairs stealthily, fists clenched, ready for trouble.

He reached the ground floor and crept along the hallway to the bar.

He could still hear nothing.

He inched his head around the doorway. As he had suspected, the saloon was completely empty. The beer glass he had emptied in the landlord's face lay on its side on the bar top. *"You'll find her quicker if you drink this..."*

And what the hell did that mean?

He had visions of being drugged by the beer, waking to find himself in some hellish place and discovering he had made the worst possible decision that could never help Aura. Or it could have been a test of his resolve, to see if he deserved to find her or not. Whatever... He would find her on his own terms.

The piece of stone that had fallen from the cottage wall resurfaced in his mind. That had been a more concrete clue, and he was sure it had come from Aura herself, even though he still had no idea what it meant.

He stepped into the bar, expecting the villagers to burst in at any minute to overwhelm him. He crossed to the main door and opened it.

He was surprised to find night had fallen outside. He could see the stars pricking through the branches of the mighty oaks that crowded up to the door. The houses that had stood opposite the pub—indeed the street itself—were gone. He stood on the threshold, and through the trees ahead of him was the clearing. He could see the stone slab where Aura had been molested by a Roman legionary over one thousand years before. Nettles grew around it. The moon shone on its uneven surface.

Billy hesitated for just a second.

Behind him, the bar had gone, too; the interior of the pub disappeared into blackness, the pitch blackness of the Darkest Bower.

Billy stepped forward into The Grove.

# Chapter Twenty-Eight
## Paper Trail

He felt sure that if he was ever to find Aura it would be here, at the heart of The Grove. At the secret place at the end of the path… Walk No. 21 had been leading him here ever since he'd seen Aura reading the guide book. Everything had been done to lure him, and here he was, "the sacrificial Billy." *Baa baaaa.*

That didn't stop him. He'd come too far now.

He walked along the path through the oaks until he was on the verge of the open space. He half-expected to see Romans hanging from the boughs, but the clearing was empty. He paused, waiting for whatever event should unfold next in this game. His fists were still clenched. His ears pricked.

Silence dominated The Grove.

He passed the shrubbery where he had lain dying over a thousand years before, moved on to stand beside the stone slab. He pictured Aura naked and lovely on its cruel surface, with a Roman soldier's defiling hands all over her.

He waited for Aura's ghostly voice to shiver through the trees and warn him like it had last time he was here.

He turned his back on the stone, searching the perimeter of the clearing. The path led away on the opposite side. A rucksack sat on the track, like the first marker in a paper trail, directing him on…toward what?

He crossed the open space, the moon full and fat above him, a cool breeze drying the sweat that had accumulated on his body from his exertions and his terrors.

He didn't recognize the rucksack. He stooped to unzip it. He found some untouched, moldy sandwiches inside a sweaty cellophane wrapping, a half-empty ginger ale bottle, and a library card with Cyril Peck's photograph smiling up benignly from the plastic.

Billy dropped the bag and continued along the path.

The oaks pushed in closer, but the feral moon prevented it becoming too dark, and he found the next rucksack easily enough. This one he recognized. The last time he'd seen it, one of the Rambling Society members had been wearing it in the bookshop, bright pink with yellow thongs. Milly? Molly? He couldn't remember her name. Just the bright and cheerful rucksack over one shoulder as she chided Billy in front of his manager.

He pushed on.

He soon came to the end of the path.

The end of Walk No. 21 was sudden and macabre.

The track led into a long, arched tunnel of warped beech trunks, the branches melding into each other to form walls and a vaulted ceiling. Bones, mostly human, dangled on greasy strings from the boughs and filled every nook and cranny. Skulls nestled with more rucksacks amongst the roots, some showing considerable signs of age. Piles of mobile phones grew like metallic ant hills beneath the trunks. Decaying corpses were half-buried, leaning up out of the soil as if to welcome Billy as he passed. The majority of the remains festooning the "temple" were skeletal, but quite a few still retained vestiges of flesh, moist with putrescence, sinking into the bark of the trees against which they lolled or growing out of the ground like obscene plants.

As he progressed further down the tunnel the decay became less pronounced, the victims more recent, and his persistence was rewarded with the sight of Cyril, eyes tugged out to dangle against his cheeks, hanging by his neck from a branch. His tattered complexion resembled an old half-chewed apple. A few paces on and there was Milly (or was it Molly?), sitting back against a beech as if quietly meditating, the lower half of her face missing. The other Ramblers were hunched around her in silent attention, though all were disfigured to some extent. Billy recognized Petunia from her bright dress rather than her face, and with good reason; her head had been removed just above her sloping chin.

He passed a blonde girl entangled in thick brambles, head down, hair covering her face. If there was something familiar about her, Billy didn't waste time finding out what it was. He knew instinctively it wasn't Aura, and that was all that mattered right now.

The scenic route of death had lost its power to horrify Billy by the time he reached what he suspected to be the end of the "temple." The passage opened up like the nave of a cathedral, pillar-like trunks towering up hundreds of feet before branches meshed overhead in an organic vaulted ceiling. A short flight of wide stone steps led up to a final arch of boughs. Beyond this arch, a plunge into utter blackness all too familiar to Billy from his adventure upstairs at the Pandemonium.

A cold wind blew from the opening. It stank of bestial, charnel things.

Billy stopped up to the threshold and waited.

He didn't have to wait long.

He could hear them approach behind him, crunching over bones as they came. Three of them. Just as it had always been.

He could almost feel the sword in his hand, a phantom weapon he'd lost over a millennia ago.

He turned to face them. Behind him, the wind from the dark whispered to his soul.

# Chapter Twenty-Nine
# "The Roman Has Returned..."

"One more dawn..."

The voice was a sword through a naked belly, a ripping of guts. It hurt Billy's ears, and it hurt his mind.

The one who had spoken moved closer, goat skull partially hidden within the depths of its cowl.

Even as it spoke, the stars faded overhead, the moon sank in rapid time beyond the loosely interlaced ceiling of branches. The sun was up in a blur of motion, and Billy could feel its warmth squeezing through the trees.

"The Roman has returned." The druid might have been talking to Billy, but it might have been addressing its two companions, or even speaking to the black void (which remained as black as ever, despite the rising of the sun) beyond the archway.

"The Roman and the Nymph." The voice carried sadistic mirth, the words ripping out of the skull as if powered by a medium far less prosaic than vocal cords and a tongue. "Even after a thousand years and more, he cannot have her."

Billy took a step forward. "Where is she?" If he was scared to see these three figures step out of his vision and into the growing daylight, he didn't show it. He could feel the sword in his hand, even though it wasn't there, and he could feel the centurion he once was, even though that man had died a millennia ago. He had a job to do back then, and he had one now, and if those missions had changed slightly over the gulf of time, then his courage and steadfastness had not. Kill the pagan cult, save the girl. Save the …

"Witch." Goat Skull spoke again, and maybe he was reading Billy's thoughts. "Witch-nymph lured you here, Roman, as the stars swing into place on Beltane Eve. Blood of the Roman shall feed The Grove. The Waiting of endless years for a long-deferred sacrifice. Our Father shall walk among us once more, the bride ready for His lust..." The druid paused, its glee evident.

"Blood and Bride, that is our gift. Are we not the Offspring of His Darke Loins? He awaits Rite's End in the Utmost Blackness Beyond, the depraved and secret heart of the woods, the Darkest Bower of All."

The sun was still climbing overhead, and Billy felt trapped in a cycle of lunacy in which time no longer had meaning. Beltane. The word came alive in his mind and brought with it associations he knew were not his, but once planted, they grew. *Beltane. The start of Summer. A time when wild things roam the Earth. Beltane... Union of God and nymph.*

*She never loved you.* This was another voice. Not the druid's, Billy knew that. Oh no, this voice was all his: *She only ever wanted to lure you...*

"The book and the Whistler played their part to summon you, too, Roman." Again, the creature seemed to read his mind, its voice a rip through mud, a tear of synapse in Billy's mind. "The book was written before Jesus flailed on his cross. It is a guide to the Darke within us and leads Everyman down the path he seeks. Any who venture upon the Way to Pandemonium shall feed with blood the Sacred Grove, where He steps Unseen. Your path led you to your thousand-year fate, Roman. Your path ends here."

At his words, the Whistler lurched forward. One arm rose, and a length of bramble snaked out from the sleeve, coiling around Billy's neck, twisting around his wrists. When there was enough bramble to bind him, the sleeve dropped again. The thorny plants writhed and cut into Billy's skin, pulling him back toward the dark void behind him, wrapping around the branches of the archway on either side, holding him in position. Blood trailed from the cruel barbs ripping his flesh. He could feel the cold wind yawning at his back. A whisper reached him, unintelligible, creeping inside his mind and hinting of terrible things. The animal stench came with the wind and the whisper.

He focused his mind on one thing: Aura.

He would not believe she lured him here for sacrifice. At first maybe… But over the short time they had together, he had seen in her eyes that she loved him, too. The bond between them after nearly two millennia was too strong. And hadn't she tried to warn him enough times to stay away?

*But where was she?*

*Beltane… the union of God and nymph…*

The whisper from behind grew stronger. He could sense the lust and hunger, although the words remained indistinct.

The three druids bowed their heads to the whisper.

The crazy sun stood overhead. Beltane was several hours away yet. Billy's hands clenched as he writhed against his thorny bonds. If he only had a sword…

# Chapter Thirty
## English Settlement

"Where you want me to park?"

Terry, the driver, stopped the minibus next to the stile and turned to face Tom, sitting in the passenger seat beside him.

Tom didn't answer for a moment. The manager looked distracted.

"Mister Lichby?"

"Huh?" Tom stared at him as if unsure where he was.

"Can't park her here, No room. I could try in the village some-where."

Tom nodded slowly. He was staring out of the window at the field beyond the stile. The guide book was clenched in his hands. He seemed perplexed by the system of low humps and gullies that formed an ancient English settlement in the field. Terry watched him open the book and flip through the pages until he came to the map. Terry peered over his shoulder, the engine idling.

"Whassup, guv?" James's bellow roared from the back seat of the minibus. "You want us all to jump out then?"

Tom didn't answer his assistant manager. He was frowning at the map, which clearly depicted the whorls and symbols that represented an ancient monument. He touched the *English Settlement* italics written next to the symbols and rubbed his forehead with his other hand. He looked a little queer, Terry thought.

The manager closed the book with a show of bravado and turned to Terry.

"Yes, we're getting out here. Park in the village if you like, or pop into Weston. Just make sure you return about five to pick us up."

Terry nodded and waited while the manager mustered his troops to climb from the minibus.

When they were all down, the driver didn't wait to watch them climb over the stile one by one but trundled the bus down the main street of Payndom, looking for somewhere suitable to park.

He drove past a purple Beetle parked outside the Pandemonium Inn and carried on until he reached the end of the main street. He turned left down a narrower road. The tops of the Tudor-style houses almost met overhead here, and Terry eased down through the gears, although there was plenty of head space between the top of his minibus and the protruding upper stories of the buildings.

He found a car park halfway down the street. There were no signs, just an open space with an overgrown village green in the middle, sur-rounded by the backs of houses. Most of the cars looked dirty and ne-glected, like it was a scrap yard or a deserted gypsy encampment, though he couldn't see any caravans. He parked in a space next to a blue Mazda, which didn't look as neglected as the other vehicles, one or two of which were actually collapsing with rust, deflated tires folded into the gravel surface.

He sat back in his seat, switched off the engine, and reached for his copy of *The Sun*. It was going to be a long day, but page three had a busty young lady that should entertain him for a while at least.

*The Wayes marked in this Booke Are not for All, though all those who touch it must follow them.*

Tom sat down on a grassy embankment that had once been a Bronze Age wall. The phrase was unbidden and kept repeating itself in his mind like a mantra.

Fact is, he really didn't know *why* he felt so compelled to come here to this weird little village in Somerset to follow a path that seemed to change from one moment to the next (and he was *sure* there had been no mention of an English Settlement on the map before, nor in the text beside it, no matter how many times James called him a doughnut). He hadn't seen any signs for paintballing either, which was the whole bloody reason why they were here in the first place.

*…though all those who touch it must follow them…*

He didn't like that phrase. Didn't like it at all. He suddenly let go of the book, as if it had given him an electric shock.

"Careful, boss. Don't wanna lose that—" James was about to pick it up off the grass when Tom stopped him. He snatched up the book again before the assistant manager could get his beefy hands on it and stuffed it in his rucksack.

"Whoa!" said James with a big grin. "Ever since you guys found out I don't wash my hands after taking a piss, you don't want me to touch *nothin'!*" His eyes beamed round at the assembled booksellers, waiting for a laugh.

Chloe, the buxom redhead, obliged him with one, a fetching giggle that seemed to be all she ever contributed to the team. Locksy, the tall brunette beside her, did her bit and pulled a face. "Gross, James."

Jerry chuckled at that, screwing the cap back on his bottle of Coke after a quick swig. "You're a dirty, dirty man, James."

"It's my generation," James admitted with a grin. "My old man never taught me to wash my hands. And anyway, footie hooligans and soap don't mix."

Jerry watched the assistant manager for a moment. The man from Liverpool had only two expressions: serious grim northerner and satirical grim northerner. Sometimes it was difficult to tell which was which. "You do realize," he said at last, "that every time we touch the staff-room kettle after you've used it, is just like touching your cock?"

"Excellent!" James looked well pleased with that notion.

"Ewww," Locksy bleated with some distress.

Tom had heard enough. The light-hearted babble had penetrated through the mantra in his head, but it also made him realize he could not ignore the call either, no matter what it meant. He stood up. "Right, guys." He pointed across the settlement to a gate in the far hedge. "Paint-ball area should be through that orchard and in the woods beyond."

He looked around at them as if checking they were all there. James, Jerry, Colesley, Locksy, Chloe, Simon, even Loss Prevention Officer Frank had come along for the ride. There was one missing, of course, and for a strange moment, Tom couldn't remember who that might be. He frowned as he made his way over the uneven ground toward the gate.

Oh yes…that was it.

Billy…

# Chapter Thirty-One
# The Centurion

And then he had a sword.

He saw it rise from the ground in front of him, a rusted blade notched by time, pushing up through the soil and grass as if a dead Roman legionary were making his way up through over a thousand years of sediment. Yet when the entire blade had emerged in an upright position from the ground, there was no bony hand clutching the hilt. The sword toppled on its side, and as Billy watched, the rust fell from the blade and the notches evened out and the steel looked shining and battle-ready.

He could feel the coils of bramble shackling him to the branches withering. He tugged, and his right hand was free.

The three druids advanced, and one of them held a staff menacingly before it in both hands, a staff with a wicked clutch of sharpened branches at one end, and at the other...

Billy could see it clearly, a lock of blonde hair wound round the staff, just above the furry right hand of the druid.

He thought of the block of masonry with the hastily scratched drawing, and he knew what he had to do, just as he knew who had returned the sword, *his* sword to him… *Witch-nymph,* the druid had called her.

With a mighty tug, he freed his left hand, too, and fell forward in a roll that brought his right hand into contact with the hilt of the Roman sword.

His roll completed in a spring, and he was back on his feet and the sword was in his fist as if it had never left it.

He crouched before the three druids, and the thousand years dissolved. He was a centurion, and the mission was not yet complete.

He screamed as he lifted the blade over his head, then swung it down. The sun, sailing toward mid-afternoon, pierced the lacing of branches above and ran the length of the blade with bright cold fire.

The sword edge slammed through the druid's right wrist like the furry limb was made of toffee. A black ichor bubbled from the stump. The druid uttered not a sound, but the staff drooped, gripped only by the left hand now. The severed hand clenched and unclenched its talons on the grass.

Billy pushed home his advantage. The sword arced again. The druid raised the staff to meet it, and the shock slammed Billy backward. He stumbled over a root, just managing to keep his balance, but the druid came on fast, thrusting the fierce end of the staff at his face with its one remaining claw. The whittled prongs dug away at his cheek, dangerously close to his eye.

Billy threw all his strength into a backhand slash that bit into the druid's good arm, releasing more black ooze. The creature tottered back, the staff lowering. Billy's blade was over his head now. "For you, Aura!!" he roared, and the Roman gladius crunched down on top of the hooded head.

The druid dropped to its knees, the staff slipping from its claw. Billy snatched it up immediately and bounded past the crouching druid.

The other two moved to block his way.

Billy didn't check his progress. He slammed into them like a quarterback, bowling them to either side. He went down, too, and the staff fell from his hand.

He scrabbled for it with his free hand, and just as he gripped it, he felt something clutch his jacket, tugging him back. Billy leaped up and spun in one move, the blade flashed and Goat Skull fell back, a gash opening up across the front of the druid's black gown. Billy was satisfied to see more black stuff dribble from the rent, but he didn't delay. He had the staff, he had the sword.

He ran.

Toward the entrance of the temple passage, leaping over corpses half-submerged in the soil or wedged between roots. Bony hands clutched at him in rigor mortis-locked greeting, brittle as twigs. He snapped through them, vaulting over Molly as she sat at her last Ramblers Meeting with her pals. He could see the entrance beyond.

And it was black.

Where the clearing at the heart of The Grove should be was only darkness, the "Utmost Blackness Beyond," which surely he had left behind at the other end of the temple, where he had fought with the druids?

He slowed as he neared the total absence of light. A portal into the "depraved and secret heart of the woods," Goat Skull had called it. Billy had already ventured inside once, at the Pandemonium. He knew salvation certainly didn't lead *that* way.

Over his shoulder, he could see the druids advancing slowly. There was no hurry. They knew he was trapped.

He hesitated. And as he did, a voice called to him. "Billy," it said.

A girl's voice. Soft, but oh so weary.

For a moment, hope leaped in his heart. Aura… But when he located the source of the voice, despair replaced the fragile hope. Another blonde. He had seen her earlier, dangling from bramble coils at the side of the tunnel. He had assumed she was dead and had barely registered her presence other than knowing it was not Aura.

Now he recognized her as she lifted her cut and filthy head to look at him. Her eyes implored with the ultimate sadness of a life betrayed. Her mouth parted, and Julie repeated his name.

Then she slowly withdrew her right arm from the retreating bramble tendrils and seized his leg. Her other hand was free, too, now and doubling the grip on his leg in a tight embrace. She would not let him go again. "Billy…" she breathed. "You always loved me. I know you always loved me."

He stared down at her aghast. The druids were nearly upon him now. Fifty yards ahead, at the entrance to the tunnel, the darkness whispered.

Julie saw her final rejection in Billy's face. She saw it and understood at last. Her half-insane face twisted into a mask of utter hatred and disgust for him. She increased her grip and called to the approaching druids.

"Kill him! Kill the fucker!"

Billy struggled in her grip, but she held on like a demented creature, her ragged, woods-stained nails digging into the calf through his jeans.

He felt the sword in his right hand tremble in his grip, but he could not use it. He glanced up desperately as the three druids closed the gap. The creature from which he had taken the staff held out its one remaining claw and flexed its talons. Billy could see the cloven hoof it used for a head, all black and glistening beneath the cowl.

He pulled frantically at Julie's grip, but it was no use. She would not release him. He lifted the staff in his other hand, ready to smash it down on her head. And as he did so, he saw the lock of hair tied to the shaft. Without thinking exactly what he was doing, he set the blade of the sword against the lock and cut it free. The twist of blonde hair floated to the ground.

Julie snarled up at him, spit dribbling from one corner of her mouth. She wanted to hurt him so badly. The way all men had hurt *her*. The nails of one hand crept under the shucked up jeans of his left leg, found naked flesh and began to tear.

Then another voice. This one female, too.

"Unhand him, you bitch…"

He looked up, and his heart expanded.

She was there.

She was there, at the entrance of the tunnel, The Grove clearing revealed behind her again where it had always been. She had dispelled the blackness that lurked there moments before, an illusion to freak Billy's mind. The real doorway to the Darkest Bower still waited for him at the other end of the temple from which he had just run, and if he listened hard enough, he could still hear the whispers creeping from its depths. But he was not listening. He was staring. At Aura. At the girl (Witch? Nymph?) he loved. She stood there glaring fiercely at Julie, the girl *nobody* loved, and Billy knew she was free. He had freed her just as she had asked him to when she tumbled that block of masonry from the cottage wall. She had shown him how.

Overhead, the sun had fallen. The first stars swung into their aligned position.

Aura remained on the threshold of the clearing, and her eyes blazed with power.

# Chapter Thirty-Two
# Bookseller Butchery

"He was right behind me a minute ago! I just don't understand it."

Frank was certainly non-plussed. They were in the orchard now, and Tom was becoming increasingly agitated.

"Well, where the hell is he now?"

Colesley had vanished. As the loss prevention officer had stated, Dick Coleslaw had been following them at the rear less than five minutes before. Tom had even heard him conversing with Frank in that haughty way he reserved for anyone he conceived to be of lesser intelligence.

As the group gathered beneath the apple trees, something else became plain to Tom.

"It's getting dark..."

James laughed. "Don't be ridiculous. It's not even two o'clock yet..."

Tom didn't lower his gaze as he faced the assistant manager. "It's getting dark."

"He's right," said Simon, the diminutive Sci-Fi buff. James stopped laughing. His jovial face tilted up to watch the skies. Darkness was filling the spaces between the apple boughs.

"What the fuck?" James checked his watch. "This doesn't make sense."

"My phone says seven-thirty." Chloe sounded scared.

"Must be faulty." Locksy checked hers. Her voice, confused, a second later: "Mine, too."

Tom opened his mouth. He almost said the words "I think we should leave," but he didn't. He stood in the center of the orchard (had there really been an orchard on the map when he first looked at it?) and wondered how he could get them to go on now.

Locksy was looking at the screen of her phone. "No signal," she said.

"Course not," James replied. "We're in 'Deepest, Darkest Zummerset,' me loverrr." Nobody laughed.

"What do we do, Tom?" Frank sounded lost, too, all his macho bravado stripped away by the impossible circumstance that was playing with this little group of booksellers.

Tom cleared his throat. "We go on," he said, although he knew in his heart it was wrong, that it was stupid. *We go back.* That's what he meant to say. What he should have said.

His staff gaped at him in amazement.

"It's half-past seven in the evening, guv. I don't know how, but it is. It's getting dark. I don't think there'll be much paintballing today."

*Paintballing?* Tom considered that concept. *But then they hadn't really come here to do that, had they? They'd come to follow Walk No.21…*

*And they hadn't reached the end of the path yet…*

"I vote we go back." James looked at his boss with mutiny in his eye. "We've already lost Dick Coleslaw somewhere along the way. If we carry on in the dark, we risk losing more. In fact, it's getting too dark to even see the way back through all these bloody apple trees." He kicked a windfall to emphasize his comment.

Nobody said anything for a handful of seconds. The stars slipped between the branches overhead. A moon, dented by clouds, limped out to greet them.

Jerry was already turning and marching off between the widely spaced apple trees.

"Liverpool lad doesn't hang around long, does he?" James nodded abruptly at Tom and started after the bookseller. "Hold up, Jerry! We're *all* coming…"

"No," Tom said, and his voice made the others pause.

"Whaddya mean, 'no'?" James turned to face him again, and his grin was one of exasperation and disbelief.

"I said no. We go on. I'm the manager here, not you, James!" His eyes were darker than usual, and it wasn't just the rush of twilight filling them.

"Seriously?"

Simon snorted in open contempt and started off after Jerry. Chloe and Locksy looked at each other in confusion. Frank folded his arms, ready to back his manager to the last, with all the loyalty of the not-so-bright.

"Anyone else wants to follow Jerry, they can. But they won't have a job on Monday."

James laughed openly. "This is a gag, right?" He saw the look on his manager's face. Tom had always been a stubborn ass, but this was crazy. He was taking his authority to surreal lengths. "It's not a gag. You are actually, fucking serious. Tom, you're losing it, man. We're not your grunts. This is a work-financed trip, but it ain't work, and even if it was, you'd still be talking bollocks. Go on to a paintball event that doesn't even exist in the middle of the night??"

Chloe was looking distinctly worried now. "It's not… It's not the middle of the night. It *can't* be!" She was dragging her phone out of her handbag again, and the dim light from the screen showed them all her scared face.

James had already seen his watch. It no longer indicated 7:30.

Chloe stifled a sob. Locksy put an arm around her, and as she did so, she saw the time on Chloe's phone. "Fuck…"

"Fuck is right," James agreed. "We've somehow lost another three hours in five minutes. This ain't right, boys and girls. This ain't right at all. Follow me and let's get out of here." He turned to follow after Jerry and Simon, who were near the far end of the orchard now. Tom's hand closed around his arm.

*"I said no!! I'm the fucking boss! You all listen to ME!"*

Tom's face was a twisted mask of rage. He squared off against James, his other hand clenched into a fist.

"You have seriously lost the plot, Tom, old son." James shook off Tom's hand. He looked around at the others. "Are you with me?"

Locksy led Chloe to stand beside James. Frank looked completely disoriented by events. He unfolded his arms and glanced from Tom to James.

"Come on, girls." James led them away. His foot stepping on a rotten windfall produced a crunch that seemed very loud in the dark. Chloe jerked in fright as she clung to Locksy.

Frank turned to his boss. "Looks like paintball's off," he said, and just as he finished speaking, two rusty prongs jutted out of his neck. Tom gaped at the naked man in a goat mask who suddenly emerged from behind a tree in the dark, clutching the gardening fork that he had slammed through the back of Frank's throat. Blood spat from the tines, momentarily blinding Tom. Frank folded to his knees. His hands came up to grasp ineffectually at the prongs in his neck, then dropped away. His eyes bugged. The tines worked in his throat, then were plucked free as the naked man balanced one foot against the security guard's shoulders for purchase. Frank flopped over onto his face.

Locksy heard Frank gag and looked back to see the naked man with the fork. She stopped walking, stunned. Chloe clung to her more tightly. James carried on, oblivious, until a portly naked woman in a leather goat mask stepped out from under a branch laden with apples to confront him.

With one hand she teased her erect nipple. With the other, she clenched a ball-peen hammer in front of her.

"What the *fuck??*" James halted in his tracks. The woman had an untamed bush of graying pubic hair and sagging breasts. He didn't know what was more unsettling: her nakedness or the goat mask. *Or the fucking hammer, for that matter...*

Before he could react, the hammer slammed forward, cracking

through his spectacles, blinding him and breaking his nose at the same time. He staggered back. Chloe was screaming now. A long, high note of total terror. The hammer came at James again, stove in his forehead, dropping him to the ground like a felled buck. The naked woman continued to hammer him, his body jumping and twitching amongst the windfall apples with each blow.

Locksy pulled Chloe after her, dodging around the demented woman with the hammer.

Ahead of them, Simon and Jerry had turned, alerted by Chloe's screams. They hesitated by the iron gate at the edge of the orchard in frozen shock.

Even as the girls stumbled toward the two men, Locksy saw another naked assailant drop from the branches of an apple tree beside them. The man was tall and wiry, carried an old ax, and even from this distance, she could see he was fully erect. Locksy stumbled to a halt, Chloe's scream still digging at her ears, her mind. Another man dropped from his hiding place in a tree just in front of them, a gardening hoe clutched in both hands. She could see the eyes beneath the black goat mask glinting with pleasure. His cock began to lift, too, in anticipation of delights to come.

Locksy didn't mess around. She shook Chloe off her and drove her boot forward into that growing member.

The villager grunted, clasping its genitals with one hand. Locksy quickly snatched the hoe from his other hand, hefted it, and then swung it into the goat head. The mask tipped sideways, half falling from the villager's head, revealing a lopsided mouth with only three or four snaggle teeth. Locksy sliced the hoe in an arc, the metal edge plowing into those snaggle teeth, gratified to see one spin out from the deformed mouth. Beside her, Chloe collapsed in the grass.

Locksy hadn't finished. She was grunting herself now as she battered the goat man with the hoe. The mask had fallen completely off his head now. Locksy saw the abnormality revealed and that irrationally made her angrier. She was cursing the freak in time with the blows from the hoe. The naked man was rolling on his back, hands out in front of his face to ward off the frenzied attack. Locksy concentrated on his now-wilting genitals, slicing them, mashing them until the man stopped squealing and lay still. She continued to destroy his private parts until two more villagers seized her from behind.

She dropped the hoe. They forced her to her knees, made her watch as they defiled Chloe.

The goat masks bobbed and jerked in glee as their hands ripped at Chloe's clothing. Her wonderful, full breasts were stripped bare. One of the goat men waved her red, lacy bra over his head in triumph with one hand while restraining her with the other. Chloe's screams had hit empty now. Just a dry tank. Though her mouth kept working at it, trying to cough up more. Her eyes were huge, focusing first on Locksy, then on the moon. They stayed on the moon as her mind lost its grasp and filthy hands pawed her breasts.

More villagers joined the fete. Most of them gathered around Chloe, and a rusted machete was passed to one of her captors. He wore a goat mask painted bright crimson and seemed to be a leader of sorts, though the bookseller was not to know she was staring at the landlord of the Pandemonium Inn. She watched as he began to pump his erect member with his free hand. The night was filled with howls and guttural, jubilant cries that sounded more animal than human.

"Why are you doing this?" It was a reasonable enough question. She voiced it with utter desperation, though it came out almost matter of fact, adding to the horrible surrealism of the scene. Over the landlord's shoulder, she could see Simon being hacked in half by a villager with an ax. His torso was free from his legs now, such was the ferocity of the attack. And Jerry… Jerry was running. It looked like he'd gotten away. He was up the iron gate and over it, dropping to the grass on the other side.

The landlord continued to pump away in masturbatory frenzy. The two holding Locksy (one was a woman, slender, with an attractive young body) forced her to watch this obscene act, though just before he reached his climax, they twisted her face toward Chloe. She was just in time to see the light go out of her friend's staring eyes as the landlord finished his exertions and played with his machete instead. Chloe's breasts were hacked free, dropping to the grass like oversized, fleshy windfalls.

Blood covered the apples. Locksy would have screamed like Chloe before her, but that just wasn't her way.

*"Fuck you!!"* she managed instead, spitting at the landlord, as he gripped his twitching member again with one hand, the bloody machete drooping in the other "I'll cut that tiny thing right off, you cowardly prick," Locksy promised him

He weighed the weapon in his right hand, taunting her, then drew it back over one shoulder, his free hand remaining on his privates.

"You want ta be murdered?" the landlord offered, then swung the machete down, silencing Locksy's curses forever. The machete went in so hard, it took all the landlord's efforts to retrieve it from the cleft in her forehead.

Tom watched him struggle.

He had wandered over to see the sights. He didn't really understand what was happening and guessed that he might indeed have lost the plot, just as James had suggested. His mind felt weird and warped. He had followed the path, as he knew he must, and this was his reward. Mutiny and blood. *If only they had listened to him, you see... None of this would have happened if they had just bloody done as they were told. They could have been playing paintball right now. Just like Billy promised them. Billy...*

*Fucking Billy. All HIS fault.*

Tom wandered through the windfalls, sliding on some of them, wet in the dew that was already forming as the world swung toward dawn on Beltane.

He passed amongst the villagers like he was untouchable. He turned in confused circles as if marveling at the spectacle, then headed away from it all, trying to remember which way the path would lead next. They let him go. At least, it seemed like they might. He was walking toward the further end of the orchard now. He really wanted to complete the walk. He wondered if they would let him.

He was still wondering when the landlord came up behind him and took off his head.

That left Jerry.

Good, old Jerry, salt-of-the-earth Liverpool lad.

He vaulted over the gate and hit the ground running. Running through the English settlement, bounding over walls, racing down into gullies and struggling up the far ramparts, emerging on top of the world for brief moments before diving down into the next depression.

He could see the stile, not twenty yards in front of him.

He could also see Colesley. The arse-licking bookseller was on a pole jutting out of the grass in a corner of the field not far from the fortifications Jerry was struggling through. Even from this distance, Jerry could see the bastard had been impaled on the pole, that the end was jousting out of his distorted mouth and that he had become a hu-man scarecrow. *Stuck there to frighten off booksellers?*

That wasn't even funny.

Jerry raced for the stile. Not far now. Ten yards. Five. He was go-ing to make it, lucky lad. Lucky grim northerner. He was going to…

Beyond the stile, there were more villagers. They moved forward out of the darkness, and the generous moon popped free of cloud to show them in all their glory. They were naked, and they all wore goat masks.

Jerry tried to reverse his sprint but only succeeded in tripping over the uneven turf of the fortification. He went down. Hard.

Even before he looked up, he knew they were coming for him over the stile.

His last thoughts were crazy. He didn't think of his mum, of his childhood, of his part-time girlfriend back at home.

He thought of Mo Salah, and how he would never see him play for Liverpool again.

Even Jerry had to admit that was an ignominious image to take with him into the dark.

# Chapter Thirty-Three
# Legion

Julie was aware in a corner of her crazy mind that her rival had appeared.

The blonde bitch who had caused her all this pain and grief. Her twisted heart, already filled to capacity with hatred, found extra space for more. She rose up from her knees, releasing Billy now, her ragged nails extending toward the beautiful girl in a gown white as a bridal dress, poised at the entrance of the temple.

Aura watched her stagger forward, half-naked, covered in mud, blood, and slime. She did not move; she just waited.

"Fucking *bitch*!" Julie was crying with rage and pain as she limped forward. She had been imprisoned in brambles as sharp and cruel as barbed wire for so many days she could barely think rationally any more. She hadn't eaten; she had drunk only the occasional raindrops that dripped down between the branch "ceiling" above; she could barely remember who she was or how she had got here. She was weak, she was exhausted, and she was half-dead. But her hatred kept her alive. Only hate, in the end, could do that. Never love. Never that...

She shoved Billy out of her way. Pathetic, weak, like all men. She would tear his eyes out like grapes later. First, she would spoil the blonde's beauty. The slag who stood in the entrance, legs apart like fucking Xena, Warrior Princess, but without the muscles and tits. She would pick out those bright blue eyes and stomp on them. She wouldn't be so pretty then. She wouldn't be so god-fucking-irresistible to men then…

She got within five yards of Aura when the druid came for her. Billy stepped forward to swing his sword, but the druid with the hoof for a head slammed him aside with its one remaining claw before clamping the same arm around Julie's throat from behind, dragging her backward. She croaked in thwarted fury and surprise. Holding her still with its claw, the druid rammed the stump of its other arm inside her mouth and deep into her throat as far as it would go while she gagged and thrashed. Black fluid, like rank pond water, bubbled from her distended lips, stretched as they were around the arm that was using her mouth like a sheath. Her thrashing ebbed. Her eyes bulged out from her white face.

Billy threw himself against the monster, his weight smashing both druid and girl sideways, dropping the staff in the process. The druid tottered, withdrawing its arm from Julie. The blonde bookseller hit the earth like a dropped sack. Billy could tell from her gaping, filth-smeared mouth and vacant eyes that she was already dead. He raised his sword to strike the druid's head from its shoulders, but Aura's voice stopped him.

"Billy!"

He whirled. She was retreating backward into The Grove clearing, her arms thrown out to either side. Behind her he could see the naked men and women of the village creeping through the trees, some pushing rusted wheelbarrows laden with the corpses of his erstwhile bookshop colleagues, the rest clutching axes, machetes, and gardening implements.

"Come, my centurion. It is time to fight with your legion once again."

He was running toward her, the sword clutched in his right hand. He saw the earth at the center of the clearing begin to pulse and heave. Fingers pushed through, followed by earth-stained arms. A head emerged, soil trickling from the open mouth. Billy recognized Sciro's brutal features immediately, even with the sheen of rot that hadn't managed to erase his identity completely, and Billy sensed Aura's influence here, too. His men, half-preserved beneath the soil where they had died, waiting for the time of resurrection. Aura had waited nearly two thousand years to bring them back to war.

The legionary burrowed his way out of his tomb of millennia, armor dented and rusted, his broken head turning stiffly. One eye was gone, but the other fixed on Billy, and there was an awful recognition in it.

Four more corpses erupted from the earth, soil and grass trickling off breastplates and shredded tunics. They stood for a moment, bearing the awful wounds that had killed them, all attention fixed on their leader and the nymph who had ushered them forth. The earth was buckling again. Swords thrust up through the grass, rusted and battered, not bright like the centurion's but weapons still, and the legionaries moved slowly to collect them.

He had reached Aura's side now. "This, their redemption," she said quietly. She didn't look at him; her eyes were focused on the heavens, watching the moon spin toward dawn.

The druids fanned out as they emerged into the clearing. Under the fringe of trees on the far side, the villagers released their wheelbarrows and froze in obvious terror at this new twist.

Aura raised her arms higher, then swept them down.

The legionaries went into battle. Like the well-oiled soldiers they were, forged in the greatest military organization that ever lived, the Romans moved into action.

Three of them split away, the giant Bellari with a crack running down one side of his head, the scrawny, faceless Martus, and the always-quiet Cartelli. They were all quiet now. They marched toward the villagers with a speed and force of intent that belied their emaciated looks, and the villagers gave way before them.

A few of them rallied, moved to meet the Romans, their gardening forks and hoes clashing against the rusted steel of thousand-year-old swords strengthened by witch fire.

Billy hesitated for only one second, long enough to see the villagers fall like wheat before the scything Romans. It was a ballet of murder. Undead legionaries trained for battle, against deformed villagers, degraded by their own perverted lusts. Billy saw the carnage, heard the screams. Heads still clad in leather goat masks rolled. Swords clashed against axes and machetes in a Punk rock chorus of brutality, a thunderous heavy metal riff of death.

Sciro and his fellow legionary, Pachellus, moved with the confidence of those already dead to take on the three druids. Billy moved with them, felt the allegiance he had never experienced in his other life, and as his sword flew toward the creature that had snuffed Julie, he felt the power and the glory of a born leader.

He had their respect at last.

His sword cleaved through the hood and furred head with a power that made his blood sing. The druid was down, and Billy's blade pulled free from the gaping cleft it had dug, moving almost of its own volition, flashing under starlight, swooping again, and the head was leaping free, rolling in the daisies…and then there were two.

He sprang to join Sciro. The brawny legionary had sheathed his blade to the hilt in Goat Skull's black ribs, bared beneath the slashed cloak. Druid and Roman made no sound as they fell in a heap together. Billy could hear only the cries of dying villagers from across the clearing and the sounds of steel on bone.

Sciro rolled on top of Goat Skull, riding him to death, his sword punching holes in the body beneath him, excavating putrid organs from within the smashed ribs. He didn't need Billy's help.

Pachellus was grappling with the Whistler. Bramble tendrils poured from the druid's gaping sleeve, cocooning the Roman's body. Pachellus's dented blade slashed and hacked at the thorny bonds, while Billy swung his sword in a perfect backhand, and Whistler's left arm spun to the grass.

Whistler turned to flee. Billy took a chunk of cloak and black flesh out of his back, but then the druid was through the entrance to the tunnel, and Billy could hear the dreaded familiar sound emanating from those pursed lips. Billy tensed to chase after him, but a hand touched his shoulder, light and crackling with energy. Aura shook her head once solemnly. Billy let the Whistler go.

When he turned back around, the battle was done. Villagers lay scattered beneath the trees on the edge of the clearing. Masks covered in blood rested in the grass or hung from branches where they had become caught in the heat of the fray. He recognized the landlord, leaning back against a tree trunk, bright red goat mask fallen in his lap. A rusted sword was buried to its hilt in his forehead.

The legionaries marched to the center of the clearing. Their rotting faces were fixed on Billy and Aura. Aura raised her arms once more, and once more let them drop.

Billy lowered his head in salute. When he raised it again, they were gone. Dust blew on the dawn breeze.

From within the temple, the whistle of the druid grew louder.

"Dawn," said Aura simply. "It is Beltane, and He comes among us..."

From inside the temple, Billy heard a growing thunder, as of something large and very terrible approaching, and the ground trembled beneath them.

# Chapter Thirty-Four
# Beltane

Aura turned to him with haunted eyes. "There must be blood *and* a bride. I was not sent here just to entrance *you*, Billy. I could change the detail, but not the outcome. The Darke Druids died before the whistle could lure Him when first we met, but now things must follow their course. It cannot be stopped a second time. This is our final dawn. Remember I loved you then, I love you now…"

Whatever that meant, he had to ignore it. Billy started toward the entrance of the temple again. This time Aura could not stop him. "*Billy*!!!" He heard her voice, but he heard that detested whistle, too, rising above the thunder of heavy steps. The whistle had haunted his dreams as well as his days, and if it was summoning something awful, it was Billy's job to stop it. The sword was still in his hand, and he would finish the job it had started.

He leaped over the paper trail of rucksacks that had led him inside the temple a day—two days?—before. All sense of time was lost. There was only now. There was only the dawn, and Beltane.

Aura followed him to the temple passage. He could smell her blossom scent vying with the stench of rot. He vaulted over corpses, almost tripping on Julie's. He could see the Whistler sprawled in obeisance before the Darkest Bower, and the whistle was more urgent and triumphant than Billy had ever heard it.

Billy slowed as he came up to the void beyond the natural arch. The black depths seemed to quiver with unnatural malignancy, in time with the crashing of heavy footfalls. He had heard that crashing before, in the darkness of the room in the Pandemonium, and he really didn't want to see whatever might be causing it.

He heard a rending of branches and undergrowth, accompaniment to the trampling footsteps.

He lifted his sword above the Whistler. The three notes defiled his brain, his soul. He would stop them... now.

And then He stepped through the arch out of the Darkest Bower.

Instinct—or was it more, was it Aura?—made Billy drop the sword and cover his eyes with his hands before he saw...cover his eyes and scream like a terrified child.

Aura was beside him. He registered her words over the whistle and the screaming in his mind that he knew was his own. *"Don't look!! Don't look at His face!"*

But he *would* look at His face. He *must*... Billy's hands began to move away from his eyes.

He had fallen to his knees without realizing it. The sword lay beside him in the grass. He was barely aware of the rust creeping along the once-shiny blade again, the steel that cracked then crumbled to dust. His eyes were fixed on those mighty hooves now as his disobedient hands fell away. Huge as elephant feet, resting on the grass inside the temple. The God was tall as the oaks, and the stink of the dark came with him. If Billy raised his head, he would see the mighty legs reaching up, all shaggy and twined with ivy and thorn. If he raised his head he would see...

*Don't look!! Don't look at His face!!*

Billy's head continued to rise. Past the shaggy thighs. Higher. Billy saw the stomach now, covered with fur, dark with blood and matted with moss. Higher.

The God from the Dark filled Billy's world. His head would explode with it all. He wanted to see the heart of the wood in that awful face, to free the bestial inside himself. But if he looked, he would see… and if he *saw*…

The whistle reached a crescendo. Billy was barely conscious of the druid sprawling next to him, its cowled head raising, too, lips pursed. When one mighty hoof lifted from the ground and hovered over the druid, Billy finally managed to drag his eyes from their inevitable climb. He focused on the hoof instead as Aura's words echoed inside his brain.

The hoof came down with an earthquake stomp. The druid's head pulped. Black ichor splattered Billy's face, half blinding him.

He fell onto his back, senses reeling. The echo of the whistle remained in his brain. Would it ever leave? The druid was unmoving, broken beside him. The hoof smeared the remains of the cowled skull, grinding them into the grass. Then there was stillness.

An awful, awful stillness.

Aura's movement broke it at last. She was walking forward, to greet the one who had arrived. Her slender hand reached out and was received by His. It was monstrous, half-covered with fur and blood. Billy's focus was drawn to the ragged nails that clutched at her beautiful fingers, took them savagely in its grip.

No.

He struggled to rise. He could sense the bestial God of the Woods about to move, ready to return to the Darkest Bower with His new bride. This Darke God, worshipped in grottoes, in caves, and in woods ever since the first man shivered with fear at what might lurk in the secret heart of the trees, where the thickest shadows lurked. This Darke God, bestial, wilder than thunder, crueler than the coldest wind and sharpest thorns, far more terrible than the blackest soul of man. This awful God, this Great God Pan.

Come to take His Bride.

No. *No!*

*NO!!!!*

He had endured too much, waited too long for this. To lose her again after a thousand years was more than he could bear.

He staggered to his feet, his hand reaching out to stop them, his head rising, and he would look upon her abductor before He turned completely and took her away forever. He would look at the Awful Face, and his mind would break, his eyes would be dust. His soul would burn. He knew this with the instinct of primitive man. Yet he would look upon the Beast...

Aura stopped him with her free hand. It rested softly on his cheek, turning his head away from its remorseless upward movement, turning it toward her instead.

Tears traced their way down her face. His heart split to see them and know she was lost. Her hair glowed pale under the last stars. Her eyes ignited with the agony of loss. She gave him a smile as beautiful as it was heartbreaking, her parting gift to him, and her voice was a ghost in the creeping dawn: "Rite complete, my centurion. The blood was not yours today. You didn't have to die. You just had to be here." She stroked his cheek, and then her hand dropped away.

He groped to retrieve it, but her back was turned. The monstrous creature led her through the arch, and she was gone.

Billy hesitated only a moment. Then he ran at the dark archway.

It was like hitting a wall. A wall of fear. He stumbled a few feet inward, the dark closing around him, just like it had in the Pandemonium Inn. He lost all sense of depth, of space, of touch and sight. Horror rushed at him out of that void, battering at his mind, the sensation ramped up a hundredfold from the last time he was lost in its darkness. The core of his being recoiled from that absence of everything he understood. A whisper crawled at him, unintelligible but patently obscene: the heart of the black wood coaxed him with insanity. He felt the skin rippling on his body, his bowels threatening to loosen.

Billy staggered back under the assault, brain yawning with terror. He was falling from a great height, falling forever.

He was lying on the grass beyond the archway. He had no idea how long he'd been out other than the fact the grass was wet with dew.

Morning had broken. He got to his feet, shivering in the gray dawn light. The archway, and the darkness beyond, had gone. In its place was a wall of foliage, and nothing else. He groped his way through the shrubbery but found nothing but more trees, more bushes, and eventually, he staggered out to the edge of The Grove itself, and there was the smooth grassland beyond, rippling in the early morning breeze. He retraced his steps, scrambling back through the trees, searching for the temple like a man searching for lost treasure.

Finally, he stood in the center of the clearing, defeated. Not just the arch, but the entire temple had eluded him; now he had wandered away from it. Even the rucksacks were gone, the trail that had shown him the way. The corpses of the villagers still lay under the trees at the edge of the clearing, however, and the booksellers with whom Billy had spent the last four years of his life lay among them. He didn't look at them.

He sank to his knees in the grass.

He didn't know how long he stayed there, waiting for her to come back to him. It didn't matter that his trousers were soaked with dew, or that his bones ached with a stiffness that would stay with him for days after. Nothing mattered. Nothing ever would again. He waited. And waited.

The day moved on around him. The sun had resumed its normal pace. It hung above his head, warming his scalp, then it was past, falling toward dusk, and still, Billy did not move. Still Billy waited.

When the moon came out to play and the stars rolled like bright dice above The Grove, Billy's head finally jerked up and around as if only just aware of his surroundings.

He got to his feet, limbs cold and heavy as stone.

He followed the path back to the village, through Lord's Wood, crossing the meadow with its tumble-down cottage from which no sound emerged, and to the stile, and, at last, Billy left the path.

He stumbled through the village searching for his car, like a man lost in a dream. His car seemed lost, too. It was no longer outside the silent Pandemonium Inn where he had parked it. He passed the empty houses, walking the deserted streets of Payndom until he discovered the carpool with its collection of dusty wrecks and a few newer vehicles. He found his Beetle with a shattered driver's side window, parked next to a minibus. He saw the minibus driver flopped in his seat wearing a livid gash like a red neckerchief, and reached mechanically for the key in his pocket.

The Beetle started straight away.

Billy moved the stick into gear and drove out of Payndom.

# Epilogue

Billy never found The Grove again, or the temple where he had seen a God.

He never found Payndom either, no matter how many times he pored over maps, surfed on search engines, or drove around the area where he had once turned off down a leafy lane. To all extents and purposes, the village never existed.

For months afterward he spent his days scouring the Somerset lanes. He retraced his route between Bristol and Weston-Super-Mare countless times, but the lane never showed itself, nor could he remember exactly whereabouts it had been. Was it just paranoia, or was there something else at work, hiding the location of Payndom, The Grove, and Walk No. 21 from his eyes?

One time, he came to the top of a hill overlooking the Somerset levels and was sure he could see The Grove far off in the mist of an Autumnal afternoon. He pulled the car over to the side of the road, heart pounding. He scrambled out and peered at the vague horizon.

He could see a copse of trees, mostly oak, but there might be some beeches (a temple?) among them. The more he strained his eyes to focus, the more the view wavered, flirting with the mist and his own sense of reality. He scrambled back inside his car and followed the road downhill in the direction in which he'd seen the copse, but the roads he chose never took him there. He drove around the levels until the daylight faded, and when he came again the next day to the same hill, all he could see on the horizon was Glastonbury Tor rising from the flat, stark countryside, and no matter how much he searched the distance, there was nothing that resembled The Grove.

Another time he saw a pub that looked just like the Pandemonium Inn. It was in a valley on the other side of a comb of trees, and he caught glimpses of swollen, whitewashed walls and black timber between the branches as he drove past. When he found a side lane that cut through the trees and down through the valley, the only pub he found was yellow and modern and filled with portly farmers supping cider. He stared up at the sign in despair. A stag's head adorned the board. One of the farmers frowned at him through the window until he eased his foot down on the accelerator and drove home.

His visits to the area grew less frequent over time. He knew he would never see Aura again, and his persistence in the face of all hope would only push him to madness, if indeed he was not there already.

He visited the bookshop one day six months after the events in The Grove to find the shop was filled with new staff, which was hardly a surprise. He wasn't really surprised to find the Guide Book back on the shelves either, although when he flicked through the pages, he could find no listing for Walk No. 21. Whatever malignant force created the book, it was done with him. Now it was some other poor soul's turn to take their chance on the paths. He considered borrowing somebody's lighter and burning the evil thing, but he had a strong conviction the next time he returned, it would be there again in its rightful place, sandwiched between *The AA Guide to Country Walks* and *Cycling Somerset*.

He noticed an Afterword he had previously missed, and the words of the druid returned to him like a blow to his soul: "*Wander at your owne Peril, for this is a Guide to the Darke within us, and leads Everyman down the path he seekes... And the Book shall find those whose fate lies along each Way...*"

A young girl with auburn hair browsing next to Billy glanced at the hardcover book in his hands with open curiosity, and Billy turned quickly away, no longer covetous of its contents, but truly afraid for any who might be lured by its sinister call.

His attention returned to the Afterword, and once again he felt chilled to the core: *"For those who walke the Paths, it shall be as if they never were."*

On his way out, Billy paused at the till until a hipster with thick, black glasses and beard all present and correct shuffled across to serve him. No, he didn't know any of the staff who previously worked at the store. He could ask his manager if Billy liked, but he was pretty sure she didn't know them either. When Billy asked if he didn't find it odd the entire workforce had vanished, the hipster looked confused and finally shrugged. "Before my time, man," he offered. "People come and go in a place like this." *They certainly did*, Billy thought.

He passed a large man in a gray suit as he left the till, and Billy recognized him immediately as the Area Manager who had been a weekly presence in the shop during his time there. Clarke looked straight through Billy with a pleasant smile on his face, the one he reserved for customers and strangers.

*For those who walke the Pathes, it shall be as if they never were...*

And Aura?

Billy would remember. He would remember her forever.

But he would not, *could* not, think of her fate at the bestial hands of the Darke God once He had taken her into the blackest heart of the Wood. Images tried to push their way into his brain regardless, only driven back by whiskey and vodka.

At nights, he would lie awake, and sometimes he was sure he heard her calling him as the wind played with the trees beyond his garden wall. Occasionally, when he did sleep, he would be woken in the dark by a scream. A fox, out in the cemetery. At least, that's what he would say to himself, and he would lie in the dark with a name on his lips and his eyes open, waiting for the dawn.

# ABOUT THE AUTHOR

Leo Darke was once famous for being sacked as a scary actor from the York Dungeon in England. His thespian efforts were so chilling as he menaced the public in between hanging Dick Turpin and describing the drawing and quartering of Guy Fawkes that girls shrieked and indignant parents wrote furious letters... His subsequent dismissal was plastered all over the newspapers shortly after. "Is this the most terrifying man in Britain?" screamed one headline. Well, he may not really be all that scary in person, without the make-up and costume, but he certainly hopes his novels are. He is also the author of *Mr. Nasty* and *Lucifer Sam*.

LUCIFER
SAM

# Chapter One

**1989**

*Barra boy no more, my son...*

Ray was staring at 15,000 upturned faces. And they were all staring at *him*.

The realization didn't hit him at first. He stood on the lip of the stage, struggling to take it all in. Proper head-fucked, as Barney, the drummer, would have put it. He was half naked, his slim torso slick with sweat. Two songs in and he still couldn't accept the enormity of it all. He stood still in the few moments grace between songs, hand unconsciously brushing at his spiky mop as he tried to get his head around it. Jezza, the guitarist, was busy tuning, head down as he concentrated so Ray couldn't see his expression. Probably thinking about playing *Dungeons and Dragons* with his Tolkien-obsessed mates, the nerdy twat. He only got hard for prog rock solos. Ray was sure his guitar mags were all very sticky. Phil, the bass player and band leader, was staring at the audience, too, a dumb grin on his square face, long, curly hair matted with sweat. Ray beamed over at him, shaking his head numbly, sharing a WTF moment. They had never been close, but this was a moment even enemies could share. This was momentous. The crowd was roaring for more, and distinct above the colossal noise, Ray could hear his name in a rising chant. He felt electrified. The vestiges of coke left in his system buzzed through his veins, boosted by his euphoria.

Then the truth of it smashed him like a hammer. This was it. He had made it. No more getting up at 5:00 a.m. to look after his old man's fruit and veg stall on Portobello Road. No more skimping on beer money to feed the electricity meter in his dingy flat off Brick Lane. No more borrowing a sub off his surly old man to take a bird to the flicks. No more scrapping outside the Ten Bells on a Friday, Saturday night cos some bastard looked at him wrong. There was gonna be no more of that shit! From now on there would be chauffeurs to every venue, drinking champers like water at top London clubs with big-breasted tarts falling all over him. He was *big time, baby!* He sucked it all in, standing on the lip of the stage. This was a fuckin' epiphany! He felt joy orgasm through his body. He spread his arms, tilted his head to one side to take in the adoration of the crowd. His name was a massive chant that would shame the rest of the band: "Starling, Starling… STARLING!!!"

Ray Starling, twenty-one years old and at the top of the world. Headlining the Frankfurt Rock Festival to 15,000 punters all screaming his name was his Mount Everest scaled. He had the voice, he had the look. He certainly had the attitude to achieve—he took no bullshit, and the desire to make it had driven him through a poverty-stricken childhood and teenage years that had seen him punch and struggle every step of the way to this moment. But it wasn't just his sheer brute willpower. His voice was unforgettable. It could chisel stars and make the Gods roar. Ray had a vocal range that allowed him pinnacle-ascending falsettos one minute and punky, thunderous growls the next. His voice had a quality that transcended the puerile subject matter Phil insisted the band concentrate on: all fantasy imagery, torture implements, and dodgy war films. It reached your soul and your gut at the same time. And not only was Ray's voice pretty damn unique, but he was also young and eminently shaggable. The first album had gone platinum across the globe, and things really couldn't get better than this.

Within two months he would lose it all.

# Chapter Two



**2014**

The punch took Ray in his left eye, and for a moment he could only see in mono.

The blow took him clean off his bar stool, dumped him on the floor of the boozer like the sack of shit the geezer who hit him obviously thought he was.

"Fuckin' rock star? More like a used-up tissue that everyone's spunked in, mate. Ain't nuffin' sadder than a pathetic Has Been who still thinks he's got what it takes. Fuckin' loser." The big man took a step back as if to deliver a kick to the fallen idol. Ray saw it coming but was too pissed to dodge it. The toe of the geezer's boot caught him on his left cheekbone, just below his foggy eye. The pain was sickening. He rolled over on his back, and the dingy pub revolved around him, darkening.

He could see a couple of faces hanging over him, repeating his name in anxious tones—certainly not the 15,000 that once roared it in exuberance. Michelle's face was tear-streaked as she knelt down next to him, her sister, Bella, turning away to scream at the man who had kicked him.

He peered up at Michelle as if wondering who she was. Was she still his bird? The last in a looooong fuckin' line of 'em. But this one had been a keeper. Before Michelle, none of 'em had meant much to him. Not really. Apart from Michelle, *nothing* meant much to him anymore.

He stared up at the cracked ceiling of the Victorian-era boozer and wondered where it had all gone wrong.


Now it was Phil Carter's face looming into vision. But Cat O' Nine Tails' bass player certainly wasn't in this back-street boozer. Nah, he'd be drinking champers on a jet somewhere on the latest leg of a world fuckin' tour no doubt…

It was just a memory. Just the same old memory that had rolled through his mind throughout the last twenty-five years like a mossy stone that could not be stopped. Phil's face was young again, just a couple years older than Ray's had been on that fateful day in October 1989 when Phil finally called time on Ray's Cat O' Nine career.

He was sitting in the EMI office again, the shades partly pulled down over the gorgeous autumn day that filled the Kensington street outside. He'd been summoned to the meeting the day before, his manager sounding curt and evasive on the blower. "Tell ya what it's all about when we see ya, Ray, old son. Gotta go."

But his manager was late. Ray had always been punctual. That was something you learned in the East End. Certainly on the fruit market. Be on time or lose your fuckin' place. Well, here he was on time…

Doug, the manager, finally showed his face, ten minutes late, and Phil was with him. They entered the office quietly, shook his hand formally, and Ray knew why he had been called before they even opened their mouths.

"Sit down, Ray, son." Doug was a tough, no-shit businessman from Essex. The band looked up to him like a father figure. He was tight as a hamster's ass with their money, but he always looked out for them and had got them where they were today. Phil might have written most of the songs, and Ray sung the fuck out of 'em, but it was Doug who had the unerring business sense to broker the deals that had sent them into metal orbit. Ray had always respected him. Which was why looking at him now and reading his fate in that boxer's mug of a manager's expression, Ray felt even more betrayed. Doug was avoiding his gaze. Something he'd never done before.

Ray dropped into a leather swing seat like he'd been felled. He stared at Doug and knew his mouth was opening to say something, but there was no breath. He coughed violently, clearing his throat, but Doug was already speaking as Phil and the manager took seats across the oval table from him.

"Ray…" Doug began, flicking a quick look at the singer, then directing his gaze to a pen he'd fished from his pocket. "I think you know why we've called you."

Ray swung his gaze to the bass player. Phil was studying the blind over the window, his stolid face expressionless.

"No," Ray said. He stood up slowly. The world had suddenly grown very small in his head. "No," he said again. "You ain't gonna—"

"Mate, you've really left us no choice!" Phil had his hands wide, and his eyes were all wide, too, in "I'm the real victim here" innocence.

Ray started to shake. He felt sicker than ever before in his life, the evilest hangover was nothing on it. His mouth wouldn't let any more words out.

Doug took over, rising from his chair to grab Ray's arm in a consoling fashion, trying to ease him back into his seat. "Ray, you know I love you like a son. You know how much it fuckin' hurts to do this to you?"

Ray looked into his eyes, and at last Doug met his gaze. The forty-one-year-old looked genuinely sad. Was that a glint of a tear in his eyes? Crocodiles cried, too… Ray began to feel the familiar anger building, replacing the shock, the hurt, the desolation. The anger that had carried him through childhood and beyond, made him the tough fucker he was today. He shook Doug's grip away and rounded on Phil.

"You cunt," he said slowly, his voice trembling with rage. "You never fuckin' liked me. I *made* this band. Without me, you're fuckin' nothin'!!"

Phil sighed heavily, studied his fingers for a minute—the stubby fingers that Ray had always thought too short for a bass player—and then sat back in the swivel seat. "You did it to yourself, mate. We can't control you. We can't take it anymore. We have to look to the future and take this seriously. Me an' Jez are always experimenting with the music. We want to push it further, but you don't give a fuck. You're just here for a ride, not to take it to the next step. And you're ruining your voice. You're always fucked out of your nut on coke or speed. And that's when you're not pouring Jack Daniels down your throat like there's no tomorrow."

Ray took that in. That was a major speech for the usually laconic band leader. He sat down again. His anger, tipped nearly to the boiling point, curdled, miraculously stalled. Phil was right; he was diametrically opposed to the bass player in literally everything. Phil very rarely drank, certainly never took drugs. He was a family man, with two babies—twins—to look after, and even when he was on tour, he would stay in his hotel room reading a Sven Hassell novel rather than boozing and shagging like Ray and whoever was brave enough to accompany him on one of his blitzes. And Phil was right about the other thing as well: they thought he didn't know about their stupid experimental sessions, but he did, and it wasn't for him—the three of them jamming together secretly without Ray, fixated on Jimmy Page, Aleister Crowley bollocks, tryin' to add some quasi-mystical, arcane nonsense to the music. He'd always just let 'em get on with it. His job was to sing, not fuck around pretendin' to be into Black Magic when they was just four ordinary blokes from the East End. To Ray, it was only Rock 'n' Roll, and he liked it. He should've seen this coming. He really should.

"But there is no tomorrow," he finally answered Phil, his voice slow and empty.

Phil looked at Doug, and then both of them looked at the table.

"We're offering you a deal, son." Doug said eventually. "Sixty grand for signing off rights to the songs you wrote for the album. It's a good deal, son. You should take it."

Ray took it.

He walked out of the office on shaky legs, but he took it. Suddenly the future didn't seem so bright, the birds wouldn't be so fit or so numerous, and the champers and the clubs would be a lot cheaper.

*But there is no tomorrow…*

The haze began to clear, the dingy décor of the back-street boozer swam back into focus. Michelle was still bending over him, tears streaking her pretty face. Ray shook his head to clear it. The five-inch metal sword on a chain around his neck jangled. He remembered the fans who'd forged it for him, gave it to him after he'd been fired, when they told him he was the best singer the band would ever have. He saw their faces now. He began to push himself up from the grubby floorboards.

"Comin' back for more, old timer?" The muscle-bound bastard who'd slugged him was grinning from ear to ear.

Ray had always been a scrapper. Outside his local down Canning Town, impressing the birds by being the hardest, the mouthiest, the meanest. Top Dog. Leader of the pack. He'd filled many a chick's panties on that rep. You had to fight to prove who you were, and Ray had instinctively understood that. He understood it now, twenty-five years older than that slim, sexy Rock God who had stood on the stage at Frankfurt and surveyed all that he owned. Except he was a bit slower now, a lot fatter, and that punky barnet had fallen to the winds. But he was still Ray Fuckin' Starling, and he'd been proving that just about every night he hit the boozers. Been fighting that memory of the office in Kensington for twenty-five long years, fighting anyone who got mouthy and called him out. Because people *always* wanted to take him on so they could tell their mates they put one over on the ex-Cat O' Nine singer. And now here was another one itching to get his bedpost notch. Ray's head began to buzz the way it always did when the Beast was coming out. Couldn't they ever let it lie…? *Couldn't HE ever let it lie?*

No. If he had to prove he was still Ray Starling, badass lead singer of the biggest rock band in the world, then a twenty-five-year-old Best Before Date wasn't gonna stall him. Ray had always been the mad one in the band. The others were boring pussies. But did he really have to point that out to every cunt in a bar who wanted some of him?

So be it.

Ray blinked to clear the haze in his left eye. He felt the rage surge through his veins, the way euphoria had done once upon a long time ago in Frankfurt.

He focused on the big man who'd started on him for no reason other than he'd once been famous. The big lug was still grinning, still waiting for Ray to get up. *Latest in a long line, son.* All the years of regret, despair, smashed dreams, oceans of booze, and mountains of drugs had led to this. Had led to every other night just like it.

Ray was on one knee now. The pain in his head was like a pile driver battering away at his skull. His left eye was half closed.

He faced the big man, swaying slightly. Then he let the anger take him.

When Ray got really mad, wise men knew to duck for cover. All hell was there, all ready for the breaking. Unfortunately, tonight's assailant wasn't too wise. "Reckon I got one more Comeback in me..." Ray said.

And suddenly everything got *very* messy.

Ray Starling had always been a scrapper.

# Chapter Three

Rose said, "I don't believe it."

Kirk said, "Fuck-ing *hell!*"

They were both watching the news in Kirk's ropey Stoke Newington flat. The TV screen showed stills of four long-haired musicians, then a video clip from one of their colossal stadium gigs. The caption beneath rolled across in the Breaking News red banner:

## PRIVATE JET CARRYING FAMOUS ROCK BAND DISAPPEARS OVER INDIAN OCEAN

Kirk started to speak again, but Rose shushed him urgently. Cat O' Nine Tails had always been her favorite band.

The newsreader was short on facts. Kirk and Rose watched breathlessly as he delivered all he had, then Rose flicked to another news channel with the same headline news and tried to pick scraps from the slight variation of detail. But there was nothing more. The facts were very minimal: the band was on the last leg of their world tour, taking them to Asia with dates in Jakarta and Japan before finally climaxing the tour in Sydney. Somewhere high above the Indian Ocean at approximately midnight GMT, Air Control had lost contact with the private jet. It had simply and inexplicably disappeared from airspace. Australian and Indonesian maritime rescue patrols were already covering the area where contact had been lost, expanding to allow for wreckage drift patterns. So far, absolutely nothing had been discovered, although, as all newscasters on all channels kept repeating, it was a vast area of empty ocean to cover. A spokesperson from EMI, the band's record label, was rolled out to completely insipid effect—Kirk wondered if he'd ever even met the band. One channel scooped Phil Carter's distraught wife and his teenage son (a younger copy of his Dad), red-eyed and devastated, trying not to fear the worst despite the words the news anchor seemed determined to put in their mouths. Baz Cropper's wife, a still-glamorous blonde with a sensitive face in her early forties, looked broken as she eulogized on how attentive and kind her husband was. And there was Jez Tweed's girlfriend, who looked remarkably like the guitarist, equally as sensible and thoughtful in appearance as her missing lover. She looked a little shell-shocked but was keeping it real. She dismissed the anchor's suggestion of terrorist hijacking as absurd. It was a private jet with the same pilot and aircrew they always used. There was no question of anybody suspicious being on board. Besides the pilot, co-pilot, and two air stewards who had been flying with the band for the last ten years, the only other occupants of the jet were the manager, Doug Roscoe, the four members of the band themselves, and a handful of road crew who, again, were loyal and trusted members of the band's entourage. Besides, she pointed out patiently, rebuffing the anchor's interruptions, Air Traffic Control had reported conversations with the pilot for the first two hours of the flight since leaving Kuala Lumpur, and there had been nothing out of order reported.

Speculation continued to fly on all the channels. Had the jet crashed, or had it indeed been hijacked, despite protestations from family members of the band? Engine failure or terrorist activity? More experts and spokespersons were rolled out. Aircraft engineers who had checked over the jet before the flight and found absolutely nothing amiss. "This craft was exhaustively and extensively serviced since the last flight," one engineer stressed somewhat defensively as the headlines unspooled on a strip beneath his strained expression. "And the service records speak for themselves. This jet was good to go." But where *did* it go, that was the question that was on all news anchors' lips.

In between footage of Cat playing Wembley Arena and happy, smiley interviews with the four musicians that constituted the band (Barney cracking fart jokes, Baz beaming in his Sherlock Holmes titfer), there were more family members dredged up. Rose was close to tears when Barney's parents appeared, looking fragile and utterly overcome with grief. The old couple clung to the hope that their drummer son would be returned safely to them at any minute. Kirk had his doubts but said nothing; he could see how increasingly upset Rose was becoming with each revelation.

Finally, the news channels appeared to have exhausted all avenues, exploited all potential resources. When they had seen the same clips of the band laughing and joking on a previous jet tour and touching down in Japan the year before three times in a row, even Rose was tiring of the repetition. Kirk took the remote from her and switched off the TV. He pulled her against him on the sofa, stroking her long brown hair, saying nothing for a while, and if he felt she was maybe wallowing, being a little *too* melodramatic in her grief (after all, it wasn't as if she knew any of the band personally), he certainly wasn't going to mention it. She was a sensitive soul, which is why he loved her.

She had dragged him to see them twice on the European leg of the tour. Once at the London O2, and again at the not-so-accessible Birmingham Arena. She had all their albums—all fifteen of them!—and while Kirk liked the band's first album well enough, the rest left him cold. While Cat O' Nine's music was undeniably appealing in a mass-market fashion with riffs and melodies as catchy as a docker's billhook, Kirk had always found their lyrics a little naff and the subject matter a trifle undergrad. Hell, that was being polite; sixth form nerd metal would be more accurate. Cat O' Nine had made themselves accessible on such a huge scale by ostensibly not being offensive to anyone, something Kirk had always struggled with. Surely, the true appeal of a band lay in their ability to challenge. To outrage as well as excite. And in his opinion, Cat O' Nine Tails (again, with the honorable exception of their first album, which, grounded by the ferocious vocal abilities and punk-rock attitude of their original singer, Ray Starling, had been vital and blistering) was anything but exciting. They had forged a career in safe, melodic metal. Pleasing to the ear, easy on the mind. Nothing wrong with that, of course, but metal had never really been Kirk's cup of tea. The genre was way too conservative despite its obsession with imagery the practitioners obviously deemed shocking. No offense, Cat O' Nine, but horror movie covers and references to stranglers and gibbets steeped in chiming guitars and twinkling solos was as far removed from shocking as you could get.

Crypt Metal was how he'd described them to Rose once, and it seemed accurate enough. The band floundered in adolescent obsessions with fantasy gore and Hammer Horror chic while lyrical howlers decimated grammar left, right, and all over the show.

It had always struck Kirk that Cat O' Nine had dabbled in pretend Crowley Satanism and dark imagery, but in a comic book fashion without ever seeming to really believe in it. He was pretty sure they didn't subscribe to the Black Arts. He'd once attended a Cat O' Nine signing with Rose, and Phil Carter had chuckled dismissively when Kirk asked him if they really believed in the Horned One as the guitarist signed a copy of *Fear Stalkers* for Rose. "Nah, mate. The missus would kill me. She banks with the other side, know what I mean?" Jez Twist had confirmed the bass player's statement in a couple of subsequent interviews, and the band's jolly drummer, Barney Smolt, had once joked on a chat show a few years back about "riding bronco with the Devil, just for a laugh like" in a mock oafish accent. It was all a piss take, window dressing. Cat O' Nine Tails were four down-to-earth geezers, cheery, a little middle-of-the-road, not to mention middle-aged; a little *conservative* with the collective imaginative powers of a squad of road menders. Long-haired, good-natured Brit rockers up for a hearty chuckle, but as boring as accountants in their private lives. In fact, Baz had been an accountant when he first left university, a fact that didn't go unnoticed by the music press eager to spotlight the new guy in town who had replaced the infamous headline bagger, Ray Starling. They wouldn't get any booze and whore stories out of Baz; no threesomes in a Premier Inn coffee lounge there. Baz was a fine vocalist, but he was dull as Dutch cheese. Then there was Barney Smolt, who had retained a hobby most boys grew out of when they were fourteen—he spent a lot of his adult pocket money buying and assembling model airplane kits. Jez Twist did role playing! Phil Carter played golf. R.I.P. rock 'n' roll. Sid and Elvis died for *this*?

But for all that, Kirk didn't exactly hate them; he'd listen to them if he had to, say on long drives with Rose or while doing the gardening at his Mum's little bungalow. Mostly only if Rose asked him to, though.

But it hadn't always been that way. He would never forget the first time he saw Cat O' Nine Tails when he was barely ten years old and visiting his big brother who lived in Germany. He had never heard of most of the bands, but his bruv was a metal fan and dragged him along to the open-air festival at Frankfurt.

What was more eye-opening than any of the raucous and wild hair bands was the sight of his brother smoking a joint with his mates as they sat in the sun watching the festival. He appreciated the way his bruv had trusted Kirk enough not to say anything to his parents. That had been mutually understood. He'd even offered Kirk a toke for a joke. And then Cat O' Nine Tails had come on stage…

It had only been about one man for Kirk; the others were just background to Ray Starling's barnstorming performance. Kirk would never forget one moment that had burned itself into his mind and chased him through childhood to the present day—an instant influence: Ray, standing on stage between songs, legs slightly apart, his shirt stripped away, chest heaving from his exertions, hair bushy and semi spiked. He was surveying the audience as if he wasn't quite sure he was really there, a "This is It" moment unlike any other Kirk had witnessed before or since (Kirk had certainly not experienced it with his own band up to this point). Then Ray had flung out his arms, head tilted to one side, Jesus on the Rock Cross, and the chanting had lifted into the sunny skies, rising, deafening: "Cat O' Nine, Cat O' Nine… CAT O' NINE!!!"

The first album was an indispensable rock classic, burning with Starling's barely contained fury and a handful of compositions that blew away Carter's songs in terms of intensity and unleashed craziness. But it had been evident then that Ray was too much of a loose cannon for his more staid fellow band members, and the signs were there that he wouldn't last if you really looked for them. After Starling's departure, the band racked up a truly impressive amount of albums and went interstellar in terms of sales. The music became less fierce, less punky and in your face. A thoughtfulness and lyricism replaced the fury (at least in the music, the lyrics themselves remained as dodgy and English teacher-baiting as ever). Cat O' Nine settled themselves into almost cozy respectability to accompany their newfound massive wealth, despite the playful gore of their cover imagery and bellicose pretense of their song titles.

As for Ray Starling…?

He had dropped out of the public arena completely. He had taken the sixty thousand pounds for the rights to the songs he had written for the band and disappeared for all intents and purposes. Although "disappeared" was not entirely true. Kirk was vaguely aware he had started up a couple of bands, attempted a solo career, and attempted comeback after comeback over the years. But all this was just stuff he'd heard down the pub; Kirk had never heard any examples of Ray's non-Cat stuff, and there was probably a good reason for that. As one of his mates had told him, "It sounds like his heart wasn't in it." And that made sense to Kirk. After seeing Ray live when he was ten and witnessing the absolute euphoria burning out from him, how could he ever truly replicate that in any other band? Cat O' Nine had been his life, even if it had only been for a short moment in time…

"I don't want to hear any more, Kirk…" Rose said, turning away from the TV.

Kirk switched off the news and pulled Rose against him.

"You don't have to, Rosie," he said and kissed her cheek fondly.

She turned to him, her dark brown eyes troubled. "Do you think they're really dead?" She sucked in a breath, and when it came out again, it trembled. "Baz is one of the nicest musicians ever. He kissed my cheek last time we saw them, remember? Such a true, kind gentleman… This just isn't right. It isn't *fair*…"

He stroked the red stripe that grew from her crown and snaked through her thick brown hair. He loved that stripe; his very own Bride of Frankenstein dipped in blood. Kirk shrugged, then leaned in to kiss her, and knowing she was sorrowful, he felt a little ashamed of his instant arousal. She always did that to him, though, and he hoped she would continue to turn him on for a long time to come. Her face was a sexy contrast of strength and vulnerability; her finely chiseled cheekbones guarded eyes that were sensual and soft, yet her lips were stubbornly firm, her nose curved, forceful. She had a temper you wouldn't want to unleash (and Kirk had set it free a few more times than he would have liked), and she was tall and imposing, maybe with half an inch on Kirk. But right now, she was bare, confused, and had never looked sexier.

So Kirk forgave himself and kissed her again, pushing her gently back on the sofa and getting to work caressing her right breast through the material of her tee. He was pulling her shirt up over her head to get at her purple bra when she stopped him.

"What the fuck!?" She pushed his hands away and sat up. "I don't fucking believe you…"

Kirk sat back against the sofa cushions, his mouth dropping, hands wide and adopting what he hoped was his best look of bewildered innocence. "What?"

"You can really be an unfeeling bastard, d'you know that?"

He shrugged again. "Thought you wanted consoling, hun."

"Do you normally console people with a hard-on? Hate to see you at a funeral."

He smirked at that, which didn't help his case. But that was another thing he really liked about Rose; she could always make him laugh.

"Sorry, Rosie." He gave her a quick kiss on the forehead. "Forgiven?"

"No. Fuck off and make me a cup of tea."

He did as he was told. He was no fool.

As he bustled around in the kitchen of the small flat, he heard the first bars of "The Stranger" start up from the living room. She'd slipped on Cat O' Nine's second album. She had always preferred the band post Starling, something Kirk could never quite understand. The volume rose as she adjusted the remote on the stereo, and he smiled. *Rosie's little tribute*, he thought fondly and put the kettle on.


"Best rock band on the planet, my arse! A fuckin' metal Genesis is all they are. *Were*. Tweed jackets and plus fours be more suitable for 'em than leathers, the phony bastards. 'Bout fuckin' time they took their last encore, if you ask me." Davey Crooked finished his tirade and took a hefty gulp of lager.

"Well, I'm not asking you. Show some fucking respect, they're dead," Kirk told the bassist before Rose could rise from the pub table and lamp him one. She could take him, too; Kirk was sure of that. Davey was a lanky streak of piss, and all the leathers in the world couldn't make him any good in a scrap. Kirk had seen him go down too many times in rucks both before and after gigs. He remembered one particularly funny moment when Davey had decided to get involved in a post-gig punch-up in a dodgy pub they'd just been playing in Cardiff. The brawl between two huge Welsh women was getting increasingly nearer the table where the members of Lucifer Sam were sitting. Davey had no idea what they were fighting about, and Kirk had no idea what made him stand up and get involved. Maybe he fancied one of the big tattooed lasses—Davey was never renowned for his refined taste in females. But there he was anyway, jumping up to part them, and he succeeded in doing so, even if only for the second it took for one of them to turn round and chin him with one meaty fist. The time between Davey rising from his feet and landing on his ass couldn't have been more than five seconds. The two Welsh gals ignored him as soon as he hit the deck and turned back to slapping the hell out of each other. Kirk and the rest left him underneath the table where he'd landed, stunned as a felled calf. Let him rot, was their motto.

"Why the fuck should I show respect? We're better off without 'em. They'd become an embarrassment. Silly old bastards pretending to worship the Devil while playing golf and selling afternoon teas to the middle class." Davey pointed a long finger at Kirk. "You do know Baz Cropper bought a cream tea shop for his Missus to run down in Devon during the Summer Season, don't ya? They're about as rock 'n' roll as my old Nan. Fuck no, she's got way more attitude and rhythm in her mobility scooter than those twats ever showed. They've been pedaling the same cartoon shit for way too long."

Even if Kirk agreed with him, he wasn't going to say so for fear of upsetting Rose again. But Rose didn't need Kirk to protect her—not when she had her own Sir Galahad in the form of Johnny Diesel (nee John Dover). The slick-haired guitarist had always been a little too quick to step in on Rose's behalf for Kirk's liking. It was probably his paranoia, but were the little conversations and smiles they seemed to be sharing all the more frequently of late entirely as innocent as Rose would have him believe? She had been furious with him the one time he'd broached it, but the paranoia remained, the little pricks of jealousy kept coming, and here was one now.

"Because they're Rose's favorite band, you dick. And if you don't respect your mates' feelings, what kind of twat does that make you?" The guitarist glared at Davey with his blue eyes (dreamy blue? Is that what Rose thought of them?), and the bass player dropped his gaze and took another gulp of lager.

Rose didn't need a knight with a gleaming Gibson right now, however. "I'll tell you why you should show respect," she said, eyes flashing with real anger. "Because not only were they a great band—yes, a *great* band, not everyone thinks *Sid Sings* is the best album ever recorded you twat—but also because they've left loved ones behind who will be in a very bad place right now. Loved ones, Davey. I know you're not familiar with the term. But you mentioned Baz's wife. Do you think she gives a shit about how musically diverse or challenging they are? She just wants her kind, lovely husband back, her childhood sweetheart who stuck by her all these years. These are *real* people who lived *real* lives. *Moron!*" She took a furious sip of her vodka, and Kirk felt his love for her swell more than ever. He put his arm around her (before Johnny could?), but she was too angry and prickly now and shrugged it off.

"Bollocks to it," Crooked muttered. "Just sharing my opinion around. No need to climb on my ass for that."

"Your ass is the last anyone would wanna climb on, cabbage head," Ned assured him. The drummer emphasized the statement with a minor twitch. His arm rose half-heartedly, as if his Tourette's couldn't really be bothered to play with him today.

"Fuck you, Brain Crack," Davey responded defensively. He never knew quite how far he could go with insulting Ned on account of his disability, no matter how minimal it was. But today he was feeling the pressure and would take on any comer. "Gonna take my head off with that tic in a minute, retard. Get your straitjacket on."

"Doesn't take a guy with Tourette's to take your head off, not when we can find any five-year-old girl to do the job."

"Fuck you all. I got better things to do than chat to a bunch of wank-cocks like you lot. Stickin' my prick in a mouse hole would be more productive."

"Way too roomy for you, mate." Ned was straight in.

Kirk could tell the bassist was feeling outnumbered, and tiring of the banter, he shut them all up with a slam of his pint glass on the table. He hadn't failed to notice the grateful smile Rose had flashed at Johnny either.

"We're not here to talk about how Davey achieves his pleasure. Or even to discuss Cat O' Nine Tails..."

"R.I.P. Rockin' in the Pacific."

"Shut the fuck up, Davey. And it was the Indian Ocean, you moron. This is supposed to be a band meeting. We need to discuss what we're actually working toward because it seems to me one or two of you seem to be losing interest." That was aimed at Diesel, though it could equally apply to Ned. Both of them had missed the last rehearsal, and Diesel had missed the one before that as well. He could feel the entire band beginning to crack at the seams, and he wasn't sure how he could reverse the situation, especially with everyone seemingly at each other's throats. Still, maybe it would be a good thing if Johnny decided to quit…

Kirk glanced at the handsome guitarist and felt guilty for even wishing it. He couldn't let himself give in to his own insecurities. Diesel was a good guitarist. Johnny blinked back at him over his beer. Even so, the man was just *way* too good looking. The bastard.

Johnny tipped him a little grin. Had he read Kirk's mind?

"Lucifer Fuckin' Sham, faggots…" Davey brought everyone's attention right back to him. Did it make him happy irritating them all the time? It seemed like it.

Kirk sighed. "Got something useful to say, Davey?"

"Yeah. Just this: you're all a bunch of pussy wipes, and I'm not sure I can be arsed pluckin' my strings for you anymore. And why the fuck does the Bride have to be at every band meeting anyway? She don't fuckin' contribute musically." He sat back in his chair, folding his arms, screwing Rose with his narrow eyes. His hair was more messy than usual. It looked like it hadn't been washed for a week or more, a spiky hay rack the color of sewage. Stubble lined his face like smeared mud. His sneer took them all in, well-practiced.

Rose yawned at him, and once again Johnny beat Kirk to the defense. "She's here to provide the elegance and intelligence you so obviously lack, Numbhead. And the only string you're good at plucking is the one between your thighs."

Kirk tensed when Rose gave Johnny that sweet smile again. The smile hurt. And it shouldn't, cos it meant nothing, surely? Kirk lost his thread, self-confidence slipping away. He stood up as if about to give a speech, but he'd forgotten the script. They were all watching him now, waiting for him to say whatever he had been about to say. Even Johnny managed to take his eyes off Rose for a second to focus on the singer.

The singer. The frontman. Leader of the band… Yeah, right. This band was a shambles. Did any of them *really* like each other? At this moment in time, that seemed a little doubtful, which was very sad, as they had all been close once. Even the slightly tubby Ned—one of Kirk's oldest and best friends whom he'd met at school alongside Johnny, and besides Rose, one of the only people he knew who could genuinely make Kirk laugh, and whom he admired greatly for not being beaten by his condition—could push the wrong buttons with his humor sometimes. And he was very critical of Kirk's songs, too. Kirk had a growing suspicion the multi-talented drummer was going to drop the band soon anyway and pursue either his stand-up ambitions or the less-stressful career of sound design. While he had a knack for twiddling knobs on a mixing board, Kirk felt the drummer was drawn more to comedy. Ned was hilarious on stage, where his firmly held belief in not trying to suppress his TS but manage it instead, and indeed use it as a comedy tool, really came to the fore. Whichever route he chose to eventually move down, Ned's boredom of the band was becoming more evident, as was his increasing indifference to Kirk's vision.

Kirk opened his mouth to speak, then paused. Why the fuck bother? He suddenly wanted to call it a day. He was getting too old for his dreams for the band to come true anyway. Thirty-three was practically geriatric in rock terms. If he—if *they*—hadn't made it by now, it was obvious they never would. He wavered on his feet, momentarily defeated.

Rose came to his rescue. "Kirk's written some new songs. Stuff you won't believe, it's that good." She beamed at him encouragingly. *That's* why he invited her to band meetings. He smiled gratefully and opened his mouth to elaborate, to tell them exactly why his new songs would go down so well live, why they should make a great new demo that would attract a manager, a deal. He was going to tell them how they would soon be playing to 200 people at their gigs instead of twenty, how they would soon be able to afford decent equipment, go on tour, hell, maybe even have a crack at America if the new album he had in his mind went according to plan, if only they could all pull together and make it work. He was going to tell them all this and more. And then just as he was about to start, Ned broke in instead with the mother of all Tourette's outbursts, his extremely loud shout of "NHS!" turning heads all around the pub, the drummer looking as completely bewildered by what was coming out of his mouth as the rest of them, and then they were all falling about laughing—all except Kirk.

His moment was gone. Rose had given him the stage, and Ned had taken it. Kirk wasn't even convinced the cry was a genuine TS tic (and felt ashamed to even think it).

"Whoah!" Johnny was clapping his hands. "Where the fuck did *that* one come from, Ned, old son?"

The drummer put his hands wide. His shaved head shone under the pub lights. "Fuck knows. New material to me, too!"

Davey was still guffawing, truly back in his comfort zone—he hated talking about the future of the band's music; he just wanted to play bass, fuck women, talk shit, and drink lots of beer. And now Ned was moving the conversation on to one of Davey's own pet topics, the state of today's music industry, and he and the bass player were almost in agreement for once, although it wouldn't last.

"That cunt responsible for the Z Factor should be hanged outside HMV for a start," Davey was proclaiming loudly, so loudly that some rock girls at the next table were smiling in agreement, which was dangerous. You should never encourage Davey Crooked. "He's turned music into puppy food for the brain-dead. Get a tramp to roast his fuckin' nuts in a brazier and sell 'em for 50 pence. Then he'd finally be contributing to society, the cum-bucket."

Ned nodded. "Set the music industry back thirty years. It's like punk never happened." When he got riled, the drummer's arm tics became a little more aggressive, which just made him madder. He could control them in the confines of a comedy routine when he was on stage, using his Tourette's to provide extremely refreshing and self-deprecating humor. But when he was angry, it became his enemy. "And as for Rap, don't even get me fuckin' started! Sexism with all the fun taken out. Calling girls bitches and lyrics about guns and gangstas…is that what kids should aspire to?" Ned's round face was getting redder by the minute. But now he had lost Davey, as the bassist liked lyrics about slapping bitches and fucking hoes. When he pointed this out to Ned, the drummer produced a physical tic that startled them both for a minute. Ned's arm tilted in a parody of a Nazi salute, while his head twitched manically.

"Cocks in orbit, man, that was a wild one!" Davey responded with his usual sensitivity.

Ned ignored both the drummer's remark and his own tic. "What do you know about music anyway, Davey? It's like talking to an eight-year-old. You've as much musical ability as a tapir. Hell, I'm sure a woodlouse knows more chords than you."

Davey's only answer was a belch that could peel the top off a beer can. It was at this point that Kirk walked away, heading for the toilet and a breath of fresh air.

By the time he'd returned, some idiot had put Cat O' Nine Tails on the jukebox and Johnny was chatting quietly to Rose while the other two argued with increasing ferocity.

He left the pub quietly and didn't turn back.

# And be sure to check out…

### THE FEAR IS GROWING

From the moment he saw the ancient castle rising out of the picturesque Scottish countryside, filmmaker Dan Martin knew he'd found the ideal location for his vampire horror movie. And nothing could make him leave. Not the eerie legends of soul-stealing beasts of the night…nor a bizarre series of freak accidents. Not even his pregnant wife's tragic miscarriage.

### THE TERROR IS BORN

Except that now there is another fetus growing in Vicki's womb. But little Darian is not going to be a normal baby. The Martins' adopted ten-year-old son Marty will soon find that out. In fact, Marty will soon know exactly what his new brother really is.

**If you can't run with the big dogs…**

It was supposed to be a corporate retreat and a series of morale-boosting exercises. It was a weekend Shawn Biltmore nearly didn't survive.

There was something else playing in the woods that night, something other than a bunch of corporate drones with paintball guns. And it had chosen Shawn as its new chew toy.

**…rip 'em to shreds.**

The local authorities chalked it up to a bear attack.
So did the doctors.
Shawn knew the truth, however, as much as he wanted to deny it.
But when one of his coworkers is viciously killed,
Shawn must face the truth…
He's a killer who needs to be put down.

www.ingramcontent.com/pod-product-compliance
Lightning Source LLC
Chambersburg PA
CBHW071743190726
48292CB00003B/856